STEALING NATASHA

VINDICTIVE QUEENS
BOOK TWO

RAISA GREYWOOD

Part I of *Stealing Natasha* was originally published in the 2024 anthology, *Pure Vengeance*, under the title *Caged Bride*.

Cover art: Wicked Smart Designs
Editing: Ellie Rose and Amy Briggs, Briggs Consulting LLC

Digital ISBN: 978-1-952596-43-8
Paperback ISBN: 978-1-952596-44-5

Part I of Stealing Natasha was originally published in the 2024 anthology, Pure Vengeance, under the title Caged Bride. Also, just so you know... I am not remotely sorry for leaving it as a cliffhanger. It was supposed to be a novella—short, dirty, and ending sweet, but Natasha and Lachlan took me on a ride I didn't see coming. And no, they didn't stop for snacks, much less bathroom breaks.

Stealing Natasha is dedicated to everyone who hung in there (heh) and begged me to give Natasha and Lachlan (less Lachlan and more Natasha TBH) a happily-ever-after.

I also dedicate this story to every man who has ever sent a picture of his poxy dick to a woman who didn't ask for it. May you soon meet someone just like Natasha.

————

*Before you continue, please protect your mental wellbeing and read the content warnings. This is a dark, **dark** romance, and some scenes may not be appropriate for all readers.*

CONTENT WARNINGS

Said in a voice like Steve Shell from *Old Gods of Appalachia*, "Reader discretion...is advised." If you like horror podcasts, you should listen to it. It's positively shiver-inducing.

Without further ado, here are all the content warnings I could think of, but I'm betting I didn't catch them all.

References to past child and animal abuse, on-page body shaming, medical play, pet play, anal play, bodily functions occurring in public, gaslighting/emotional abuse, on-page violent death of a human caused by a dog, mention of illegal drug use, on-page sexual scenes involving dubious consent/nonconsent, public degradation, explicit language, social alcohol use, references to and on-page violent crime, forced body modification including piercing and branding, on-page life-threatening illness of a pet, suicidal ideation, on-page murder.

———

PS: The dog will never die. Ever. He will live forever with his kitten, and drive-thru attendants will always give him chicken nuggies for being handsome.

PART ONE

CHAPTER ONE

An Ashland does not flinch.

Not ever.

Even when she's being forced to marry a man she's never met.

I didn't have anything old or borrowed but I had plenty of blue. Well, black and blue anyway. There was even a little purple under my right eye to make things festive. The makeup artist was careful, but it still hurt when she tried to cover the bruises on my face with concealer.

The thick paste wasn't even really concealer. It was theatrical paint I would probably need a sand-blaster to remove. At least I wouldn't have to worry about smudging it. The artist was incredibly talented too. Aside from the rose-pink lip stain and skillfully applied smoky eyeshadow that lightened my brown eyes into golden amber, I looked like I wasn't wearing makeup at all.

My curly brown hair even looked good. Somehow, she'd managed to tame my usual frizz and create glossy waves trailing to the center of my back.

"Ten minutes, Tasha!" my father shouted as he pounded on the door with a meaty fist. "Get your fat ass moving."

Considering he'd have found something derogatory to say regardless of my weight, the jab didn't bother me, but I bit my tongue before I reminded him that my name wasn't Tasha. It was just another of his power plays—as if by shortening my name he could make me feel small.

Too bad it usually worked.

Hell, he'd barely given me time to throw a few outfits into a small suitcase before hustling me to the church.

The stylist flinched, then tugged me to my feet and led me to where my wedding dress waited. The gaudy mass of embroidered lace, tulle, and satin would have looked better on a taller, slimmer bride, but I wasn't given a choice in the matter. It was the first dress I tried on that didn't need alterations.

I sent my best to the curvaceous bride who had managed to escape my fate.

Sometimes I wished my mother hadn't died when I was a baby, but mostly not. She might have been able to stop my father from treating me like dog shit, but it was more likely she'd have been abused too. Of course, knowing my father, I was pretty sure her death hadn't been an accident.

I had always been little more than a financial asset—something to trade in exchange for money or power—and I wondered what my future husband had promised him.

At least I knew his name, but aside from that, I was clueless about who Lachlan O'Donnell was or what he did. I hadn't even seen a picture of him, which meant he was either old enough to be my grandfather, or too unpleasant to get a wife without buying one.

Not that it mattered.

He was probably at least as bad or worse than my father, but maybe he wasn't. Instead of bitching and grousing, maybe I should've thanked my lucky stars I was getting out from under my father's thumb, but it was damned hard to keep a positive attitude.

Heck, if I was entertaining pipe dreams anyway, maybe Lachlan would let me go to college. I swallowed a laugh. Women in my father's world didn't go to college. They learned how to do lunch, plan parties, and direct housekeeping staff.

Most importantly, they learned to keep their mouths shut and stay out of their husband's way.

And if Lachlan had made a deal with dear old Dad, he was probably the same. I'd be thankful enough if he didn't hit me and doubly blessed if he got himself a mistress and left me alone after I gave him his heir and spare.

I didn't look at the stylist or the makeup artist as they zipped me into my dress. There wasn't any point, and I hadn't bothered learning their names. Lucky for them, they weren't my friends, and I'd forget what they looked like before I cut my wedding cake.

And no way would I ever let them know how much it hurt when they squeezed my bruised ribs into the tight satin bodice. I felt like a fucking sausage.

"You look so pretty, Ms. Ashland," the stylist

murmured as she draped my veil over my face. "Mr. O'Donnell won't be able to take his eyes off you."

Yeah. He's going to wonder whose curtains got used to make this horror of a wedding dress.

"Thanks." I slipped my feet into the crystal-encrusted heels and straightened my spine. "I guess it's showtime."

I picked up the end of the chapel-length train before I tripped on it and opened the door leading from the small dressing room. To my surprise, a woman waited outside. She wore a pale-pink bridesmaid dress with a sweetheart neckline and cap sleeves. A silky shawl in a slightly darker pink covered her shoulders and arms, and her blonde hair was pinned into a neat chignon.

"Natasha, hi!" She carried a bouquet of white roses and nearly dropped them when she hugged me. "You look so beautiful! I hope you like the flowers. Lachlan is such a man and didn't ask for your preferences, so I had to guess."

I had no idea who she was, but nobody had greeted me like they were happy to see me in years. Giving her a tentative smile, I said, "Hi. I...um—"

"I'm so sorry! Gosh, I swear, my brain sometimes. I forgot to introduce myself." She held out the bouquet. "I'm Lachlan's sister, Saoirse, and I'll be your bridesmaid."

"Wow, okay. Thank you. The flowers are perfect."

"Yay!" She hooked her arm through mine. "We're going to be great friends. I just know it."

Maybe things were looking up. I'd been issued a groom and a stupid ugly dress, but once I was out of my father's reach, I could make friends. My future husband's sister seemed like a good place to start.

I would probably melt if Lachlan shared Saoirse's charming Irish accent.

As if to remind me I didn't get to hope for nice things, my father stormed toward us.

"Beat it, stupid bitch," he rasped, pushing Saoirse out of the way.

She planted her feet and shook her head, her cheerful smile fading. "I'm afraid that doesn't work for me, Stevie. Consider yourself lucky you're being allowed to escort Natasha down the aisle as it is."

I gasped and tried to find an escape route, knowing Saoirse would suffer for daring to call him anything but sir, but I was determined to get help before he hurt her too badly.

My father might have been handsome once upon a time, but the years of cruelty had left their mark on him. Deep lines scored his face, surrounding soulless brown eyes.

His cheeks reddened and he clenched his fists as he glared at her. "Someone needs to teach you some manners. Maybe it should be me."

Sighing, Saoirse rolled her eyes and reached down toward her hip. To my shock, she pulled a slim steel dagger from a slit in her dress, then flipped it expertly. She caught the hilt and positioned the sharp tip under my father's chin. "I recommend against it, but you're welcome to try."

"You little bitch."

"So good of you to notice." She gave him a delighted grin and curtsied before the smile and the dagger vanished. "Now, move before you get blood on my dress."

I kept my face clear of all emotion and didn't even ask why Saoirse was carrying a knife to a wedding. Not a single giggle, chortle, guffaw, or the slightest hint of a smile would mar my features, even though I was dancing a fucking jig inside. When I heard organ music from the sanctuary, I said, "I think that's our cue."

After giving Saoirse one last poisonous glare, my father stomped off.

Unable to help myself, I snorted, then clapped a

hand over my mouth before a laugh escaped. "Wow. I think I have a girl crush now. You're my new best friend."

"Oh, cool!" She grinned, revealing a dimple in her cheek. "I've never been anyone's girl crush before. We're definitely going to be besties, and I'm thrilled to have a new sister."

"Me too."

Arm in arm, we walked to the end of the yellow carpet stretching to the altar in the sanctuary. Ignoring my father, Saoirse gave me a tight hug and kissed my cheek. "I'll go first, and you follow when the wedding march starts, okay?"

"Got it."

I ignored my father's tight grip on my arm, knowing he was taking one last shot at hurting me, but nearly stumbled when I saw my future husband.

Although I didn't know Lachlan's age, he definitely wasn't old enough to be my grandfather. He was tall and fit, and while there was a definite family resemblance between him and Saoirse, his features were harder, with sharper edges. Blond scruff decorated his jaw as if he'd forgotten to shave. I liked it though. It made him look...

Maybe more approachable, like he wasn't a hundred percent perfect.

He smiled and my heart fluttered as I walked toward him. After one look into his sparkling blue eyes, I was head over heels in lust for my new husband.

———

LACHLAN

"I can't believe you're marrying that inane little cow," my sister whispered in Gaelic. To her credit, the sneer behind her words didn't appear on her perfect face.

I'd spent twelve years waiting for the right moment to strike back.

Four thousand, three hundred and eighty days of unclaimed vengeance eating me from the inside. Maybe it was old school to visit the sins of the father upon his child, but Natasha Ashland would pay for every single one of them.

"We've been through this already, Saoirse. Drop it."

"Fine," she grunted sourly, then added, "The thought of being tied to the Ashland family makes me sick. I can't even imagine what Darragh—"

"I said, that's enough." I refused to have our

brother's name mentioned while the physical manifestation of over a decade of planning and work walked toward me. "As long as you did your job and convinced her to come to me willingly, your part is almost done."

"I can't believe I agreed to this, but I'm finished after tomorrow, right?"

"Yes, just as I promised."

"Good." She huffed and seemed to glare at me while smiling at my bride. "I told the bitch I couldn't wait to have a new sister. She swallowed the lie whole."

In her white dress and veil, Natasha looked deceptively innocent, but I knew what lurked inside. She was Steve Ashland's daughter, after all. Despite her beauty and heart-stopping curves, her soul was as black as his was.

Even now, Steve seemed reluctant to let her go as he led her up the few stairs to the altar. He didn't release her until I leveled him with a hard stare. I hadn't left him with a choice. I'd bought up all his debts, and he was well aware of what I'd do if he didn't give me his beloved little brat.

Her days of being her father's pampered princess were over, and Steve would watch while I knocked her off the lofty perch he'd put under her delicate feet. She'd crawl for me and beg for even the tiniest scrap of kindness.

If Steve was very lucky, I'd send her back to him in one piece after I got my fill of vengeance. Well, her body would be more or less intact. I didn't plan to leave her mind that way.

At first, I'd considered getting an heir from her before I broke her, but Saoirse had a point. I didn't want my bloodline contaminated.

Steve swore she was a virgin, but there was no telling how many men had come before me. Thankfully, the blood test I'd demanded had come back clean. She'd also gone off the script and gotten a birth control shot.

I wasn't sure how I felt about that. Part of me was glad I wouldn't have to worry about getting her pregnant, and another was furious that she'd taken the choice from me. Knowing I was being ridiculous didn't soothe my irritation.

"Lachlan, do you take Natasha to be your lawfully wedded wife?"

Realizing I'd spaced out on most of the ceremony, I focused my attention on the minister. "I do."

"Natasha, do you take Lachlan to be your wedded husband, to have and to hold from this day forward, for better, for worse, for richer, for poorer, in sickness and in health, to love, cherish, and to obey until death do you part?"

Her lips twisted at the old-fashioned wedding vow I'd instructed the minister to use. She lifted her chin, then said, "I do."

I wasn't at all pleased at the sudden surge of arousal in my gut at the sound of her soft, husky voice. Maybe I'd keep her gagged. I didn't want to hear anything that came out of her duplicitous mouth anyway.

Finn, my second, and best man for this farce of a wedding, handed me the plain gold wedding band I'd had him pick up at a pawn shop, and I slid it over her left ring finger as the minister droned on.

The minister smiled and closed his bible. "By the power vested in me by God and the State of California, I now pronounce you man and wife. Lachlan, you may kiss your bride."

Gritting my teeth, I lifted her veil to perform the distasteful act, then pulled her into my arms. Her big brown eyes widened, and I almost laughed when she blushed. I hated that she smelled delectably like citrus and vanilla, but the perfume hid putrescence.

It didn't matter. Her scent would soon match what lived inside her.

She stiffened and a tiny gasp escaped her

rosebud lips. Despising myself, I lowered my head to kiss her. Heated electricity shot through my body at the first touch of her lips against mine, and against my better judgement, I deepened our kiss, tasting lemon candy and something spicy I desperately wanted to consume.

Strangely, she didn't seem to know what to do with her tongue when I coaxed her to open her mouth. She kept it tucked firmly against her bottom teeth until I tipped her head to the side and traced the edges of her straight, white teeth with the tip of my tongue. Whimpering softly, she finally relaxed and let me kiss her like I wanted.

Saoirse cleared her throat, reminding me of my purpose. Reluctantly, I eased away from Natasha, but the feral beast inside me reveled in the sight of her glazed eyes and swollen lips.

"Ladies and gentlemen, it is my great honor to present Natasha and Lachlan O'Donnell."

The few guests rose and clapped politely. They all knew this wedding wasn't a joyous occasion.

When the applause faded, the minister said, "If you'll follow me, we'll get the marriage certificate dealt with."

"All right."

I took Natasha's elbow and scowled when she

jerked out of my reach to pick up the back of her dress.

"Sorry. I don't want to trip over this thing." Carrying the mass of lacy fabric over one arm, she followed the minister into a small office.

The minister handed her a pen and laid the certificate on the desk in front of her. Watching her hand tremble as she signed her name soothed my irritation at having to marry her in the first place, but it flared anew when she smiled as she handed me the pen.

Once the marriage certificate was signed by both of us and witnessed by Finn and Saoirse, she gave me a tentative smile. "I... Sorry I'm so weird. Are we having a reception?"

This shy, awkward young woman wasn't the bride I'd expected. According to rumors, she was arrogant and rude, with a streak of entitlement a mile wide. Considering the gossip came from her father's guards, who had known her from birth, I was inclined to believe it, except it didn't explain what I was seeing.

I hid a frown and nodded, then offered her my arm. "Of course. Only the best for my beautiful bride."

Surprisingly, Natasha clenched my arm tighter

as we approached her father and moved out of reach when he lifted a hand to get her attention. I almost stumbled when she pressed herself against me as if she wanted my protection.

When she tried to increase her pace, I wrapped my arm around her, forcing her to slow down as we walked past her father to my town car waiting at the curb. He gave me an evil scowl before turning away.

As we left the church, her shoulders slumped. "We're legally married now, right?"

I had no idea why she'd ask such an odd question. She had to know our marriage wouldn't end well for her, given the animosity between her father and me.

"As soon as the minister files the marriage certificate, yes."

To my shock, she said, "Thank god."

CHAPTER TWO

NATASHA

Held in the private dining room of a posh hotel I'd heard of but never visited, my wedding reception was small and intimate—exactly how I'd have wanted it if I'd been given the choice.

Thankfully, my father decided to skip the party, and I didn't think any of the few guests were acquainted with him, although I didn't know for sure.

The thought of never seeing him again made me giddy, as did the delicious Malbec served with my meal of beef Wellington alongside tender grilled asparagus, and purée of celeriac topped with scads of butter. Maybe my luck was changing. My father was out of my life, and aside from my ugly dress, I'd gotten the perfect wedding, including a handsome husband with an Irish accent.

Heck, I didn't even care about the obey part of our vows—well, not much. Obedience to one's husband wasn't really a thing anymore. For all I knew, Lachlan was a traditionalist, or it was a thing with Irish weddings.

Lachlan didn't say much, seemingly content to let Saoirse monopolize the conversation, but I liked his deep voice. His accent made me all shivery inside.

"I think I forgot to do whatever thing is supposed to happen with your dress train to keep you from tripping on it," Saoirse said.

I laughed, then slapped a hand over my mouth when everyone looked at me. My belly clenched and my supper roiled in my stomach. My father hated it when I showed any kind of emotion, and it took several seconds to remind myself that he didn't get to say whether I could laugh or not.

Hashtag no contact.

"It's okay," I finally said. "I was actually thinking of asking for scissors to cut the darned thing off."

"Don't brides usually keep their dresses for their daughters?"

"Ew." I grimaced and took a sip of wine. "Not this dress. It looks like something made out of kitchen curtains scavenged from a whole bunch of houses belonging to old women."

"Well..." Her lips twitched into a smile. "At least the shoes are cute, and whoever did your hair and makeup is the bomb."

"Right?" Unwilling to spoil the party, I didn't tell her what the makeup was hiding. Lachlan would find out soon enough, and I still had no idea what I'd say when he saw the bruises.

"So, why did you pick it?" she asked.

My face heated under the thick coating of paint. "It was the only one that didn't need alterations. I'm guessing some other short and chubby woman decided to skip her wedding."

"Hush, you. You're gorgeous and you know it. Actually..." She stood and tugged me to my feet. "I have an idea. Let's visit the little bride's room."

"Um...sure?"

Still holding my hand, she led me to a beautifully decorated washroom with a lounge. When the door shut behind us, she pulled her dagger free and walked toward me with dark intent in her eyes. I froze, wondering if my escape from my father would end in a hotel ladies' room.

Honestly, it wouldn't surprise me at all if dear old dad contracted a hit on me. Maybe the animosity between him and Saoirse was just an act.

Instead of sinking the blade into my heart, she knelt before sawing at the skirt, cutting it off at my knees.

"This is better," she murmured as she tugged the frilly crinoline free. She got to her feet and tossed the wads of fabric into the wastebasket. "So much better. It looks like something someone might actually wear without being forced into it."

Unable to stop myself, I hugged her and tried not to cry.

"Thank you," I whispered once I thought I could speak without sobbing. "All the thank yous forever and ever."

"It was nothing." She pulled away.

Realizing I'd made her uncomfortable, I dropped my arms. "Sorry. I know I'm weird, but still, thank you."

"Yeah." She cleared her throat and cocked her head toward the door. "Ready to go back?"

I nodded and led the way from the bathroom, enjoying the absence of that stupid dress as I sat comfortably for the first time since the stylist zipped me into the awful thing.

Strangely, Lachlan's face darkened, and he tilted his head to look at me, but didn't say anything.

He was probably already having second thoughts. I crossed my fingers and prayed Lachlan would give me a settlement large enough to allow me to get as far away from my father as I could. He probably wouldn't, but I'd fucking walk and eat out of restaurant dumpsters if it meant staying out of my father's reach.

My heart sinking, I made the best of it and tried to be a good host to the guests until Lachlan asked, "Are you ready to go, Natasha?"

No. "Yes. Thank you for planning such a wonderful day." I held up my hand and smiled at the tastefully understated gold wedding band adorning my left ring finger. "Even this ring is perfect. How did you know exactly what I wanted?"

He shared a glance with Saoirse. I didn't know either of them well enough to identify the perplexing mixture of anger and confusion on their faces. Leaning close to him, Saoirse whispered something in a language I didn't recognize and scowled at his soft reply in the same language.

"You're welcome," he finally said without

answering my question. After rising to his feet, he offered his arm.

I stood and laid my free hand in the crook of his elbow. For better or worse, as the minister said, I was married now. Maybe it wouldn't be roses and happiness, but I had to look on the bright side of things.

Lachlan seemed kind, and I was out of my father's reach. I even had a new friend, and she didn't seem to care that, aside from what I'd seen on television and movies, I didn't know what friends did together. Of course, I wouldn't get to keep her. The minute her brother decided to end our marriage, my friendship with Saoirse would end too. At least it wouldn't end violently.

"Shall we?" Lachlan asked, pulling me from my thoughts.

"Yes, of course." I matched my pace to his as he led me to the black town car waiting outside. The driver held the door as Lachlan helped me into the vehicle.

"I'll be back shortly." He shut the door, cutting off my reply, then went to talk to Saoirse.

They appeared to be arguing, and I frowned, wondering what they discussed. Lachlan held a hand up and shook his head, then turned on his heel and returned to the car.

After seating himself next to me, he said, "Take us home, please."

His spicy cologne and the heat of his body cocooned me, and I inhaled deeply, finally able to breathe without worrying about being punished for it.

From his spot behind the wheel, the driver said, "Yes, sir."

LACHLAN

It was all a lie.

After growing up with Steve Ashland, Natasha couldn't possibly be so cluelessly sweet and innocent. Worse, my own sister was beginning to question what we were doing.

Saoirse agreed to the fucking plan and went even further when she suggested befriending Natasha to make her fall from grace even more painful. And now she wanted to bail because Natasha had gaslighted her into thinking she wasn't a spoiled, materialistic bitch.

I knew better.

Oh, this ring is perfect, I mocked inwardly. *How did you know?*

All bullshit. There was no way Steve Ashland's daughter would accept a pawned wedding ring. She'd learn soon enough that whatever she thought she'd gain by aping manners and gratitude would get her exactly nowhere.

My lips curved into a smile, and I resisted the urge to rub my hands together. Natasha would have plenty of diamond-encrusted platinum jewelry. Sadly for her, none of it would be on her slim fingers.

At least her dress looked better with the bottom half missing. Natasha had great legs, but I hated that I noticed how truly beautiful she was. Then again, I wouldn't have to put a bag over her head so my dick would stay hard while I fucked her.

"I'm sorry," she said, interrupting my plotting. "I don't know where your house is. There wasn't time... I mean..." She sighed and looked out the window. "I'm sorry I'm so awkward. I'll try to do better."

Better at trying to make me think you're not a conniving little cunt.

"It's okay. Our wedding must have taken you by surprise."

"That's putting it mildly," she muttered under her breath. In a louder voice, she added, "I really like Saoirse. She's so nice. Do you have other siblings? I'm an only child, and my mom is gone. I'm also sorry you had to meet my father."

I'd say one thing for her...the girl was good. If I didn't know better, I'd have almost believed she was exactly as she appeared—naïve and too stupid to live.

Not surprising, since according to the dossier I'd compiled, she hadn't bothered with college. A lack of education didn't make her stupid, but given her father's assets, there hadn't been anything aside from entitled laziness stopping her from getting a degree.

"It's just me and Saoirse," I replied.

"Oh, okay. Sorry, I—"

"Stop apologizing," I snapped.

Her shoulders went up around her ears and I kicked myself for deviating from the plan. I was supposed to get her to like me before I yanked everything away and treated her like she deserved. It was no wonder Saoirse was having second thoughts. Thankfully, I knew better than to think Natasha was genuine.

"I'm the one who's sorry," I said, softening my

tone. "I shouldn't have yelled at you. Our parents died in a plane crash several years ago."

To my shock, she reached over to squeeze my hand. "It's hard to lose a loved one. It won't make anything better, but I'm so sorry for your loss."

"Thanks." Deciding to get my head out of my ass, I added, "Anyway, our house is an hour south on the coast."

She grinned and her eyes sparkled as she turned to face me. "Can you see the beach from it?"

"Yes. There's a great view from the second floor."

"I can't wait to see it." Natasha let go of my hand and sighed happily. "I know I'm being completely socially inept again, but I'm so happy you picked me to marry. I just…never mind."

She trailed off, and for some inexplicable reason, I wanted to know what she'd say in that soft, husky voice that seemed designed to make my dick hard.

"Just what?" I asked.

"I don't have any right to ask, but…" She turned in her seat and took my hand again. "Please be patient while I learn to be a good wife."

"Don't worry." I brought her hand to my lips and kissed her knuckles. "I'll teach you everything you need to know."

"Thank you." She glanced at our entwined

hands, then leaned close to kiss my cheek. "I promise I'll do my best to make you proud of me." She yawned, belatedly covering her mouth with her hand. "Sorry for being rude. It's been a busy day."

Pulling her close, I let her put her head on my shoulder. "Rest for a while. I'll wake you when we get there."

"Okay. Thank you."

To my surprise, she did indeed fall asleep almost as soon as the words were out of her mouth. I nearly applauded her performance but let her rest. I told myself I welcomed the silence, but part of me missed the sound of her voice.

As we drove through the gate and on toward the house, I tapped her shoulder, and she jerked awake with a cry of surprise.

"Sorry to startle you, but we're almost home."

Her brilliant smile nearly stopped my heart as she leaned over me to look out the window.

"It's so beautiful!" She clambered across the seat, nearly kneeing me in the crotch in her excitement. "My gosh, you live here, like, all the time? Can we walk on the beach?"

"Perhaps we'll pack a lunch."

It was a complete lie, of course. If she tried to walk on the beach, she'd have to take a swan dive off the cliff first. Even if she survived the fall, the sharks would get her before she could find a way out of the water.

By the time she figured it out, it would be much too late for her.

CHAPTER THREE

NATASHA

Knowing I was making Lachlan uncomfortable, I tried to control the verbal diarrhea pouring out of my mouth.

His house was just so beautiful, I couldn't help it. The recessed landscape lighting sent a golden glow over the Victorian mansion and seemed to touch on the gorgeous gingerbread architectural features. My father's house was modern glass and steel, and arguably nice, but it lacked the warm charm of Lachlan's.

It looked like a princess house, and the cool

ocean breeze smelled fresh and clean with touches of the redwood forest surrounding the property. As he helped me from the town car, I heard dogs barking close enough that I didn't think they belonged to a neighbor.

"What kind of dogs do you have?" I asked, turning in the direction of the barking. "I've never had a pet before. Will I get to meet them tomorrow?"

"No pets?" He cupped my elbow and led me up the short flight of stairs to the charming wrap-around porch complete with rocking chairs.

"No. My father—" I cut myself off before I went down that brutally dark path. "He didn't like animals."

"I keep Mastiffs, and yes. You'll get to visit the kennel tomorrow."

He opened the stained-glass door, and I bit back a gasp. "Oh, wow."

Soaring at least two stories, the front entryway was illuminated with a large crystal chandelier. My heels clicked on the marble floor as I turned in place to take everything in. A tiled fireplace was next to a low table bracketed by two leather club chairs, and there was an antique mahogany hall stand with a large, beveled mirror and several umbrellas in the side racks. A man's raincoat hung from one of the hooks next to the mirror.

The sweeping twin staircases leading up to a landing with a carved railing stole my breath. It was like something out of a fairy tale with thickly carpeted treads and a wooden banister that begged for someone to slide down it.

"Wow?"

"Yeah. I mean, it's really nice." My face heated and I resisted the urge to curl in a ball and die of embarrassment. "No. It's the most beautiful house I've ever seen, but I'm trying to act like a normal human and not go overboard even though I still can't believe I'll be living here."

His laughter surprised me with its warmth. "And you've only seen the foyer."

"I know." I shrugged and looked up into his sparkling blue eyes, wondering if my hot cheeks would melt the theatrical paint off my face. "Sorry."

"I'll give you the grand tour tomorrow." He took my hand and led me to the staircase. "You've had a busy day, and I'm sure you want to shower and rest."

Gulp.

My core clenched as I ascended the stairs. I didn't know if my physical reaction was from nerves or desire. Lachlan was so damned gorgeous. How was I supposed to know how to please him when I'd never even kissed someone?

Except that wasn't quite true. Moisture pooled between my thighs as he escorted me to a double door at the end of the hall. That one kiss Lachlan had given me after our wedding...

I resisted the urge to fan myself as he opened the door. Lachlan's suite was decorated lavishly, with a massive bed made of dark wood piled high with pillows and a burgundy coverlet. A leather couch faced a large television centered between two floor-to-ceiling windows, and there was a small Queen Anne table with two chairs in a corner near a wet bar.

"The bathroom is through that door, and there's a robe for you," he murmured. "Your suitcase has already been unpacked into your dressing room, and we'll have more things delivered tomorrow."

"I have a dressing room?" My heart rate quickened, and I wondered if I'd faint. "Really?"

"You'll see everything tomorrow." Lachlan encouraged me to walk into the most beautiful bathroom I'd ever seen. "Take some time for yourself and relax."

"Sorry... I mean, yes, thank you."

"My pleasure."

He shut the door behind him as he walked out, leaving me to wonder how the hell my father had managed to do one decent thing in his long, evil life and marry me off to such an amazing, kind man. Biting back a hysterical giggle, I stripped out of my dress, tearing it in my haste when I couldn't get the zipper by myself. Using ties I found in one of the drawers, I secured my hair and stepped into the marble and glass shower enclosure.

There was also a sunken tub surrounded by candles and expensive bath products. The bathroom in my father's house was small and utilitarian with a shower stall, sink, and toilet. I hadn't taken an actual bath since I was a kid, but I'd save that treat for when I didn't have a beautiful husband waiting for me.

I giggled but caught myself before I stuck my head under the spray. I didn't dare risk rinsing the makeup off until I had products to replace it. The last thing I wanted was for Lachlan to see what my face looked like.

LACHLAN

Although it didn't happen often, I could admit when I was wrong—not that I'd tell my sister that.

I stripped off my tie and jacket, then rolled the sleeves of my dress shirt to my elbows. After kicking my shoes into a corner, I sat on the edge of the bed and tried to think about what I'd observed.

There was no way Natasha's behavior was fake. She was truly astonished and delighted by something so small as a private dressing room and acted like she'd never seen a bathroom before.

It was more than odd and raised questions I couldn't afford to have answered. Aside from that, her naivete didn't matter. She was simply a means to an end.

However, I could give her one thing. I'd give her the wedding night she'd deserve if I wasn't me, and she wasn't Steve Ashland's daughter. I'd just have to remind myself to treat her like a cherished bride instead of the instrument of my revenge—at least for tonight.

She'd find no succor here. Not from me or Saoirse, or from any of my staff. I'd give her one night of joy before ripping it all away, and I wouldn't allow myself to feel a single bit of guilt.

It would hurt her even more when I introduced her to her new life, which played into my future plans perfectly.

The shower cut off, and a scant few moments later, Natasha opened the door and crept from the bathroom as if she expected me to bite her. My dick hardened at the thought of nipping her tender skin.

"Thanks," she murmured as she approached the bed where I sat waiting for her. "I...um... I tried to leave plenty of hot water for you."

"It's fine." I patted the mattress next to me. "Come. Sit with me."

"Yes, sir."

My cock throbbed at her address, and I swallowed a groan. Fuck. I was beginning to have dangerous thoughts already and I'd known Natasha less than a day.

She would have been so perfect if not for...

Everything.

Damn Saoirse for being right.

Natasha sat on the edge of the bed with her knees pressed together and her hands on her lap—the very picture of a nervous virgin.

Maybe the rumors of her promiscuity had been

wrong too, but even that wasn't going to stop me. In fact, it would make the outcome even better if I took Steve's precious little girl's virginity.

After getting my head on straight, I said, "I know you provided a health screening, but I have one too if you want to see it."

"No, that's okay." She peered up at me through her lashes. "I...um... I also got a birth control shot. If you'd rather start a family right away, it'll wear off in a few months."

Stupid, trusting little bitch.

With that one comment, I hardened my resolve. There was no way in hell I'd breed her and risk bringing another Ashland into the world. Once I thought I could speak without strangling her, I said, "That's a good choice. We'll wait until we're ready."

Deciding to get it over with, I turned to face her, then cupped her cheek in my hand and kissed her. Strangely, she hadn't taken off her makeup, but I didn't care. She tasted just as sweet as I remembered from our wedding, but I missed her citrus and vanilla perfume.

Her cute little whimpers enflamed me as she clutched at my shirt. In a desperate attempt to remain in control, I said, "Stand up and take off that robe. I want to see my wife."

With exquisite obedience, she rose to her feet, then looked at the floor as the robe slid down her curvaceous body. She was made for fucking, with generous hips and a slim waist. The dark curls on her mound would be removed soon enough, but I was surprised to find hair at all—much less the natural bush she sported.

Her tits were more than a handful with brown nipples that hardened to stiff points under my avid gaze. Her alabaster skin was flawless without even a single freckle, save for extensive bruising on the right side of her torso.

She flinched and tightened her hands into fists when I touched one of the marks. "What happened?"

"I...um... I'm just so clumsy." Her husky voice squeaked, and she smiled brightly as she lifted her gaze to my face. "I fell down the stairs."

Christ. If that wasn't the most obvious tell ever...

Considering I'd watched her navigate stairs in four-inch heels without a single misstep, I didn't believe the lie for a second, but I didn't care enough to ask for the truth. Instead, I nodded agreeably. "Poor thing."

"It's okay. It barely hurts at all."

And yet another lie. Judging by the marks, I

wondered if she had a few bruised ribs. I'd just have to be reasonably gentle when I fucked her—at least until those bruises faded.

In six weeks, she'd be gone anyway. I couldn't allow myself to care where they came from.

CHAPTER FOUR

NATASHA

I hated lying to Lachlan, but I couldn't bring myself to tell him the truth. It wasn't because I wanted to protect my father. Far from it, in fact.

Shame kept my lips sealed.

His touch almost seemed to soothe the lingering pain and I relaxed under the gentle glide of his fingertips over the bruises.

"Better?"

I startled at the sound of his voice and quickly nodded. "Yes. Thank you."

"It must have been a heck of a fall."

"I trip over air if I'm not careful."

He laughed, but I wished I could shut up. The last thing I wanted was to draw attention to my flaws.

"I'll kiss them better." Still dressed, he lowered himself to his knees and kissed a path across the marks on my ribs, turning pain into pleasure.

Being naked in front of him while he was clothed did something to me. It was decadent and so achingly good...almost as if he was worshipping me.

Unable to help myself, I threaded my fingers through his thick blond hair and let my head fall back as his kisses fell on my hip, then down to my thigh. Slowly, and ever so gently, he encouraged me to widen my stance, then brushed soft kisses over my belly.

Oh, god. Was he...

"I'm your husband, but you can call me your god all you want. And yes, I am."

Before I could be embarrassed over speaking out loud, he spread my folds with his thumbs and licked my pussy from bottom to top before sucking my clit into his mouth.

I cried out as my knees buckled. Somehow, he managed to hold me up, but I could barely stand as heated shards of pleasure coursed through my body. Instead of yelling at me for making noise, or for the death grip I had on his hair, Lachlan eased a finger into my channel.

The penetration into my virgin hole should have hurt, but the faint sting was quickly subsumed by excruciating pleasure. Without warning, I clamped down on his finger and screamed as I dragged his face closer to where I needed him the most.

My vision flickered into darkness, details of the room swimming out of focus as I came. I couldn't stop the surge taking me down, nor did I want to.

Laughing softly, he rose to his feet and cradled my jaw in one large hand before kissing me. The salty taste of myself on his lips should have been disgusting, but it wasn't. In fact, I wanted more.

"Yes, Natasha. We're definitely doing that again. You won't even need to beg, but I love hearing you scream my name when you come."

"I..." I blinked and tried to make words work. "Wow."

"Only wow?" He unbuttoned his shirt, revealing a muscular chest dusted with dark blond hair. "I'll have to up my game."

"I think I might die of a stroke if you do."

He smirked as he slid his trousers down over his lean hips. "But what a way to go."

My knees wobbled as I stumbled to the bed, desperate to sit before I fell. His cock was...

God, would that massive thing even fit?

"There's my good girl," he crooned as he stalked closer. "Lie back, but don't bother thinking of England. You'll be too busy screaming my name."

"Why would I think of England?"

"Never mind." His smile made me utterly convinced he was a fallen angel. "It's an old cliché Victorian mothers used to tell their daughters on their wedding nights."

"Oh. Sorry."

"I told you to stop apologizing."

"Yes, sir." I bit my lip before another *sorry* came out.

"I forgot one thing." Without waiting for me to answer, he got a small bottle from the nightstand drawer. "Lube to make your first time easier."

I slid up the bed and covered my face with my hands. "So, so humiliating. How did you know?"

"I didn't." He crawled up the bed and pulled my legs apart, then wedged his hips between my thighs. "I guessed, and you confirmed it."

"I'm so—"

He gripped my chin before I could finish and said, "I told you not to apologize. Especially not for being a virgin. It's the best gift I could have ever asked for, and I promise you won't regret marrying me for a single moment."

Trying to relax, I hauled in a breath and nodded. "I trust you."

"Good girl."

He lowered his head and licked my nipple, then pushed my boobs together to suck both of them at the same time as his thick cock bumped against my entrance. God, it felt so good. I lifted my hips, hoping to encourage him, but he didn't take the bait.

Instead, he lavished attention on my breasts, driving me even crazier than I already was.

"Please, Lachlan!" I finally cried.

"Just getting you ready."

He tightened his teeth on my nipple, and I gasped as pleasure shot into my core.

"I'm already ready!"

Giving me that sexy, deliciously naughty smirk, he lifted himself off me until he rested on his knees, then slicked his thick cock with a generous coating of lube.

"I'll go slow and try not to hurt you."

"You won't."

There were all kinds of hurt, and yeah, getting my cherry popped probably wouldn't be comfortable, but I'd embrace the pain. Heck, I didn't truly need the lube because I was already dripping for him.

True to his word, Lachlan was almost too slow, and I pressed my lips together before I begged for more. Instead, I decided to take my fate into my own hands and sank my nails into his taut backside.

Meeting his gaze, I lifted my hips as I pulled him down, making him impale himself inside of me. The pinch of pain was gone before I recognized it, and I cried out as he finally filled me.

For once in my life, I'd taken what I wanted. And god, it was fucking amazing—especially when he glared at me and hissed out a curse before surging into me with hard, consuming thrusts of his magnificently huge dick.

The bed creaked under us as he made love to me, and I wanted it to slam against the wall. I wanted everyone in the house to hear us, but my climax came too fast and too hard to give me a single second to breathe—much less ask for what I wanted.

Lachlan cursed again and stiffened above me. His cock swelled and I felt every single quiver as he erupted inside me. His heavy body fell to mine and I wrapped my arms around him as I sighed happily.

The day finally caught up with me and my eyes closed with him still inside me.

"Totally worth it," I slurred, unable to shut my stupid mouth. "I'm so glad to be your wife."

———

LACHLAN

Damn her.

Natasha fucked me stupid and unconscious, then left my bed. Worse, she'd been a virgin. The pinkish tinge of blood on my cock put paid to my insistence that she wasn't.

I couldn't decide how I felt about it, yet part of me wanted to preen at giving her pleasure for her first time.

Sunlight streamed through the windows, and I cursed softly before getting up to shower and dress in jeans and a worn T-shirt. As I slipped my feet into my shoes, a knock sounded at my door. Thinking it was my errant wife, who would soon take her place where she belonged, I said, "Come in."

To my surprise, Chelsea, my cook, walked in and said, "Your wife is in the kitchen making French toast stuffed with mascarpone, wild berry compote, and grilled sausage. There is also a pitcher of mimosas with fresh orange juice."

"All right. Thank you."

She nodded and took off her apron, then laid it over a chair. "Mr. O'Donnell, I'm not going to stop what you're doing, but I won't help you either. I've arranged for a meal delivery service to meet your future needs."

"Wait." Frowning, I held up my hand to stop her from leaving. "Are you quitting?"

She gave me a brief, humorless smile and patted a stray hair back into her customary gray chignon. "Let's call it a leave of absence. I'll return when your common sense does."

Without another word, she walked out.

"Fuck." I scraped a hand through my hair and texted Saoirse, instructing her to meet me for breakfast, then went downstairs.

It was time to get things started, and judging by Chelsea's behavior, not a moment too soon. Natasha couldn't be permitted to charm anyone else on my staff.

I found my sister already seated at the breakfast table with a plate of food in front of her. Natasha hovered nervously, still wearing a full face of makeup and a T-shirt over leggings.

"Is it good?" she asked after Saoirse took a bite. "I can totally make something else."

Saoirse waved her hand and shook her head as she chewed. After swallowing, she said, "Do not even dare. This is amazing."

"It certainly smells amazing," I said.

Natasha squeaked and rushed to the stove. "Have a seat, Lachlan. I'll make you a plate."

Christ. She was just as dumbly innocent as Saoirse thought. I was going to end up burning in hell next to her father, but I couldn't let my revenge fade just because I was having second thoughts.

I poured myself a mimosa from the frosty pitcher, then leaned close to Saoirse. "Her appointment is in less than an hour. I don't want to hear a word from you. Just take her and get it done."

Before she could reply, I handed her the small box containing the jewelry Natasha would wear for the next six weeks. "Don't fuck up."

"And a happy good morning to you too." Glaring at me, she broke a white capsule over Natasha's drink and swirled it until the powder dissolved. "Also, fuck you without lube."

"Here we go!" Natasha laid a plate in front of me, then fidgeted nervously before I took a bite of sausage.

"Delicious, sweetheart. Thank you." I cut a piece of French toast and nearly moaned at the taste. "You're a wonderful cook."

Her delighted smile nearly stopped my heart, but I ignored the twinge of guilt in my gut.

"I poured you a glass," Saoirse said, holding the doctored mimosa out for her. "And also, I'm low-key kidnapping you for the day. We're going shopping, and maybe to the day spa for mani-pedis."

"Oh, my gosh. That sounds like so much fun." Natasha perched on the edge of a chair and lifted her glass to her lips. After taking a sip, she turned to me. "Do you mind if I go, Lachlan?"

"Not at all, but you should eat first. Saoirse's shopping expeditions resemble a military invasion."

"Gosh, I got so excited, I forgot my own breakfast!"

She returned quickly with another plate, but before she could sit, I asked, "Could I get more of that delicious sausage?"

"Sure thing! I'll be quick."

When her back was turned, Saoirse scowled and broke a second capsule over Natasha's food. In a soft poisonous whisper, she said, "This is so wrong."

"Get over yourself and remember our brother."

"Fuck you."

Smiling happily, Natasha laid a plate full of sausage on the table, then sat next to me. "Please, enjoy. I love cooking, and I'm so glad you like it."

Her eyelids drooped before she finished her meal, and she sagged in her seat. I caught her before she faceplanted into the remains of her breakfast, then tossed her over my shoulder.

"It's time. Let's go."

CHAPTER FIVE

NATASHA

My head ached and I struggled to open my eyes. Brilliant light sent agony through my skull, and I squeezed them shut.

"Should we dose her again?" a male voice asked. "She's waking up."

"We can't," another man said. "She's supposed to feel everything."

Someone touched me between my thighs, and I gasped when I couldn't close my legs. Cold restraints kept my ankles stretched apart, and my wrists were immobile too. My vision hazed and wobbled as I tried to figure out who was holding me.

There were two men and a woman, all dressed in dark blue scrubs. I had no idea who they were.

"Wha—What's happening?" My throat felt thick, and I slurred my words. "Who—"

"Shh." A woman said. "Relax, and this will all be over before you know it. Just be glad we managed to get the laser hair removal done before you woke up."

"You'll feel a pinch, sweetheart," the second man said.

Without warning, a sharp stab of pain pierced my most private spot and I cried out. Before I could try to struggle free, the first man laid a hand on my breast. "Nipples next."

"I'll get her tongue and septum when you're done," the woman replied.

"Vertical and horizontal. He wants four on her tongue," the second male added.

"Christ. Sick bastard."

"We don't judge," the woman said. "We do what we're paid for."

Oh, god. Had my father come back? Lachlan wouldn't hurt me like this, and I couldn't think of any other explanation.

I felt a sharp tug on my right nipple, then a terrible stab of pain. Scant seconds later, my left breast suffered the same fate. I wanted to look down and see what they'd done to me, but my head felt too heavy to lift.

"No, please—" Before I could finish speaking, something hard pinched my tongue and pulled it from my mouth.

I screamed as a flood of agony erupted. Choking, I cried weakly, feeling hot tears on my cheeks as someone pushed gauze into my mouth to soak up most of the blood.

"Could you hand me the makeup wipes?" the woman asked. "I need to clean her face before I do the septum piercing."

I smelled lavender as the woman removed my makeup, exposing what I'd tried so hard to keep hidden.

"Fuck's sake," she muttered as she dabbed gently at the paint. "Next time he asks for an appointment, tell that sick bastard we're busy."

"Please stop," I whispered. "My husband won't let you do this to me."

"Oh, honey." The woman shook her head sadly, sending her blonde ponytail waving. "Who do you think paid for our services?"

I stilled and didn't react when she pushed a needle through the cartilage separating my nostrils. I didn't resist when they flipped me to my stomach and set an electric branding iron to the outer curve of my ass.

Despite my determination to stay silent and unmoved, tears coursed down my cheeks as I screamed.

They released the restraints and helped me to my feet before leading me to stand in front of a mirror. My nose had a ring through it like I was livestock, and matching rings dangled from my nipples. My clit hood had a fucking bell on it that chimed with every step. Even my pubic hair was gone, taking away what little protection I had.

A white bandage covered the brand on my ass, but I didn't want to know what it was. Probably Lachlan's initials. When I took the gauze from my mouth, the studs in my tongue clicked against my teeth and I forced myself to swallow the blood pooling in my mouth.

My stomach gurgled in warning, giving me only a few seconds to drop to my knees next to a wastebasket before everything came up. When I was done retching, the woman cleaned my face and gave me a cup of water.

"Here. It's just saline. Rinse out your mouth and spit in the sink," she said quietly. As if she thought it would help, she patted my back when I obeyed, then replaced the gauze.

I should have known better than to hope.

I should have fucking *known.* God, I was too stupid to live. Why, for a single second, did I think something good could possibly happen to me?

Naturally, no one offered me anything to wear. The dumbass heroine in a dark romance was always naked, and my level of dumbassery reached critical mass the minute I married Lachlan.

To no one's surprise, Saoirse strode into the room but refused to meet my gaze. Without a word, she attached a thin chain to the ring in my nose as one of the men locked shackles on my wrists.

He pulled my hands behind my back, and I heard a soft click as he linked the shackles together.

Gazing at me sadly, the woman affixed a steel collar around my neck and locked it with a hex key, then mouthed, "Sorry."

To Saoirse, she added, "You already have the aftercare instructions. Bring her back if there's any sign of infection."

"Got it." She tugged gently on the chain, making the pain in my nose flare. "Let's go."

I should have poisoned their breakfast.

I couldn't do anything but follow her unless I wanted that fresh nose piercing yanked out. Of course, given my current state of undress, and the fact that my wrists were restrained, I wouldn't get far if I tried to run.

Didn't stop me from thinking about it though.

She led me outside into bright sunlight, then to Lachlan's town car. I couldn't decide whether to be happy it was parked in an enclosed lot where no one could see, or wish it wasn't.

After opening the back passenger door, she laid a thick towel on the seat, then pointed at it. "Get in."

It was hard to talk through the gauze, but I asked, "And if I don't?"

Saoirse shrugged, then pulled a small, black device from the pocket of her slacks. "I really don't want to do this, but you'll get tased and I'll put you in the trunk."

Maybe I should have tried to run, but I didn't delude myself into thinking Saoirse wasn't completely serious about tasing me. I'd long since learned that being conscious and able to see was better than not.

———————

LACHLAN

"I think I might hate you as much as Natasha probably does." Saoirse shook her head as we watched Jerome, my kennel master, lead Natasha to her new home. "She truly thought you'd come rescue her until the piercing artist told her you were the one paying for everything they did to her."

"So?" I shrugged and kept watching as Jerome opened the chain link kennel door and pushed her inside. "It just means I did my job and fucked her well enough to convince her I liked her. Hell, she made us breakfast."

"Don't be crass and stop deflecting." She turned to face me. "I know I agreed to your plan, but Natasha isn't like Steve. It's not right what we're doing to her."

"And you know this after one day?"

My sister laid a hand on my arm and sighed. "Let me ask you something. Were you too busy gloating to look at her face?"

Unwilling to admit I'd been paying too much attention to her curvaceous backside and wishing the brand was healed enough to uncover, I asked, "What about it?"

"Someone..." She hesitated, then added, "Did you beat her last night?"

"No. Why do you ask?"

"Well, someone did," she retorted. "Her face is black and blue. It must have happened either the day of or the day before the wedding. The ones on her ribs are faded a bit, so I think they came earlier."

For a moment, I wondered if Steve knew someone had touched his precious daughter but shook the thought away. Whoever had beaten her wouldn't get another chance, and I liked knowing Steve would never get his own vengeance over the person who hit my wife.

Although Natasha's immediate future would be filled with humiliation, degradation, and debasement, she wouldn't be physically harmed. After I set her free, she could remove the piercings, and her brand would eventually fade. Steve might even be able to find her another husband who would accept my sloppy seconds—especially after I trained her for obedience.

It was more likely she'd find another husband quickly. After all, it wasn't every day a man got to marry a trained slave who was also competent to navigate society. Then again... I wondered if *I* ought to choose Natasha's next husband. I wanted someone who would understand the value of the time investment I'd be making.

I considered a few gentlemen of my acquaintance and made a note to present Natasha to them at her pseudo coming-out party. Fuck, that day couldn't come soon enough, but for now, I had a sister to placate.

After kissing her cheek, I pulled her into a hug. "You know why I'm doing this, but I'll understand if you don't want to watch it happen."

"I've already had the pilot file a flight plan for Boston. I'm leaving as soon as I pack."

"Of course." I accepted her kiss on my cheek, then added, "You'll be back in six weeks, right? I don't want you to miss the look on Steve's face when he sees Natasha."

"I'll be there," she promised. "I just hope you can live with yourself afterward, because I think you're crossing a line."

"Don't worry." I allowed myself a small smile as I gazed at the kennel. "It'll be worth it."

I waited until Saoirse's driver took her out of sight before making my leisurely way to the kennel, but Jerome met me halfway.

"Did she say anything?"

"No, sir. I kept expecting her to beg for her no-account father, but she hasn't said a word." He shrugged. "There isn't much we can do while she heals from the piercings and brand."

"You're the only man I'd trust to take care of her."

"I'm honestly not sure why, sir. I seriously considered strangling her."

Darragh wasn't our only loss that day. Ben, Jerome's oldest son, had died trying to protect my brother.

He scowled, then added, "I'm not inclined to beat on a woman's face but looks like someone already taught her some manners. Maybe that's why she's quiet."

Jerome didn't question me like Saoirse had, but I knew what he was thinking. Unfortunately, I had no idea who hit her. My ignorance irritated me more than it should have.

"Just imagine the look on Steve Ashland's face when he sees her." I slapped his shoulder companionably. "We don't have much time, so get her bathing protocols started today. If she misbehaves, use the strap on the backs of her thighs, but be careful not to hit the brand."

"The dragon tongue is easier to handle and hurts

more, so I doubt she'll act up after the first time I use it."

"I bow to your wisdom, but remember, I don't want her to know why she's here."

"She won't hear it from me." He grinned, then added, "Would you like to watch me work?"

"Wouldn't miss it for the world."

CHAPTER SIX

NATASHA

The concrete was cold under my bare feet, and a breeze from the ocean I'd probably never see raised goosebumps on my exposed skin. In an effort to stay warm, I sat on the floor and leaned against the back wall, doing my best to keep my weight off the brand as I brought my knees to my chest and wrapped my arms around my calves. It didn't help much, but the coolness eased the pain.

Maybe I should have questioned the tall man who had locked me in a dog kennel, but I doubted I truly wanted to hear the answers about why I was here. Besides, I was pretty sure I already knew.

I was here because of my father. He wanted me gone, but he'd also want me to suffer. What better way than to force me into marriage with a man who would treat me like an animal? For all I knew, our marriage wasn't even legal. The document we signed looked like a marriage certificate, but it could have been fake. I wouldn't have known the difference.

At least no one had hit me—yet—and the tall man had unfastened my cuffs from behind my back. They were probably just waiting for all the piercings to heal up before they hurt me again. The thought didn't bring me much comfort, but it was all I had.

Tears burned and I lowered my face to my knees as I wondered if I'd ever be free of people who wanted to hurt me.

I heard voices that grew louder as Lachlan and the tall man walked toward me. God, I was stupid. I almost opened my mouth to beg them to let me go.

"Bath first?" the tall man asked. He was older, maybe around my father's age, with gray hair and hazel eyes. He wore jeans with a leather belt, a plaid flannel shirt, and thick-soled brown boots.

"Yes. I want her prepped when I take her out for her walk," Lachlan replied without looking at me. "Do you have everything you need?"

"Her tail is in my office. If you don't mind getting it, I'll put her in the wash bay."

"No problem."

Wash bay? Tail? I peeked up through my lashes, trying to understand, but all I saw was the tall man unlocking the door to my kennel. As if he didn't have a care in the world, he strode inside, then hauled me to my feet before attaching a chain leash to the ring on my collar.

"Let's go, pet."

When I didn't move, he scowled and spun me around before pushing me against the wall. I heard a crack a split second before a pinprick burst of flame erupted on the back of my left thigh. The pain nearly dropped me to my knees, and I cried out when he jerked on the leash, forcing me to remain on my feet.

"I said, let's go, pet. Don't make me tell you again."

Shivering, I scurried after him, not daring to disobey.

Except...

Compared to what my father would have done, that single blow was negligible. Although I knew it was yet more evidence of a continued too stupid to live moment, maybe whatever Lachlan planned for me wouldn't be so bad.

I wasn't about to press my luck though.

He grunted and led me further into the kennel to what looked like a bathing area for animals. A hose was on a reel next to a rack with long-handled brushes and pump bottles of what I assumed was soap. Rubber matting covered the floor, but the rough surface wasn't any easier on my bare feet.

Lachlan lounged in a chair well out of reach of the bathing area. Strangely, he held something furry in his lap and smirked wickedly at me as he petted it. I took no comfort from the expression as the last bit of my hope faded.

I hadn't even realized there was any left, and losing it hurt more than all my bruises combined. Maybe it was better to give it up. After all, if I didn't have anything left to lose, Lachlan couldn't hurt me again—at least not mentally. I was sure he'd do plenty to my body, but I was used to that already.

The tall man grabbed my right wrist and shackled me in a cuff chained to the ceiling above our heads, before repeating the process with the left. I twisted and tried to free myself, but the cuffs were too tight.

"Bath time," he announced as he picked up the hose nozzle.

Cold water hit me in the chest, and I bit back a

scream. He paid me no mind, and after donning nitrile gloves, proceeded to wash me with a rough sponge and unscented soap. Although his touch was impersonal, he was strangely gentle with my piercings and covered the fresh brand with a towel to keep the dressing dry.

After rinsing the soap from my body, again with icy cold water, he pinched my chin between two beefy fingers and made me look at him. "I'm Jerome, your kennel master. You will call me sir when I tell you to speak. Be good and you won't be hurt. Misbehave, and that will change."

I swallowed hard and tried to nod.

"Good puppy."

I stilled with horror as everything clicked into place in my mind. Lachlan treated me like an animal because, to him, I was. And now he was going to make me act like one too.

Why did he hate me so much?

Before I could react, Jerome loosened the cuffs from the chains attaching me to the ceiling, then pointed at a strange metal bench across the bathing area from Lachlan. It looked like a sawhorse with an extra crossmember about knee-high. "Bend over that bench. Knees spread as far as you can on the bottom bar, and your arms down in front of you. I'll give you a treat if you don't make me tie you down."

Still smirking, Lachlan watched me as I trudged across the wet floor. Gingerly, I rested my knees on the cold steel and bent over the top bar. It pressed into my stomach, making me glad I'd already lost my breakfast. As soon as I dropped my arms in front of me, something cold touched my ass and I clenched as it prodded my back passage.

Jerome slapped the back of my thigh, then said, "Relax, puppy. Breathe in, then let it out."

I blinked back tears as he pushed something hard and unyielding into me, then swallowed a moan when warm water filled my bowels to bursting.

My belly swelled uncomfortably, and I squirmed, trying to decide if it hurt or felt good. Maybe the pulsing fullness was a disconcerting mixture of both, but my pussy clenched and released with filthy need I didn't dare reveal.

Why?

God. Why was I getting aroused by being treated like an animal? I might have been able to handle my father's physical abuse, but this...

This broke my very psyche.

I... God help me, I *liked* it. I especially liked the way Lachlan watched.

"Good puppy." Jerome patted my hip. "Now, after I take out the enema nozzle, you will walk to that toilet and sit before you relieve yourself. I suggest you do your best to keep everything inside until then."

The praise shifted something inside me, breaking me into tiny pieces I wasn't sure would ever fit together again. I tried to ignore the flood of warmth growing in my chest. This was wrong. So, so wrong.

I staggered to the toilet and sat, not a moment too soon. Fouled water rushed from my body and ignoring the constant thrum in my pussy, I breathed an imperceptible sigh of relief as my bowels emptied.

Hopefully, I could remember how wrong this was if... no, *when* Lachlan decided to let me go.

———

LACHLAN

Natasha wouldn't believe me if I told her, but she was absolutely perfect. I'd never seen anyone take so well to pet training. If I hadn't known better, I'd have said she was a fully consenting slave who had enjoyed daily enemas for years.

She didn't even protest the thick, bushy tail attached to a larger than average butt plug. Fuck, she barely winced when Jerome shoved it in her ass and tightened the harness around her hips to keep it in place.

A dark thought intruded into my attempt to understand what I was seeing. What did I truly know about her?

Nothing, aside from rumors and gossip, most of which I'd already learned wasn't true. For all I knew, someone else had been training her. Maybe it was the person who gave her all those bruises.

I shook the thoughts away. If she'd been in train-ing, she sure as fuck wouldn't have been a virgin.

As much as I wanted to see how far I could take her, I needed her to hurt. I needed Steve Ashland to see empty desolation in her eyes and know it came from me, and for that, I needed her broken.

And I had six weeks to do it.

She stood docilely and looked at the floor as Jerome fitted her hands with mitts, but twitched her left shoulder until her long hair covered her breasts.

"Oh, puppy," I murmured softly. "You don't get to hide."

Before Jerome could section her silky tresses for the ponytails that would resemble floppy dog ears, I rose to my feet and went to the supply cupboard for a clipper motor. Without letting her see, I handed it to him.

"Sir?"

"Shave her," I ordered. "I want her head as bald as her cunt."

To my delight, she was already crying when I positioned my chair where I could watch her face. I even got to hear a tiny sob over the sound of the clippers.

Mission accomplished. I leaned back and smiled as hair fell to the floor around her trembling body. Disappointingly, she stopped crying long before Jerome finished. In place of sorrow, her face was an expressionless mask of placidity, which wouldn't do at all.

Jerome shook his head and used a towel to brush off the last bits of hair from her body. "Will that be all, sir?"

"Yes. Thank you."

The click of the chain leash on her collar garnered nothing more than a faint flinch, making me frown. Breaking her had been too easy, but I had plenty of other ways to make her soul bleed.

Smiling brightly, I tugged on her leash. "Ready for walkies, puppy?"

She followed but didn't look at me until I led her to the garden, where several of my men waited. Her chest flushed a brilliant red, but the bruises covered the blush on her cheeks.

Such a pity.

"Time to do your business," I said.

"I—" She peeked up at me and licked her lips. "I don't understand."

I pointed at the ground, then snapped my fingers. "Puppies pee in the grass. Squat and tinkle like a good girl. Make sure to hold your tail out of the way."

"But I..." She bit her lip and glanced at my men, who watched her impassively. "I don't have to go."

"Then I guess you'll squat until you do." I held up a waste collection baggie containing a wipe and a nitrile glove. "Don't keep me waiting."

Tears dripped from her chin as she obeyed, holding her tail up behind her. After several minutes, a small trickle of urine finally fell to the grass.

"Who's my good girl?" I called as I clapped my

hands. My men joined the applause as I put on the glove and cleaned her with the wipe. "Such a good girl to tinkle for Master."

Tears clumping her thick eyelashes, she looked up at me. "You lied to me."

"Oh? When did that happen?"

"You said I wouldn't regret marrying you."

"I said you wouldn't regret marrying me for a single moment," I corrected. "You're going to regret it every moment of every day."

CHAPTER SEVEN

NATASHA

"You're being such a good girl for me, puppy." Lachlan's hateful voice slid over my skin like acid as he thrust his erection into my mouth. "Aren't you glad your piercings are healed? They feel so good when you suck my cock."

I worked the four little balls along the thick length of him, wishing I had the nerve to bite it off.

"Now, swallow and open up. I want to see my cock moving in your throat."

Tears filled my eyes as he cut off my air, but I didn't dare blink. That usually brought a few new stripes from a cane.

Maybe I'd get lucky this time, and he'd decide I didn't do well enough for a reward.

Then again, luck had nothing to do with it. My reward depended on how many people were watching. If it was more than five, he'd make me come. Less than that, and he'd give my ass a benevolent pat before returning me to my kennel.

The whole crowd was watching today.

Hooray.

Hissing out a curse, he stilled inside my throat. His shaft pulsed as thick cum filled my empty belly, making it roil with nausea. As usual, he didn't pull out until my vision darkened and lack of oxygen drove me to the brink of unconsciousness.

"There's a good puppy," he finally said, his breaths slowing as he wiped his dick on my face before tucking it away and zipping his pants. "That does deserve a reward."

He smirked as he touched my dripping core, then held up a wet hand as everyone laughed. "And as usual, my puppy doesn't need lube. She just loves having everyone watch her come for me."

God, I hated that he was right.

I steeled myself as he slid the diabolical toy into my sopping pussy and turned it on. Curved to hit my g-spot and clit at the same time, it was one of very few things that made me struggle to maintain my vow of silence. It was on the highest setting today, meaning I was in for a ride.

The asshole wanted me to beg, but he would be disappointed. Again. All I had to do was hang on. The highest setting meant it would be over soon, and I could go back to my kennel.

The toy vibrated hard against my g-spot as the other end went to work on my clit.

"Think we can make her squirt again, gentlemen? Betting pool is open on how far it goes."

I tuned out the laughter at Lachlan's sick joke, desperate to reach the finish line as my inner walls clamped down on the toy. My belly tightened with the start of my climax, and I gritted my teeth.

Without warning, the vibe stopped. Lachlan pulled it out and shook his head sadly. "Too bad. She didn't want it enough to beg."

God help me, I almost did, but caught myself before a single syllable escaped my lips. It wasn't the first time he'd edged me, but it was the only one of his games that got me even close to breaking.

Using my collar, he pulled me to my feet and traced the red marks on my belly from the steel sawhorse. Tsking softly, he nudged me into my kennel. As he shut the door, he said, "You just had to say please, puppy."

My pussy aching, I laid on my back and stared up at the corrugated steel awning over my kennel, trying to pretend the tail in my ass wasn't there. Thankfully, the weather had warmed enough that I didn't freeze overnight. The thin blanket Jerome had given me helped, but it didn't ease the pain in my hips and back from sleeping on concrete.

He and Lachlan had fought about that blanket. Jerome won, but only because he reminded Lachlan that I might die of hypothermia. Guess my sadistic bastard of a husband didn't want to go that far.

Go figure.

This was my fifth week of confinement. At least, I thought it was. Maybe it was the sixth.

The lengthening days were beginning to run together, but the brand and piercings were healed, so it was probably closer to six weeks.

I wanted to say Lachlan wasn't as bad as my father. Aside from a few whacks with a cane or strap, he never hit me, but what he did was worse than my father could have dreamed.

When the daily enemas and pissing in front of his men stopped bothering me, he made me play fetch on my hands and knees for hours but stopped when my knees started getting scraped up.

Next was the pony cart designed for a person to pull it. There was even a harness with straps to support my breasts when I jogged. That was almost pleasant because I got a chance to walk upright for a change, but the rubber bit made my jaws ache. God, I dragged his ass all over the property in that thing and even got to see the ocean on occasion. It was a great leg day too.

Lachlan had lied about the beach. It was a hundred-foot drop to the surf below. Might have been fun to jump and see if I could drag the cart behind me, but he never let me get that close.

He almost had me with the sensory deprivation tub. Being blindfolded and restrained in a water-filled chamber with a small tube providing oxygen… well, I didn't like it much, but I didn't panic uncontrollably anymore—not even when he randomly shut off the air. It was peaceful in the dark with nothing but the sound of my own heartbeat. Sometimes I held my breath just to see how long I could.

And sometimes I wondered what it would be like to open my lips and let the air tube fall into liquid blackness.

Eating ground chicken cooked with chopped

vegetables and lentils from a dog bowl didn't bother me either. I barely even noticed when Lachlan set up a table and ate in front of me a few times a week. Usually, it was steak, but he had a gorgeous sashimi platter once that almost made me drool. He offered me a piece but took it away when I wouldn't say please.

I hadn't weighed myself in ages, but I was willing to bet I'd dropped at least twenty pounds. Then again, maybe not. I'd put on some muscle, and it wasn't as if I had clothes or a mirror to judge.

Even my new hairdo was growing on me.

Get it? Growing on me? Ba-dum tiss.

Jerome still shaved me a few times a week. I liked not having to mess with my formerly thick and unruly hair, and nobody could use it as a handle to haul me around like my father used to do. Best of all, no more headaches when I put it up, and the constant frizz was a thing of the past.

Heck, Lachlan and Jerome were more diligent about putting sunscreen on me than I'd ever been. For the first time in my life, I had an even, golden tan, and they never let me get sunburned.

The one thing I did not do was speak. Lachlan didn't get a single goddamned word from me. After all, puppies didn't talk.

But Jerome did. He said a lot—especially to a huge Mastiff he called Dante. Although Dante terrified me, I couldn't help watching him launch himself at the training dummies Jerome set up for him.

Jerome would say a single, unintelligible word and all I could see was my father's neck between Dante's powerful jaws. Maybe Lachlan's and Jerome's too. For a moment, I wondered if this was another form of torture, or maybe a reminder of what would happen if I tried to run.

It was probably just more mindfuckery, but I practiced the new word anyway.

I doubted I'd ever find out what it really meant, but to Dante, it meant killing.

Maybe, just maybe, it meant a chance for me.

LACHLAN

"She's been watching me work Dante," Jerome said. "She doesn't do much else anymore."

"I noticed she's stopped pacing," I replied. "Has she said anything?"

"No, sir."

I'd long since given up on trying to make Natasha speak. She refused to say a single word—not even for the promise of a steak dinner seated in an actual chair. None of the other treats I'd tried worked either, and no amount of edging would force a single whimper from between those lush pink lips.

Despite her refusal to talk, and the ever-present mask of patient equanimity I was almost desperate to destroy, she never missed a beat throughout her training.

Holding a ball balanced on her nose? I'd clocked her at almost half an hour before letting her release the position.

She moved like a fucking dressage horse when I hitched her to the pony cart and had learned to eat from her dog bowl without a single scrap of food getting on her face.

I hated it but I hated her more.

Thankfully, she'd be gone in just a few more days. I planned to leave her on her knees for her father to deal with. The divorce papers were already drawn up, and once she signed them, I could forget she existed.

Fitting, considering she refused to acknowledge my existence at all unless I was actively training her.

"Put Dante in the kennel with her until it's time

to send her back to her father," I finally said. "We'll see if that scares her enough to beg."

"Sir, I…" Jerome hesitated, then nodded. "Of course, sir."

The next morning, I got out of bed with a spring in my step and hurried to the kennel. I hadn't met my goal of making her hurt, but I'd settle for fear. Besides, turning her into an obedient slave puppy would drive Steve Ashland over the edge.

If I was very lucky, he might do something that would give me an excuse to cut his miserable throat.

Best of all, once I got rid of Natasha, Chelsea and Saoirse would come back. I was tired of frozen meals and I missed my baby sister.

Jerome had taken the morning off for an appointment after feeding Natasha but would return soon enough to get her ready for her grand entrance. I snickered as I approached the kennel, but my steps slowed when I heard soft, sweetly poignant singing. I didn't recognize the song.

Keeping my steps quiet, I sidled around the corner until I could see Natasha's kennel.

My favorite dog—the one I'd raised from a puppy, and who had thousands of hours of advanced security and defense training—was on his back with his head in Natasha's lap. He gazed at her adoringly as she sang while feeding him her own breakfast.

"God damn her to hell," I whispered.

"Okay, buddy." She scratched his belly and laughed when his leg kicked. "I love you to pieces, but we better get up before the assholes catch us snuggling. If they think I don't hate you, they might not let you stay with me."

That fucking bitch. After almost six weeks of silence, she decides to make friends with *my* dog?

I took a deep breath and walked away. With so little time before she was gone, I just didn't care anymore, and I certainly wasn't going to let her know she'd gotten to me.

There was just one more thing I could do. I couldn't wait to see the look on her face when I took her new friend away.

CHAPTER EIGHT

NATASHA

These days, the only difference between me and Dante was the chain leash attached to my collar—the end of which Lachlan kept wrapped around his fist.

According to my husband, Dante didn't need a leash and got to sit in the front seat because he was a *good boy*.

Hubby dearest wasn't wrong.

Dante was the best dog in the world—at least to me—and I didn't even care that Lachlan had probably wanted him to scare me when he made us share a kennel.

Where most people would see a ginormous

trained killer, all I saw was flappy jowls, more tongue than any one dog actually needed, and kind brown eyes full of love. I was head over heels from the moment he licked my face.

I was so, so careful to never let Lachlan see how much I adored Dante, and Dante seemed to understand the dangers too. He didn't come near me when Lachlan or Jerome were around.

The town car pulled to a stop in front of a large Tudor home with several old-growth redwoods scattered around the outside. Motion-activated floodlights illuminated the property in yellowed patches, but I couldn't see much of the landscaping from my position in the footwell of the back seat. About the only thing I knew of our location was that it was several miles south of my prison.

Dante bounded out the minute the door opened. Before I could follow him, Lachlan held up a hand to stop me.

"You may walk until we're inside. The driveway is gravel, and I prefer my pets unmarked."

He scowled and jerked on my leash when I nodded and didn't reply.

"A thank you would be in order right now, puppy." He tugged harder on the leash, forcing me to my tiptoes. "Or would you rather crawl on the gravel?"

Before I could decide whether or not to answer, he cursed under his breath and strode away, pulling me along behind him.

It was dangerously passive-aggressive, but Lachlan didn't get my words.

Despite being mostly inured to Lachlan's treatment of me, I almost hesitated when he led me through the foyer into a large, open-plan living room. I hadn't been indoors in weeks, and I wasn't sure I liked the walls closing around me.

All the guests were men, and judging by their effusive greetings, they were obviously acquainted with him.

Saoirse was there too, dressed in a gorgeous green cocktail dress that did amazing things for her athletic figure. I hated that she looked so good, but the frown on her face when she gazed at me spoiled the aesthetic. Her mood didn't matter to me though. It wasn't as if my presence in her life was my fault. I'd happily remove myself from the situation if her brother would let me.

I'd been to many parties in my past life. I used to wear couture. The overpriced wine and delicate hors d'oeuvres sometimes made up for the insipid conversation. I never listened to it anyway because I was always too busy making sure my father couldn't fault a single moment of my performances.

And this was a performance too.

I supposed I should have been thankful there were fewer than a dozen attendees, and I wouldn't be asked to speak to any of them. I tried not to notice them watching me, but the gossip would make the rounds before midnight. Thankfully, I didn't see any cell phones catching my ignoble path toward the buffet table.

It wasn't as if anyone could miss a bald woman crawling at a man's side wearing nothing but a nearly sheer black leotard with a hole in the back for a butt plug to which a fluffy tail was attached.

At least he'd had Jerome use actual hot water and decent soap to bathe me, so I didn't smell like the dog kennel I'd been living in since my wedding day.

Lachlan would take any opportunity to humiliate me, and this must have been his crowning achievement. He had a goal though, and I had a good idea what it was.

"Is he here yet?" he asked one of the men.

"According to the guards, his car just pulled into the driveway."

"Good."

God, I hoped I was right about the person Lachlan was talking about.

He hated my father—maybe as much as I did, although I didn't know why. He probably thought presenting me in a dog costume with mitts on my hands and a tail shoved up my ass would drive my father nuts. I might have laughed if Lachlan's plot wasn't at my expense.

The word I'd memorized, and only practiced when I was absolutely sure no one could hear or see slid across my lips, tasting both sweet and bitter. Sweet, because I might finally be in a position to achieve the first part of my goal, and bitter because it would cost me my only friend.

A scant few moments later, my father strode inside, then stopped in the middle of the room when he saw me. He paled and his hands tightened into fists as his eyes narrowed.

"Come, puppy." Lachlan tugged on the leash, making me crawl as fast as I could. "I'd hate for you to be naughty and miss your reunion with your father."

With an especially violent yank, he pulled me along until we were within feet of my father.

I lowered my head and sat back on my heels

with my mitted hands on my thighs as Lachlan dropped my leash and moved ahead of me. Instead of following Lachlan, Dante sidled closer as if to give me comfort.

Or maybe he thought he was protecting me.

"Shouldn't pets be left outside?" my father asked.

"My wife, my rules." Lachlan shrugged, and I was glad I couldn't see the smirk that probably decorated his too-handsome face. "I thought you might want to say hello."

"I don't talk to animals; much less useless little sluts like her."

"Dad?" I lifted my mitted hand to touch his knee, but he pulled back his leg to kick me.

"Don't touch me, bitch."

Dante bared his teeth and growled, obviously sensing my intent. I lowered my head before I let the word I'd practiced leave my lips on the faintest breath of a whisper, audible only to my one friend who didn't deserve what would happen to him. I'd live with the guilt forever.

———————

LACHLAN

Before Steve's booted foot could connect with Natasha's face, Dante lunged for his throat.

"No!" His eyes widening with fear, Steve threw up an arm, but there was no stopping almost two hundred pounds of trained guard dog. Steve had just enough time for one last terrified scream before the sound cut off with a wet gurgle.

Despite years of training and impeccable obedience, Dante killed Steve without his cue word. He didn't make a sound. I heard not a single growl or snarl as he took my greatest enemy to the floor and tore out his throat.

Steve passed from this world almost as quickly. It seemed the devil already had a place for him in hell, but I had to admit to some disappointment. I'd planned to let him spend years thinking about what I'd done to Natasha.

Except... Judging by the things he said, Steve was happy to see Natasha on her knees. Aside from that, he would have hurt her badly if Dante hadn't stopped him. His reaction didn't make sense at all. Hadn't he loved her?

His muzzle and chest covered in blood, Dante returned to his position next to Natasha and sat on his haunches—the perfect picture of canine submission—and also without his cue to stand down. I'd been too shocked to say it, and Dante hadn't given me time.

Natasha didn't move. She kept her head bowed and her hands on her thighs while my men silently waited for my reaction.

None of them were sorry to see Steve Ashland dead, but as usual, Natasha's inexplicable behavior irritated the fuck out of me. Saoirse didn't say a word either, but her hands shook as she poured herself another cocktail.

Why wasn't Natasha crying? Her father was dead, so there should have been tears. For that matter, why wasn't she cowering away from Dante?

"Don't worry about the mess," Finn said, drawing my attention from my perplexing wife. "We'll get it cleaned up and arrange trash disposal."

"Thanks."

Finn hesitated and glanced at Dante. "I know he's your favorite, but he attacked without his cue. We can have the vet out to put him down in the morning."

There it was.

If I hadn't been looking at her, I'd have missed the muscles tightening in her back. She hadn't moved a goddamned inch over her father's death, but Finn's suggestion to have Dante destroyed made her react.

And why the fuck was I seeing the knobs of her spine? Considering I trained her every day, I wasn't sure how I'd managed to miss the absence of her soft curves, but she was all hard edges and angles, with wiry muscle under silken skin.

"I'll take it under advisement. Muzzle him and put him in the front seat."

"Yes, sir."

I couldn't dispel the picture of Steve's foot aimed at Natasha's face, or his vicious scowl when he looked at her. With a start, I remembered the bruises covering her face and body on our wedding day. Swallowing hard, I pushed down my nausea.

How far did his perplexing animosity go? Had it spread to the guards?

They'd lied to my face about Natasha's behavior and personality, telling me the exact opposite of who she truly was. They probably thought I would harm her, and they hadn't been wrong. Even after knowing everything they said was untrue, I'd continued toward my goal.

I caught Finn's arm as he turned to leave. Leaning closer, I lowered my voice to ensure

Natasha didn't hear me. "Catch Steve's driver before he escapes. Show him Steve's body. I want him to know exactly what will happen to anyone who tries to harm my wife. Make sure he gets the message."

To his credit, he didn't react to what must have sounded like an odd request, Instead, he said, "Yes, sir."

I snapped my fingers and crouched to pick up Natasha's leash. Before she could get to her hands and knees, I pulled her to her feet and wrapped my hand around her wrist. "We're going home."

Something was off about this whole situation, and I couldn't abide not having the whole story. A story I should have learned before I married her.

I let her maintain her silence, and her spot at my feet in the footwell, until we got home. Dante was safely muzzled in the front seat with my driver.

There would be plenty of time to get the answers I wanted. I laid my hand on the back of her neck as I thought of all the ways I'd extract information from her.

My town car slowed and stopped close to the steps leading up to my house. When my driver opened the door, I said, "Take Dante to the kennel. I'll deal with him in the morning."

Natasha flinched under my touch, but I let her

reaction slide without commenting. When she turned to follow my driver to the kennels, I tugged her leash and guided her into the house.

And still, she said not a word.

Malicious compliance, thy name is Natasha Ashland O'Donnell.

She could give a fucking masterclass.

With Steve dead, there wasn't any reason for me to keep her anymore. Considering she wasn't even ten when Steve put the hit on Darragh, she bore no guilt herself and was just a means to an end.

Except I couldn't let her go until I knew all her secrets.

And maybe I would think about sharing one or two of my own.

Of course, I was already doing that to some extent. She hadn't been inside my house since our wedding day, but she didn't react to that either. She kept her eyes on her feet as I led her up the carpeted steps to my suite.

Still silent, she followed me to the center of the room. Before she could drop to her knees between the bed and the ensuite, I shook my head and got the hex key for her collar from my pocket.

After unlocking her collar, I let it drop to the floor and took off her mitts, then turned her to face the bathroom. "Remove your tail and wash off the blood. There's a robe hanging on the door. You may wear it when you finish."

She nodded but didn't speak as she walked into the bathroom. I had to treat her like a person, and not only because I needed some answers.

When the door closed behind her, I went downstairs to the kitchen for a bottle of wine and some snacks. She'd be doubly appreciative for the chance to eat something from a plate instead of from a steel dog bowl.

After that?

I wasn't sure. With Steve dead, my taste for revenge was gone. I had no reason to keep Natasha, and a hundred reasons to set her free.

Obtaining a divorce would be easy enough. She'd be so glad to get out, I was betting she'd walk away with nothing but my bathrobe and never look back. If I was feeling very generous, I might arrange for her to inherit what was left of her father's assets. There was probably enough for her to buy a small house and start over.

Except...

I didn't want to let her go.

CHAPTER NINE

NATASHA

Although I wanted to stand under the hot water forever, I rinsed and turned off the taps. I tried not to look at the sumptuous bathroom while I dried off but almost burst out laughing when I spotted a hairbrush on the sink vanity.

I most definitely did not look at the mirror. It was bad enough to know the brand on the outer curve of my ass was there, as were the piercings in my tongue, nipples, and clit hood. I didn't need to see them or my bald head.

It would serve no purpose to get used to such luxury, so I resolved to enjoy it as a one-off experience. Lachlan would move me back to the kennel soon enough. I glared at the tail resting on the sink vanity, wishing I could throw it out the window.

Not that I would. Oh, no. I'd washed the fucker instead, knowing it would be back in my ass before I crawled to my cage.

There'd even been a razor next to the expensive bath products. After gazing at it for several seconds, trying to decide if I could break it apart for the blades, I left it alone. Lachlan didn't seem to care that I looked like a sasquatch. My pussy and head were the only places Lachlan didn't want hair, and after multiple laser treatments, I doubted my pubic hair would come back anytime soon.

Honestly, not having to shave every other day was about the only good thing to come from being married to him.

And Dante too.

I wouldn't let myself forget him. He deserved so much better than me. I sent up a silent prayer, hoping Lachlan didn't hurt him when he...

Squeezing my eyes shut against tears, I took the robe from the hook on the back of the door and put it on. The silk robe would have been the height of decadence to past Natasha. Present Natasha, who hadn't worn clothes in weeks, shuddered under the heavy, scratchy weight of unfamiliar fabric.

Knowing I couldn't delay any longer, I opened the door and crept from the bathroom.

Funny, I'd expected his private space to smell like brimstone, but all I smelled was laundry detergent and lemon furniture polish mixed with his spicy cologne—just as it had on our wedding night.

Lachlan occupied one of the chairs near the wet bar, and there was a bottle of wine on the table in front of him, along with a tray of snacks. My mouth watered, but I didn't look at the food. It wasn't as if I'd get any of it.

"Come sit, Natasha. I bet you're hungry."

How long had it been since I heard my own name?

My toes curled in the thick gray carpeting, but I trudged toward him and perched warily on the edge of the chair facing him, keeping my hands in my lap and my head down.

I heard the rasp of porcelain over wood and hid a flinch when he said, "Eat."

Glancing up just high enough to look over the edge of the table, I saw a serving platter filled with a variety of cubed cheese, olives, glistening purple grapes, and whole-grain crackers, along with slices of what looked like Parma ham and cured salami. I caught the lower edge of a stemmed wineglass and lifted my gaze higher to find it filled with wine.

"Help yourself," Lachlan said before tossing a grape into his mouth.

Whatever he was planning wouldn't end well for me, so I decided to take the offer. At least I'd get a decent meal before I went back to the kennel.

Willing my hand to remain steady, I ate a piece of cheese, and almost moaned. The rich, slightly salty Manchego was like heaven after weeks of eating unseasoned ground chicken cooked with peas, chopped broccoli stems, and lentils. For all I knew, it was the same food Dante ate.

I fucking hated peas.

Belatedly, I wondered if Lachlan had poisoned the food, but he was eating from the same platter. Of course, I hadn't seen him pour the wine.

Fuck it. I lifted the glass to my lips and drank several swallows of a wonderful pinot grigio. Despite knowing I was about to be the recipient of yet another mindfuck, I was going to carpe the shit out of this diem. After all, I had good reason to celebrate. The price would be painfully high, but my father was finally dead.

Lachlan didn't eat much past that one grape, but

kept my wine refilled while I devoured everything in sight. When the platter was finally empty, he divided the last of the wine between our glasses and lifted his in a toast.

After so long without a drop of alcohol, the wine went straight to my head, erasing my sense of self-preservation along with my silence. I probably should have kept my mouth shut, but Lachlan seemed different somehow—like maybe he'd actually listen. Touching my glass to his, I asked, "What are we drinking to?"

He smiled—and it wasn't one of the nasty smirks he usually gave me either. Weird, but probably just more gaslighting to encourage me to let my guard down. Even stranger, he didn't comment on the first words I'd spoken to him in weeks.

"We're drinking to questions asked and truths exchanged."

LACHLAN

"Huh."

I didn't stop her while she finished the last of the wine. After drinking most of the bottle, I doubted she was entirely sober, despite the food she'd eaten. Of course, I wanted her that way. Alcohol tended to loosen reluctant tongues, and I wanted her to speak without measuring her words.

There were some truths I wouldn't ask about. I already knew how wet she got when I took her for walkies and made her squat to relieve herself in the grass where everyone could watch her. I'd heard her breathless whimpers as her bowels filled when Jerome administered her daily enemas. She dripped liquid heat every time the bell attached to her clit piercing chimed, and I knew what she sounded like when she came.

Natasha would deny how much her body loved being degraded, and I wanted deeper truths.

"Huh?" I asked.

"I'm just wondering who should go first in this little game, and what the rules are." She frowned at her empty glass, then added, "It's probably one of your mindfucks anyway, so I guess the rules don't matter."

Hiding a smile, I cocked my head. "You're being very brave right now."

"I'm being very drunk right now," she retorted. "I might as well get some enjoyment out of the game since I already know how it ends."

"Oh? How does it end?"

"It ends with a tail in my ass, and me sleeping on concrete in a cage." She lowered her head but lifted it almost as quickly. "It ends with you torturing me for something my father probably did, and then you'll sleep like a baby in that big, comfortable bed without a care in the world."

"Well—"

"So, I'll go first with my question. Now that Steve is dead, will you let me go?"

"We'll save that one for later," I countered. "Why have you lost so much weight?"

Her cheeks turned pink, but she didn't avert her gaze or try to hide herself. "You've been feeding me the Keto diet from hell for over a month, plus two or three hours of cross training every day. What did you expect?"

"That's fair." And it explained why she'd devoured the snacks. She must have been starving for the fat, salt, and carbs.

Before I could formulate another question, she asked, "Are you going to let me go?"

"Again, tabled until later. I'll tell you when I'm ready."

"Fine." She toyed with her empty glass. "What did my father do to you?"

It shouldn't have surprised me that she suspected the reason behind our marriage. "Twelve years ago, he paid to have my older brother murdered when he signed a contract to buy a piece of property your father wanted. Jerome's son, Ben, died as well."

She winced and her hand moved across the table toward mine, but she pulled back before touching me. "I'm sorry."

"I don't need your pity. I—"

"Stop right there," she interrupted. "I'm sorry he did that, and I'm sorry for your loss, but don't you dare attribute me with an emotion I'm incapable of feeling for you."

I didn't know why her words made me so angry. I didn't want or need her pity, and I certainly deserved her animosity. My hands clenched, but I forced myself to remain still instead of taking my belt to her ass.

After all, I'd wanted her to speak.

"Fair enough. How do you feel about your father being dead?"

"Relieved." She rose to her feet and went to the sideboard, then returned with a bottle of my best scotch. After breaking the seal, she poured a few fingers into her wineglass and sipped it. "Also, sad, but not for him."

My suspicions regarding her relationship with her father grew. Although it was probably the booze, I'd managed to relax her enough to start giving me the answers I should have found weeks ago.

"Why are you sad?"

"Tabled for later."

Her retort came too quickly, and I decided not to push—at least for now.

"Okay. Why didn't you go to college?"

"Also tabled for later."

"All right." I studied her for a moment, then said, "It must be hard to lose your father, especially so violently."

"Nope." She scowled at the scotch in her glass, then went to the wet bar for water. After adding a few drops to her drink, she said, "It was easy as pie, and very satisfying to watch."

I poured scotch into my glass but didn't drink. Instead, I asked, "Where did the bruises come from, Natasha?"

"Which ones?"

"The ones you had on our wedding day."

She snorted and laughed bitterly. "As if you don't know."

"I don't," I lied. I was almost certain I knew

where they'd come from, but I wanted to hear it spoken out loud. "Answer the question, please."

"Huh. That explains why you kept asking." Her brow wrinkled into a frown. "You're apparently too slow on the uptake to figure it out, but my father beat the shit out of me when I refused to marry you."

Fucking bastard.

I should have known—especially after Steve tried to kick her in the face. Before I could think up a reply, she said, "Look. I'll give you all the truths you want, but I truly don't care about yours unless they involve you letting me go."

"Natasha—"

She ignored the warning in my tone. "I got accepted to Stanford to study biochemistry. Dear old Dad found my acceptance letter and broke three of my ribs, then beat me again after I got out of the hospital."

"Jesus."

"You're so cute when you think a leash and public humiliation is going to break me." She laughed and rolled her eyes. "When I was six, I had a kitten. She was just a little stray that found her way onto the property. I called her Floof because she was light gray like a dust bunny. My father eviscerated her in front of me and laid her on my breakfast plate the morning after my teacher reported the whip marks he'd left on my legs. He said it was all my fault because my uniform skirt wasn't long enough to cover them."

"Natasha, stop."

"Spare me the crocodile tears, Lachlan. You asked the fucking questions, so now you get to hear the answers." She pinned me with a derisive glare. "When he was feeling particularly lazy, he'd have his guards whip me instead of doing it himself. The housekeeping staff we used to have looked the other way and pretended they didn't hear me scream because he would have hurt them if they tried to help."

My throat worked as I attempted to swallow the bile filling my mouth. Maybe I was as bad as her father, but the thought of someone touching a child made me sick. "Did they... Did the guards touch you?"

If they had, they'd be dead before they knew it. Knowing Natasha had been abused so horribly was bad enough.

"No. They all said I was too fat and ugly to fuck. Besides, you knew I was a virgin when you married me." She waved a dismissive hand at me as if she was brushing off the abuse she'd suffered. "The teacher's name was Mrs. Price. She had a new baby and a husband who picked her up from school. The day she reported the whip marks on my legs was the last time I saw her. I'm pretty sure my father had her murdered because we had a new teacher the very next day, and nobody at school mentioned Mrs. Price's name even once. When I was eight, he did the same thing to the gardener's puppy after he caught me playing with it. I was in middle school when the cello I used to love ended up in the fireplace along with my favorite teddy bear. He fucking toasted marshmallows over it, even though I never practiced where he could hear me."

"Stop." I held up a hand to cut her off, but she wasn't done. It didn't seem to matter that I didn't want to hear any more. Shame ate at me from the inside. I might have lost Darragh, but she'd suffered a lifetime of systematic abuse at Steve Ashland's hands.

Instead of saving her, I'd continued Steve's despicable work and destroyed an innocent soul.

"Every single thing or person I paid even the slightest bit of attention to ended up destroyed or dead. I didn't dare make friends, much less try for a boyfriend, so you don't get to be surprised about me being a virgin on our wedding night." She leaned back in her chair and studied me with emotionless eyes. "I don't have any proof, but I'm willing to bet he murdered my mother too. So, when you ask me if I'm happy he's dead, the answer is a resounding yes. I want to spit on his fucking grave."

A slow, insidious thought intruded into my brain and I almost gasped when I realized she'd spent days with a dog who should have terrified her, and according to Jerome, had watched his training for at least two weeks.

Hoping to catch her off balance, I asked, "What's Dante's cue?"

Her lips bowed into a faint smile, but I didn't miss the satisfaction gleaming in her brown eyes. "How should I know your dog's cues? I'm just thankful he's a good judge of character."

She was lying. Somehow, she'd figured out Dante's cue to attack and managed to whisper it at just the right moment.

Fuck, I thought I was the cold-blooded one.

"Natasha, I am so—"

"Didn't we agree to no pity?" she interrupted. "I will give you one more truth, and then I want your answer about when you're letting me go."

CHAPTER TEN

NATASHA

Although Lachlan hadn't put away nearly as much booze as I had, he poured himself a double shot and drank it, then poured another.

Strangely enough, I felt almost completely sober. Maybe unloading on him with all the words I hadn't spoken in so long drove the alcohol from my system, along with the poison that had festered in my heart for almost my entire life. It was too bad too. Being drunk might have made it easier to return to the kennel after the tiny taste of humanity he'd shown me.

"All right." He put his empty glass to the side

and folded his hands in front of him. "What's your final truth?"

As much as I wanted to, I didn't touch the last of my scotch. I'd had quite enough already. After taking a deep breath, I said, "I'm sad for Dante because I love him, and I know you're going to put him down. All I ask is that you do it humanely and let me hold him while he passes."

He studied me intently for several seconds, his piercing blue gaze seeming to burrow into my chest. "I'm not your father, Natasha. I'm not going to destroy an animal for doing exactly as he was trained. Your feelings for him are irrelevant."

"Yeah." The answer disappointed me, although I had no idea why. I should have been happy to learn he wouldn't harm Dante. Besides, my feelings had never mattered to anyone in the first place—least of all to the man who only married me to exact revenge on my not-so-dearly departed sperm donor.

"I also know you're lying," he said, surprising me from my morose thoughts. "How did you learn his kill cue?"

"If I tell you, will you let me go?"

"I'm still thinking about it."

Although his answer was better than an outright refusal, I bit back a sigh. He might have been willing to give me this moment before I went back to my regularly scheduled public disgrace and humiliation, but I'd never be free of him unless I could make him let me go.

Then again, I'd done it with my father already. It would just take time to work out another plan for Lachlan.

"I listened to Jerome when he worked Dante with the training dummy. It's not English, so I practiced before I used it."

He barked out a dry laugh. "It's the Gaelic word for rabbit."

"Have you decided if you'll let me go?"

"If I do, what are your plans?" He gave no indication that he cared about my answer.

"I'll go home long enough to pack a suitcase. I don't know what will happen after that."

It wasn't exactly a lie, but even if I had a plan, there was no way in hell I'd share it with Lachlan O'Donnell.

Tucked into plastic zipper bags taped to the underside of a loose floorboard in my closet, I had almost five thousand dollars saved from a decade of lunch money and the pittance of allowance my father usually forgot to give me. I'd also have whatever I could get from selling my jewelry, and there might even be something I could sell in the safe in my father's office. I'd never dared open it. My father would have killed me for knowing the combination in the first place.

Assuming everything was still there, I would have enough to get me far away from California. I wished I had a passport though. A whole ocean separating me from my asshole of a husband sounded like a damned fine idea.

"And what would you want from me?" The skin around his eyes crinkled and he laughed mirthlessly. "We didn't sign a prenup, and I imagine you'd be able to impoverish me after you tell the judge what I've done to you."

"That's certainly a tempting offer." I stood and went to the window overlooking the expansive lawn. It was dark, but I could almost see the tree at the back of his property where he usually took me to *do my business*. How many times had I watered that tree?

Even more stupidly, I had to remind myself how to pee without an audience when I sat on the toilet in his bathroom.

"Natasha?"

"I don't want your money," I finally said.

"Then what do you want?"

"I want Dante." I felt no need to add that I didn't trust Lachlan not to hurt him the minute my back was turned.

"Done." He rose to his feet and crossed the room to a dresser, then tossed a pair of gray sweatpants and a dark blue T-shirt on the bed. "I'll have someone take you home."

He walked out, leaving me stunned. Although I knew he was probably setting me up, I grabbed the clothes and strode into the bathroom. After hanging the robe on its hook, I stared into the mirror, trying to make myself remove the piercing jewelry.

He will hurt you when he finds out...

As much as I wanted to, I couldn't do it. My hands refused to move toward any of the piercings.

If he wasn't trying to fuck with my head, I'd sleep in a comfortable bed with real sheets tonight. I could watch television or make a cup of chamomile tea to help me sleep and soothe my turbulent stomach. I could call a friend and arrange a lunch date—not that I had any friends—and I wouldn't need to worry about my father harming them.

My pussy clenched and moisture dripped down my inner thigh when I thought of how Lachlan smiled when the bell attached to my clit ring chimed. I'd never hear him gasp when my tongue piercings hit just the right spot on his cock. All the times he'd beam proudly when I learned a new trick would never happen again. God, I hated myself even more than I hated Lachlan.

Shamed beyond measure at my body's reaction, I grimly wiped the mess with a tissue and threw it into the wastebasket. The sweatpants were way too big and I hated the way they felt between my legs, but they hid the brand on my ass. It was the only thing I couldn't erase and would forever be a reminder of a man I wished I'd never met.

As I slid the T-shirt over my head, Saoirse entered the bedroom without knocking. She'd changed out of her green cocktail dress into black jeans and a dark gray sweater. Looking me up and down, she said, "Are you ready? I'm supposed to drive you home."

"Yes. Where's Dante?"

"Waiting by the car."

Barefoot, I followed her from the room, down the stairs, and outside. Just as she'd said, Dante sat on his haunches, alive and well, next to a sleek gray Mercedes. His leash was attached to his collar but rested on the ground next to him, along with a canvas shopping bag of dog food. Someone had even cleaned my father's blood off his fur.

"There's my good boy." I knelt and wrapped my arms around him as the tension leached from my spine. A part of me hadn't quite believed Lachlan when he said he wouldn't harm my dog. "Ready to go home?"

He licked my face, making me giggle. After loading him into the back seat, I got in to sit next to Saoirse. Without a word, she drove away from the source of my torment. She didn't speak for the entire drive to my father's house.

Neither did I. I couldn't think of a single thing to say to the woman who had aided and abetted my torture and degradation.

Well, nothing polite anyway. Besides, I didn't want her to change her mind and take me back. It was bad enough that I didn't have the nerve to take out those damned piercings.

She parked close to the steps leading to the front entrance. The house was dark, and I couldn't see any guards.

Maybe it was just as well. I'd intended to fire the guards anyway. I had Dante, and I wouldn't tolerate them anywhere near me—not after all the times they'd watched and participated in all the awful things my father did to me.

Before I could exit the vehicle, she said, "I saw what you did."

"Excuse me?" I turned slightly to look at her but kept my hand on the door. "What are you talking about?"

"Does my brother know you gave Dante his attack cue?"

"Yes."

"Interesting." She turned to look at me, and to my shock, a tear left a silvery trail down her cheek. "Why didn't you have him kill Lachlan?"

"Because I hated my father more than I hate your brother." I opened the door, but didn't get out. "Or you."

Shivering, she pulled a large manila envelope from the slot between her seat and the armrest and held it out. "Your phone is in here with keys to the house and a document transferring ownership to you. There's a debit card too. Don't know how much is on it, but the banking details are there."

I took the envelope and tried not to show my surprise. Things like debit cards and property transfers took time. Had Lachlan planned to let me go all along? I felt some kind of way about that but didn't have the emotional strength to parse through my feelings.

"Thanks, but I'm not staying."

"For what it's worth, Lachlan and I loved our brother. I tried to stop him, but..." She shrugged and didn't look at me. "I'm sorry you got caught up in it. We thought—"

"Does your brother love you?" I interrupted.

"What?"

"Answer the question. Does Lachlan love you?"

"Of course, he does. Why are you even asking me that?"

"Loving someone makes a person vulnerable, don't you think?"

"I have no idea what you're talking about."

"Sure you do. You and Lachlan thought my father loved me. You thought you could hurt him by hurting me." I paused and met her gaze, letting my lips turn up into a smile when she blinked nervously and looked down. "Why are you sweating, Saoirse? Why do your hands shake so badly?"

"I—"

"Ask yourself what I might do to make your brother hurt." Leaning close, I tucked a lock of hair behind her ear and felt her tremble when I stroked her cheek. The perfume of her fear smelled so damned good. "Tell Lachlan I just learned how to give him more pain than he could ever imagine. Most importantly, tell him I'll like it."

Hoping my threat would stick, I got out, then grabbed the shopping bag and opened the back passenger door to let Dante out. We walked away without looking back.

———

LACHLAN

The legal-sized manila folder rested on my desk, but I didn't open it.

Not yet.

I knew what was inside though. It was the much-amended document that would end my marriage to Natasha.

Behaving true to type, she stubbornly crossed out and initialed every line item regarding transfer of assets to her. She'd even caught the generous alimony I tried to hide in another section. I couldn't go outside the legal dissolution of our marriage and put money into the bank account I'd set up for her either.

The disagreeable brat closed it and mailed me a cashier's check, along with the debit card shredded into razor-edged confetti—probably in the hope I'd nick an artery on one of the pieces. She hadn't spent a penny of it—not even for the fee to cut the check. It was more than odd. I'd have sworn I left Steve Ashland without any assets, and I couldn't figure out how she was supporting herself.

I didn't blame her for the other package she'd sent containing all her piercing jewelry, her wedding ring, and a large pile of dog excrement.

Although I still had the video feed from cameras I'd placed around the property, judging by the sale sign at the end of the driveway, she didn't plan to stay.

I couldn't even track her phone anymore. As if she'd known I'd added a hidden locator to the device, she set it in the driveway and drove over it several times with a large SUV. On a whim, I decided to try the number, only to find it had been disconnected.

At least she hadn't found the GPS tracker on her vehicle—not that she went anywhere. Aside from weekly supermarket trips, she didn't leave the property. Instead, she played fetch with Dante and took him for long walks while workmen hauled out her father's tacky furniture and replaced it with more tasteful selections.

She was probably staging the house for sale, but I couldn't help hoping she'd stay. It would be safe for her now that her father's guards were nowhere to be found. Fuck. They didn't deserve to breathe her air, much less breathe at all, but my warning, given to Steve's driver before he could escape, would keep them far away from her.

Only one person visited her. A middle-aged Japanese woman came every day at nine in the morning and left at noon. According to the magnet decal on the back of her minivan, she was from a mixed martial arts studio. A bit more research revealed her to be a Krav Maga instructor—which explained Natasha's significantly more muscular figure and all the gym equipment she'd had delivered.

God, I missed her lush curves. At least she was gaining the weight she shouldn't have lost in the first place. Her hair had grown back into a short cap of bouncy curls that highlighted the chiseled bones in her face. The new hair suited her, but I missed her innocently rounded cheeks.

As I watched her make the trek to the mailbox at the end of her driveway, Saoirse walked into my office without knocking. I scowled when she arched a brow at what I was watching.

"Christ, Lachlan. Aren't you bored yet? You've been creeping on that poor girl for six months."

"Shut it." I leaned closer to the monitor and narrowed my eyes when Natasha pulled something from the mailbox and jumped up and down before crouching to hug Dante. "Don't you ever fucking knock?"

"No."

Resolving to ignore my annoying sister, I turned my attention back to my laptop. "What the hell is she so cheerful about?"

I liked seeing Natasha happy but hated it at the same time. After everything I'd done to her, I had no right to feel that way either. Worse, I was self-aware enough to know what I was doing was beyond toxic for both me and Natasha. I just... I couldn't let her go.

When had she become more than a means to an end?

"Still don't know why you're so damned curious when you know she hates you." She propped a hip on the edge of my desk. "If you have to keep digging into Natasha's private business, catch a screenshot of the video and enlarge it until you can see what she's holding."

When I didn't immediately reply, she rolled her

eyes and turned my laptop to face her. Within moments, Saoirse had a somewhat blurry still image on the screen. She squinted at the laptop, then laughed. "Looks like Natasha got herself a passport. Guess that's your sign to stop tormenting yourself with what you'll never have."

"Piss off, Saoirse."

"Gladly. I'm tired of seeing you all butthurt over something that's entirely your fault—particularly after I begged you to stop." She sobered and touched my shoulder. "A word of advice first. I want you to remember in vivid, technicolor detail what Natasha did to Steve Ashland. You need to remember she was virtually naked, leashed, and powerless when she had her dog rip out her father's throat, and you *especially* need to remember how much she wants us both dead."

"Dante wasn't hers," I muttered, refusing to acknowledge Saoirse's point—especially since I was wrong. The damned dog had been Natasha's from the moment I forced them to share a kennel.

"That's what you got out of everything I said? For fuck's sake." Saoirse closed the laptop and wrapped her arms around herself before moving to the window overlooking the tree where I used to make Natasha piss like an animal. "You didn't see her face, but I watched her. She was so cold. No emotion, no surprise. No...nothing. And when she looked straight through me with those utterly expressionless brown eyes like I'd be next if I didn't stay perfectly still... Well, I get nightmares sometimes, which would probably delight her to no end."

"Saoirse—"

"You didn't hear her tell me she'd make you hurt." She shuddered and her breath hitched. "God help me, I believed her. The whole way home, I felt like there was a monster built of Natasha's rage hiding in my back seat. Fuck, I still sleep with my Ruger—when I can sleep at all."

I rubbed my forehead and sighed. "I'm sorry."

"You know what really keeps me awake at night? I could have been Natasha's friend, and you could have been a good husband to her. Helping Steve's daughter live a safe, happy life without fear of mistreatment would have been the worst thing we could have done to him." She laughed bitterly. "Instead, you took a horrifically abused little girl and turned her into a sociopath. Congratu-fucking-lations."

As I was wishing I'd never told her about Natasha's past, she shook her head and walked to the door. She stopped and laid her hand on the doorframe, then added, "Coulda, shoulda, woulda, I guess. I've already lost one brother, Lachlan. Let her go before I lose you too."

"Leave. Close the door behind you."

She slammed it, and I winced at the sharp crack before opening my laptop. I loved my sister. We were all each other had left. As much as I hated her words, she was right.

I'd gone too far. My actions forced Natasha to kill, and she was training her body to do it again if I dared come near her. She had no idea about the turmoil she caused, and no idea how my heart leapt and sank every time I saw her.

And I could not stop. She was worse than cocaine in the way she sent me to the height of ecstasy, only to kick me into blackest despair. It was only fair, considering I'd done the same to her multiple times a day for weeks.

The cameras followed as she skipped up the driveway to the house, Dante at her heels. I didn't have audio, but I could almost hear her laughter.

CHAPTER ELEVEN

"So, where do you think we should go, Dante?"

My dog didn't answer. Instead, he resettled himself in his jumbo-sized memory-foam dog bed and let out a loud snore as he tucked his stuffed bear under one paw. I smiled and reached down to scratch his ears.

I might have been training my body to kill, but he wouldn't be asked to do it again.

With the funds from the offshore bank accounts I'd found in my father's safe, I could go anywhere. I could finally attend college, travel, or even just buy a house somewhere far away from the almost ex-husband I refused to name and be a hermit for the rest of my life.

Some days I could forget what he'd done to me. Mostly not, although every day he didn't show up to take me back to the kennel made it easier to think I'd be okay. At least I'd finally gotten up the nerve to take out my piercing jewelry and send it to him with a pile of Dante's shit.

And some days, I could even get myself off without thinking of all the depraved things that used to make my pussy clench with the visceral need only he could assuage.

I had a service dog vest for Dante so he didn't have to travel in a crate. Granted, he wasn't exactly a service dog, but he was extremely well-trained. Besides, my anxiety spiked whenever I couldn't see him, so I supposed that made him an emotional support animal with better manners.

After sitting on the comfortable microfiber couch, I spread printed travel brochures across the elegant French provincial coffee table. Although I told myself the furniture was only for staging the house for sale, I loved the new décor. Now that every trace of my father was gone, I almost wished I could stay.

Unfortunately, his poison permeated the walls

and spread into the soft furnishings. If I looked at it sideways, even the neatly manicured lawn appeared to bubble with tarry black, and the landscaping seemed to wilt more with every passing day.

The house needed to go to a new family who could replace his evil with happiness.

"Maybe we should take this transatlantic cruise to Greece," I mused out loud. "I'm thinking do the whole *Mama Mia* thing. It would totally count since I'm your mom, and I'll be single when your former dad gets off his ass and signs the papers. All we'd need is a run-down inn."

When Dante didn't answer, I added, "Or how about Iceland? I've always wanted to go there."

The doorbell rang and I glanced at the time on my phone before rising to my feet. "Misaki is way early. We'll have to decide on our destination after lunch."

Before opening the door, I checked the video from the security feed and froze, my belly clenching with a mix of fear and anger.

Mostly anger.

I slid my new shotgun from the umbrella stand, then unlocked the multiple deadbolts securing the door and slowly opened it.

"Jerome."

Dressed in his usual faded jeans and plaid flannel shirt, the kennel trainer kept his eyes fixed on the shotgun.

"Hey, Natasha." Swallowing hard, he took a step back. "I...um—"

"Since when do you use my name?" I interrupted. "Did Lachlan send you?"

"No!" He shook his head vehemently. "I didn't come because of him."

I caressed the trigger guard with my thumb. "Then what do you want?"

"I'm going to put my hand in my shirt pocket." When I nodded, he pulled a gray tabby kitten from his pocket and held it out to me. "It won't make up for what we've done, but I hope you like her."

"You're giving me a cat?" I blinked at the tiny mound of fluff curled up asleep on his large palm. "Why?"

"We took your kindness and destroyed it, Natasha," he said quietly. "I'm hoping the kitten will help you get it back. Cats are good at doing that sometimes."

Stunned, I took the baby from Jerome and decided to cancel my training, so I could figure out how to take care of her. "Wow. Okay. Thanks, I guess."

"You're welcome." Jerome hesitated, then asked, "How's Dante?"

"He's good." I heard the click of Dante's nails on the hardwood and pushed the door with my shoulder to let him out.

Strangely, Dante stumbled, his front legs almost buckling when he tried to reach Jerome. His head listed to the side, and he panted heavily as his pupils narrowed to pinpricks.

"Dante?" Trying to control my panic, I slammed the shotgun into the umbrella stand and set the kitten on the floor as I dropped to my knees. "C'mon, buddy. Tell me what's wrong."

Jerome nudged me out of the way, then crouched to examine my dog. "Go on and bring my truck close. We need to get him to the vet."

"What's wrong with him?" I asked, swallowing the tears thickening my voice.

"Move it, Natasha. Now."

The barked order got my feet moving before I realized it. Although I hated my body for its automatic obedience, I couldn't deal with it now. My baby was in trouble.

Thankfully, the keys were in the ignition. Blinking rapidly to stop my burgeoning tears, I moved the truck as close to the stairs as I could get. I got out to help, but Jerome simply grunted and lifted Dante into his arms before laying him carefully on the bench seat.

After covering him with a blanket, he got behind the wheel and rattled off an address. "Follow me and bring the kitten."

Without waiting for an answer, he drove to the end of the driveway and waited for me.

I darted inside for the cat and slammed the door behind me before racing to the garage. Every mile sent a fresh shard of terror into my heart, and I was sobbing long before I pulled into the lot and parked. Jerome's truck was empty, meaning he and Dante were already inside.

The SUV's engine ticked as I sat frozen. I needed to get to Dante, but I couldn't see...

Couldn't make my feet or my brain move to the logical conclusion. Could barely breathe through my sobs.

From the passenger seat, the kitten made a tiny peep, forcing me from my mental stalemate. I swept her up and forced myself to walk into the clinic.

Jerome rose from a chair next to an elderly woman who had a poodle on her lap. After wrapping a thick arm around my waist, he led me to sit next to him, then handed me a threadbare bandana.

"Doc's got Dante. They think he had a stroke." He took the kitten and tucked her into his pocket.

"He's not..." I coughed to ease the thick wad of tears from my throat. "Will he be okay?"

Jerome sighed but didn't immediately reply. Finally, he said, "Dante is almost eleven."

"That's young, right? He's going to be okay."

I said the words with every bit of conviction I could muster, but they sounded false.

He turned to face me and shook his head sadly. "Natasha, he's old. Large-breed dogs rarely live more than ten years or so. Might be best to—"

"No! That is not fucking happening!"

My scream startled the elderly woman. Her eyes wide, she clutched her dog to her chest and hurried from the clinic.

Dante's illness wasn't Jerome's fault, but I had no other outlet for my rage. Fixing my helpless fury on Jerome, I wrapped my hands around his thick neck and squeezed. "This is your fault. Your fucking fault!"

LACHLAN

Although I shouldn't have come, I parked next to Jerome's truck and got out.

I was the last person Natasha would want to see—especially when she was grieving her beloved dog—but I couldn't stop myself.

Natasha had already been through too much, and I couldn't stand the idea of letting her lose Dante without at least trying to help her. Jerome's call just gave me an excuse to see her, but he hadn't mentioned why he'd been at Natasha's house in the first place.

Thankfully, Saoirse hadn't been around to talk me out of it.

Maybe the vet could bring him back, but I doubted it. Dante was old, and although he had no health issues aside from a touch of arthritis, he'd been living on borrowed time for over a year.

Before I could enter the clinic, a police cruiser pulled in and stopped in the middle of the lot. Two officers exited the vehicle and strode to the entrance, then opened the door, allowing a feminine scream of rage to escape.

As I hurried across the parking lot, the officers carried Natasha, who was kicking and shouting a virulent stream of curses, to the cruiser. She was dressed in a pair of tight spandex shorts and a sports bra, and her feet were bare.

One of the officers held her bent over the hood while the other slapped cuffs on her wrists as he read her Miranda rights. Ignoring her angry screeches, they locked her in the back of the cruiser.

Jerome walked from the clinic. Rubbing his throat, he veered off to intercept me.

"The staff called the cops," he murmured, his voice hoarse and scratchy. "She tried to strangle me when I told her Dante probably won't make it."

"Not your wisest moment," I replied. "I'll take care of it."

"I'll just stay out of range." Despite his words, he followed me at a distance. "At least she left her shotgun at home."

"Officers," I called as I strode to the cruiser. "I'm very sorry for the inconvenience. My wife's dog is dangerously ill, and she's understandably upset."

From the back of the cruiser, Natasha narrowed her eyes at me, then turned away, making her feelings clear. I was guessing she'd rather go to jail than talk to me, but I could give her something she'd be a fool to refuse.

Unfortunately, I wasn't sure if her common

sense would outweigh her sheer, bloody-minded obduracy. She'd cut off her whole damned head to spite her face and throw it at me like she was a major league pitcher.

"Mr. O'Donnell, sir," the taller of the two said, obviously recognizing me, "people generally don't commit aggravated assault while their pets are at a vet's office."

"We just lost our old mutt," the second officer replied. "It's never easy."

"It isn't," I agreed. "So, what do you say we forget this happened? I'll take care of Natasha while we deal with our loss."

"I'm very sorry, sir," the taller one said. "Unless the victim decides not to press charges, we have to take her in."

"I raised Dante from a puppy. I can't be upset with Mrs. O'Donnell because I feel the same. He was —" Clearing his throat, Jerome corrected himself. "Dante *is* a fine dog."

"I'll make sure Natasha stays calm and give her as much support as she needs. Do we have an agreement?" I asked.

The officers shared a look, and the taller one nodded reluctantly. "I guess we can do that," he said. "We don't want any trouble with the O'Donnell family, but I doubt the staff will let her in again."

"Thank you. I appreciate your service and your understanding during this difficult time."

I waited—not very patiently—while they helped Natasha from the back of the cruiser and removed the cuffs from her wrists. Hate filled her brown eyes, and she tightened her hands into fists, making veins pop in her arms.

Before she could escape, I pulled her into a tight hug and positioned my lips next to her ear while her scent of vanilla and citrus filled my lungs, making it hard to breathe.

She stiffened, her muscular shoulders bunching under my touch, but didn't try to get away. I hated that she felt like she had to prepare her body for battle.

Fuck, I missed her so hard it hurt.

"Don't speak. I need you to listen. If you want to see Dante again, you're going to chill the fuck out and pretend to be my doting wife."

"And if I don't?"

I should have known she wouldn't make things easy, and I had no idea why I still hoped for a more positive outcome when she had every reason to want to dismember me and throw the pieces off a cliff. Although I didn't want to antagonize her, I decided to give her a few hard truths in the desperate and probably futile hope that she'd listen.

"You go to jail, and you don't get to see your dog. Choose wisely."

CHAPTER TWELVE

NATASHA

My wrists still tingling from the touch of cold steel handcuffs, I braced myself and tried not to vomit when I kissed Lachlan's cheek.

It was a momentous occasion, after all. We hadn't kissed since our wedding day.

Didn't stop me from wishing I had a knife to slip between his ribs, but the scent of his spicy cologne made my belly quiver as my pussy spilled a flood of moisture into my panties.

I couldn't decide if I hated him, or if I hated myself for what he made me feel. It would take a lifetime of therapy to help me figure it out.

"I'm so sorry for my behavior, officers." Giving the cops a smile I hoped didn't look like a grimace, I pretended to wipe a few tears from my eyes, then turned to Jerome. "And I'm really sorry for trying to hurt you, Jerome. You were only doing your job, right?"

Judging by the expression in his dark eyes, he knew exactly what I was talking about. He probably also knew I was only sorry for not popping his head like a fucking grape.

"We're good, Mrs. O'Donnell." He shuffled his feet, then added, "I'll go check on Dante."

"We'll go with you," Lachlan said, keeping his arm around me. "Dante will need his family close by while he recovers."

Somehow, I managed not to laugh. We were not, and never would be, a family. The only reason we were still married was because Lachlan was being a stubborn bastard and hadn't signed our divorce papers yet.

Pushing the hateful thoughts aside, I tried to calm down and focus. Lachlan was right about one thing. Dante needed me. He'd need his mom to help him over the rainbow bridge and into heaven where he belonged.

A tear—a real one—slid down my cheek, and I

prayed. I could not think about Dante leaving me, and if Lachlan got me back into that clinic, I might possibly consider the idea of letting him keep breathing.

I didn't protest when he kept an arm around my waist as he escorted me inside, where I gave my most heartfelt apologies to the staff.

They were real ones too. I shouldn't have tried to end Jerome in their presence.

Once the staff were assured I wouldn't go postal again, they let us back into an exam room. Dante was nestled in a mound of soft blankets and had an IV line running from his left foreleg. A respirator was fitted over his blunt muzzle, but he appeared to be resting comfortably. To my surprise, the kitten was curled up next to his head. Her little tummy was round, and I heard her purr as she made biscuits in Dante's blankets.

"We didn't think you'd mind," the vet, a middle-aged woman, said. "Dante's heart rate stabilized when we put her with him."

"Is he—" More tears flowed, and I covered my mouth with one hand as I stroked his coarse fur with the other. "Will he get better?"

She glanced at Lachlan and stepped out of my reach. "He had a stroke, Mrs. O'Donnell. We're keeping him under mild sedation to give his brain a chance to recover."

"Will he... Will I have to..." I squeezed my eyes shut and resisted the urge to curl up on the exam table with my baby. "Will I have to let him go?"

Her gaze softened and she shook her head. "No, not at this time. We don't know his prognosis yet, but he's not in any pain. It's possible he'll recover."

She smiled and gave the kitten a gentle pat. "This little one is helping, and since she needs some care as well, we'll keep them together. If you could bring one of Dante's favorite toys and maybe a blanket he uses, that would also be helpful."

"I'll have someone deliver a few of his toys," Lachlan replied.

"No!" When the vet flinched, I added, "He'll want his stuffed bear. He likes to cuddle it when he sleeps. And his memory foam bed too because his joints get stiff, and—"

"Shh, love." Lachlan pulled me against his chest and rubbed my back. I hated how nice it felt. "We'll get everything."

"Nothing from his kennel," I warned. I didn't want those horrible hard rubber toys that looked like human limbs. I refused to tolerate anything that would remind either of us of when Dante was a trained killer.

"Okay." Lachlan didn't stop stroking my back. "Just his bear and his bed."

"And we'll care for him to the best of our ability." The vet bent to kiss Dante between his ears. "I've been taking care of this old gentleman since he was a pup, and I promise I won't let him go without a fight."

My sobs burst free, stealing my ability to breathe. Crooning softly, Lachlan supported my weight when I would have collapsed and just held me while I cried.

The tears were for Dante, but even more for myself. For once, I might get to keep someone I loved.

———

LACHLAN

"I want around-the-clock care for Dante at my house."

To her credit, Dr. Mendez didn't blink at my request. "He'll need a vet plus a tech and equipment. It'll cost you."

I picked Natasha up to carry her from the clinic, but she wouldn't stop crying, and kept her arms wrapped tightly around my neck. "Talk to Jerome to arrange payment. I'm taking my wife home."

Every one of her tears sent a vicious pulse of agony into my chest as if she was trying to carve out my heart.

I could have been her friend. You could have been her husband.

Coulda, woulda, shoulda, indeed.

My sister's words driving into my brain, I carried Natasha from the clinic. I wanted my wife and her dog home where they belonged, and neither of them would be living in that goddamned kennel.

They'd have the largest guest suite, including everything Dante needed to get better—at least for long enough to allow Natasha time to come to terms with losing him. Sadly, it was part of sharing one's life with a pet. They never seemed to get half as many years as we wanted them to, and it was especially true for large-breed dogs.

As I settled her into the passenger seat of my car, I wondered if she'd come back to me if I showed her I wasn't a complete asshole. I had to try, even though the idea was completely self-serving. If I did it right, I might, just maybe, get my wife back.

I'd have to be careful though. Instead of throwing her into the deep end of my sexual depravity, I'd have to coax her gently, without force, and remind her of how good it had been.

All of that could come later—after Dante was better.

"Where are we going?" she asked without looking at me as I turned left out of the lot.

"I'm taking you home."

"You're going the wrong way."

"If you plan to stay with Dante, you'll be doing it at my house. I already set things up with Dr. Mendez."

Her face reddened and I steeled myself for the oncoming storm.

"If you think for one goddamned second that you're putting my dog into that disgusting kennel, I will—"

"No. He's going to share your suite."

She opened her mouth—probably to tear me a new asshole—then shut it. "Not your room?"

"You'll have your own on the other side of the house."

After several seconds, she said, "Fine. I want a deadbolt on my door. I also want a gym installed to my specifications at your expense before the end of the week. My trainer visits every day between nine and noon. Until the gym is installed, you'll clear the west lawn for my use."

"Done. Anything else?"

"Yes. I don't want to see you. I don't even want to know you're alive. That goes for Saoirse too, and I'll be carrying a weapon at all times in case either of you decide to fuck around and try for me."

Because I was a sick bastard, my cock thickened as I imagined her armed and ready to kill.

Her phone rang, cutting off my agreement. She hadn't left me much choice. If I wanted her back, it had to be on her terms.

"Misaki, hi. I'm sorry I was a no-show for training today. Dante got sick."

She glanced at me as her trainer replied, then said, "Thank you. I'm hoping for a good outcome. Anyway, I'd like to move my lessons to another address if that's okay. Also, bill me for the missed lesson, but that one and all future bills go to Lachlan O'Donnell until I say otherwise."

Ouch.

I didn't protest though.

After giving her trainer my address, she ended the call. "When can I expect my dog?"

"Probably not until late this afternoon. It will

take time to get the equipment in place and work out scheduling for the staff."

"Okay. I want someone to get my car from the clinic."

"All right."

"Good."

"Are you planning on going somewhere?"

"Yes."

And...we were back to monosyllabic answers. Deciding to pick my battles, I let her lapse into silence until we got home.

CHAPTER THIRTEEN

NATASHA

Keeping space between us, I followed Lachlan into his house. Sadly, he didn't seem to be afraid of me, but he was definitely wary. I supposed that was good enough.

"I sent all the staff home," he said as I followed him to a ground-floor guest room. "This is yours. I'm afraid we're on our own for cooking and cleaning."

"It's okay. I'll make sure I stay away from the vet. It was pretty obvious I scare her."

"You're not going to hurt the person who can make your dog better," he replied as if he truly believed it.

Before I could respond, he added, "There's clothes in the dresser to tide you over until you can get back to your place."

"Okay. I'm going to clean up."

I walked into the room and shut the door in his face, then turned the lock set into the knob. It wouldn't keep Lachlan out if he really wanted in, but I'd have plenty of warning if he decided to invade my space.

The guest suite overlooking the woods to the south wasn't as large as Lachlan's room, but it was comfortable and decorated in soothing shades of pale green and gray with oak furnishings. The dresser was full of unisex clothing in assorted sizes and colors, socks, and both men's and women's underwear still in their packages. There were even several pairs of new slippers in the closet.

After grabbing fresh clothes, I went into the bathroom and locked that door too. Wrapped toothbrushes, toothpaste, and bathing products were in a large basket on the sink vanity, along with a small first aid kit containing a few basics.

"Amateurs," I muttered. There wasn't even a suture kit. After growing up with Steve Ashland, I was probably as well-trained as a military field medic, so the one I had at home was in a rolling tackle box.

I showered as quickly as I could, and after drying off, I dressed and gave my short curls a quick scrunch with my fingers.

God, I loved my new hair. It was probably stupid to look for silver linings in my unwanted marriage to Lachlan, but my therapist encouraged it. Surprisingly, it even helped sometimes.

She wanted me to think about what my life would look like if I forgave him for what he'd done to me. Sometimes, when I thought about Dante, I could almost picture it.

Without Lachlan, I wouldn't have met Dante, and my father wouldn't know I was the one who killed him.

Big, sparkly silver lining right there!

My stomach rumbled, and I snapped my fingers for Dante before I remembered he wasn't around to have lunch with me. Tears burned and I wiped them hurriedly before finding a pair of slippers in my size. I couldn't think about losing my baby dog.

Steeling my spine, I left my room. Oddly enough, I remembered the way to the kitchen.

Before I reached it, I heard the blare of a smoke alarm and broke into a run. I stopped cold when I found Lachlan spraying the stove with a fire extinguisher.

"Shit!" He set the extinguisher on the counter and sighed as he opened a window to allow the smoke to escape. "Goddamnit. What a mess."

"What happened?"

"Nothing." Using a potholder, he grabbed a blackened skillet dripping with foam and tossed it into the sink.

"Um..." I moved closer and peered at the stove. The cooktop didn't appear to be damaged, but it was crusted with burnt food. "This doesn't look like nothing."

"Fine." Still glaring at the skillet, he crossed his arms over his chest. "I was trying to make French toast, but the fruit stuff boiled over, and then the sausages decided to catch on fire."

My mouth fell open, but I couldn't think of a single thing to say when I realized he'd tried to recreate the first and only meal I'd ever cooked for him.

"French toast." Some odd sort of sound bubbled in my chest, and I coughed to dislodge it. "French toast?"

"And that fruit stuff you made, plus sausages."

Scowling at the stove, he added, "Guess we're having sandwiches instead."

"French toast." I coughed again, but the sound escaped and turned into hysterical laughter before I could stop it.

"That's all you have to say?" His cheeks reddened and he turned his glare on me, but a faint smile blossomed on his lips. "You forgot the sausages and fruit stuff."

Unable to control it any longer, I sank into a chair and kept laughing.

———

LACHLAN

Her giggles eventually faded, but I didn't want her to stop laughing—even if it was at my expense. I had no idea what the hell I was thinking when I tried to cook actual food. I was lucky I hadn't burned the house down.

After wiping the tears of mirth from her eyes, she snorted out another giggle, then said, "Well, let's hope you're better at cleaning than you are at cooking. When you're finished, make sandwiches. Lettuce, tomato, and mayo on mine, please."

"You're not going to help?"

She shrugged and went to the wine fridge for a bottle of chardonnay. After uncorking it, she got a glass from the overhead stemware rack and poured herself a drink without offering me one. "Nope. Not my mess."

"It'd get done faster with two of us."

"And?" Leaving me to it, she spent several minutes looking through the fridge and pantry while I got to work scraping the burnt berries from the cooktop.

The woman in my kitchen wasn't the same one I'd married. This Natasha was confident and self-assured, with a dry, somewhat acerbic wit I enjoyed. I especially liked that she wasn't bending over backward to please me out of fear, or because she thought she had to. Of course, her attitude probably had a lot to do with her newfound combat skills. I also watched her make a note of where all the knives were as she got her wine.

And because I was still a sick bastard, I loved it.

"As my lady commands," I murmured as I got cleaning products from under the sink. "What are you planning for supper?"

She got a large steel bowl from the shelf under the kitchen island, then added yeast, water, and a healthy dollop of honey. "Herbed Focaccia, salad, and I think pastina with parm and chopped kale. I'll make plenty for all of us, plus leftovers because I'm not cooking when I should be spending time with Dante."

"All of us?"

"You, me, the vet, and her technician." She dumped flour into the yeast mixture without measuring it, then mixed it with a wooden spoon.

"Where did you learn to cook?"

Natasha's spoon stilled for a moment before she started stirring again. "My father used to hire undocumented workers for housekeeping staff. He paid them a pittance and threatened them with deportation or worse if they tried to report what he was doing to me. Sometimes the cook would let me watch her. They finally managed to get out a few months before our wedding."

"How?"

"My father took me and the guards to some fancy hotel for a party. Nobody was there to stop them. After that, I watched cooking videos on the internet."

"So glad he's dead."

"No kidding. Anyway, I assume Saoirse won't be joining us."

"No." I hesitated, then added, "You scare her."

"Good. I meant to." She spread olive oil on the kitchen island, then turned the dough out. "As long as you don't fuck with me again, she's in no danger from me."

I nodded and scrubbed the wall behind the stove. "I get it. I... Everything I did to you was to make your father hurt. I can't exactly blame you for turning it back on me."

"I don't want to harm her, Lachlan." She kneaded her dough in silence for a few seconds. "But she will die if you try to force me into that kennel again."

Natasha's words, spoken in a flat, emotionless monotone, chilled me. "I understand. You have every right to protect yourself, and I won't touch you without your consent."

"Good." She slid the smooth ball of dough into the bowl and coated it with more oil, then covered it tightly with plastic wrap. "I do want to thank you for something."

"What's that?"

"You gave me the means to finally end the old bastard." She grabbed a rag and cleaned up the last traces of flour and oil from the kitchen island, then washed her hands. "And once Dante is well, we're leaving California. You'll never see us again."

"For what it's worth, I wouldn't have done any of it if I'd known."

"Considering you still haven't signed our divorce papers, it's not worth much." After drying her hands, she added, "Forget the sandwich. I'll be back in a few hours to make supper."

I didn't want her to leave, but I couldn't physically stop her after promising I wouldn't touch her. Before she could walk away, I asked, "Natasha, what would it take for you to let us start over?"

"It would take a miracle, Lachlan, and I think we're both too old believe in them." She smiled, but her thickly lashed brown eyes seemed to look right through me. "Sign the papers and let me go."

Without waiting for me to answer, she walked out. However, she left me with probably more information than she intended.

The kitchen wasn't the only thing I needed to clean up, and I'd already put it off too long.

After wiping my hands, I got my phone and tapped Finn's contact. He answered on the first ring.

"Do you need us to return, sir?"

"No. I have a job for you."

CHAPTER FOURTEEN

NATASHA

"Look at you, my beautiful baby boy," I crooned, encouraging Dante as he tottered toward me. The kitten kept pace with Dante, her purrs seeming to reassure him.

"He's doing really well," Dr. Mendez said as she knelt next to me. "All the exercises are helping."

"So is Angel," I replied, pointing at the kitten.

Jerome had been right. Cats—at least the right cat—helped people find kindness. Despite Lachlan's continued presence in my life, Angel and Dante healed my spirit more than any amount of therapy or Krav Maga training.

Dr. Mendez laughed and held out her fingers for the kitten to sniff. "Can't forget Angel."

We'd somehow become friends during Dante's recovery, and Teresa wasn't afraid of me anymore. It was nice, but very strange to have a real friend—not one who only pretended to make it easier for her brother to abuse me.

Bitter, much?

"You helped more than anything," I replied. "I don't think he'd have made it without you."

She smiled and wiped a bit of drool from his jowls. "Natasha, he is doing better, but I wouldn't be doing my job if I didn't remind you—"

"I know." I kissed my baby dog between his ears, then sighed. "He's almost eleven, and I can't move across country without risking his health. I bought a house about ten minutes from the clinic. It's handicap accessible and doesn't have stairs."

Although small with only two bedrooms and one bathroom, the Craftsman bungalow was perfect for me and my baby dog. I especially loved the gourmet kitchen with its original cupboards and hardwood flooring, and I absolutely would not paint over the height markings carved into the bathroom door frame from the previous owner's grown children. They were incontrovertible proof that some families got to grow up happy.

Thankfully, I'd managed to unload my father's house quickly, and at a fair price, but I wondered if I should find an exorcist or something to cleanse the place of lingering evil before the new owners took possession.

Ack. Don't mention possession.

"Sounds perfect." Teresa gave Dante a pat and scritched Angel under her chin, then rose to her feet. "I need to get back to the clinic, but text me if you need anything."

"I have leftover sweet potato gnocchi if you're interested in lunch. You could take it home to Vince if you don't have time now."

"Tempting, but no." She sighed and patted her stomach. "My scrubs are already too tight from your cooking, and Vince is threatening to divorce me so he can marry you for your food."

Laughing, I got up and escorted her to the door. "Fair enough. Are we still on for that wine tasting Friday?"

"You know it! Vince will be our designated driver."

"Sounds perfect."

Look at you, scheduling outings with friends and shit.

I waved as she got into her truck and drove away, then trudged to the kitchen. As usual, I found Lachlan at the table waiting for me.

"You're worse than Dante," I muttered as I pulled the pan of leftover gnocchi from the fridge. "Always begging for table scraps."

"You know what they say..." He grinned, reminding me of the man I'd once thought he was. "The way to a man's heart—"

"Is through the fourth and fifth ribs with an eight-inch carving knife." I scooped a helping to a plate and put it in the microwave, leaving the gnocchi out for him to heat up his own. "Have you signed my divorce papers yet?"

"Are you going to quit refusing alimony?" he countered.

"No."

The jackass had the nerve to smirk at me. "Then I'm not signing them."

"You're an asshole."

"I know." He warmed a plate for himself, then grated a generous amount of parmesan on top. "But I'm an asshole who truly wants to do right by you."

I sighed and ate my food even though my

appetite fled. Why the hell was I even fighting about this? It was like my subconscious was looking for ways to stay married to him.

Ugh. No, thank you.

Besides, letting him give me alimony didn't mean I had to use it. I didn't even have to keep it. Hiding a smile, I carried my empty plate to the sink and rinsed it.

"You win. Bring me the damned papers."

"I never thought you'd give in," he murmured as he crowded me at the sink.

His warm breath tickled the back of my neck and I shivered, hating that I wanted him to touch me. "Actually, you're going to double your original offer."

"I'm not complaining, but why?" He reached around me and took my plate, then rinsed it.

"I'm donating it to a women's shelter."

He stilled, making me dart out of reach before he lashed out. Instead of chasing me, his shoulders shook with laughter.

"Touché, Natasha."

———

LACHLAN

I laid our divorce agreement on the table in front of her before handing her a pen.

"Put in the amount you want and initial it," I said.

Natasha's hand didn't shake—unlike when she signed our marriage certificate. I couldn't decide if I was happy or not.

Win the battle, lose the war.

At least my sister would be happy.

Despite my best efforts, Natasha was just as antagonistic as she'd been when she moved in with Dante, and I still didn't know how to fix us.

I truly fucking hated how she flinched whenever I broke her six-foot bubble of personal space. I would have given anything for a do-over so I could have ended her father twelve years ago.

For a moment, I wondered if I should tell her about the real wedding gift I'd arranged, but it wasn't quite finished. Finn hadn't been able to locate three of her father's former guards, and I didn't want to say anything until they were all dead.

"There you go." She returned the pen and folded her arms over her chest. "Your turn."

Hiding a grimace, I put my initials next to the

change and signed the bottom. "I guess that's it. You're a free woman."

"Thanks." Rising to her feet, she added, "I'm moving out tomorrow."

"Where to?"

"I bought a house close to Dr. Mendez's clinic."

"I—" My phone chimed with Saoirse's ringtone. "Sorry. It's my sister."

"Perfect timing." As she strode to the kitchen door leading outside, she added, "You can tell her it's safe to come home."

I nodded and tapped the screen to accept the call. Before I could say anything, Saoirse screamed my name loud enough for Natasha to hear.

"Saoirse? Are you okay? What happened?"

Frowning, Natasha returned to sit next to me, then leaned closer.

I heard low male laughter. "Just the man we wanted to talk to. Have you heard from your old friend Finn lately?"

Natasha paled and her throat worked as she swallowed. "Oh, god. George."

"Why should I care? He'll turn up sooner or later." I laid my hand on Natasha's knee and tried to project a calmness I didn't feel. "I'm looking for Enrique and Matt too. You've somehow managed to crawl into the sewers like diseased rodents, but I got everyone else."

Natasha blinked and her lips parted as she stared at me. George interrupted before she could speak.

"Nice. I hear you still have that little cunt Tasha with you. Might as well put me on speaker so she can hear what happens to uppity bitches who don't do as they're told."

My phone threatened to crack under the pressure of my grip, but Natasha eased the device from me and set it on the table before tapping the speaker icon. I could hear my sister crying softly and my blood iced.

"We're listening," Natasha said softly. "What do you want?"

"From you? Nothing right now, so be quiet and let the grownups talk." He laughed again, and I heard a crack of sound before Saoirse screamed again. "I'm thinking Lachlan might want something though."

"What are you talking about?" I asked.

"See, I'm thinking you might be interested in a trade. You give us Tasha, and you get your sister back. She'll even be in one piece, more or less."

Natasha stiffened and all the fear faded from her

expression. She looked at me with dark brown eyes that seemed to have lost even the smallest trace of humanity.

"Tell him yes," she whispered softly.

I muted the call, then grabbed her shoulders and shook her. "You are not fucking giving yourself to them."

"Not even to save your sister?" She smiled, but it was as if an automaton moved her facial muscles. "You surprise me. Think of all the money you'd save if you didn't have to pay me alimony."

"Fuck the money. We'll find another way. I am not letting you go."

Before I could pull her into my arms, she shook her head and took a step away from me. "Trust me. Tell him yes."

"No. I—"

A flicker of irritation flashed in her eyes but disappeared almost as quickly. "Lachlan, trust me. Please."

"Fuck!"

Natasha didn't say please. She didn't beg and had asked for nothing except her dog's life—even when she had the means and motive to destroy me altogether.

I did trust her. With my life. But the cost was too

high. I couldn't lose her—but I couldn't lose Saoirse either.

"Lachlan..." She moved closer and brushed a kiss over my cheek. "Trust me. I'm not going to let anything happen to you or your sister."

My shoulders slumped and I tapped the mute icon. "You have a deal. Where and when?"

"We'll meet in two hours at your house," George snapped. "No guards, and if I see the dog that killed Steve, your sister is dead."

The call dropped and I blinked to hold back tears of fury. Once I had myself under control, I looked up at my wife. "God, Natasha. I hope to fuck you know what you're doing."

Ignoring me, she tapped her phone screen and held it to her ear. "Hey, Teresa. I need a huge favor. Can you come get Dante and Angel? I have a slight emergency, but I'll pick them up in the morning."

Her eyes twinkled as she listened to the reply. "Thanks. It's nothing serious. I just don't want to leave them alone. I'll give you some of that lemon cannelloni I made too. See you soon."

Nonplussed by her cheerfulness, I followed her into the kitchen and waited while she pulled a large aluminum baking tray from the freezer and placed it in a canvas shopping bag.

Dr. Mendez didn't waste any time, and soon had Dante and Angel loaded into her truck. Giving us a wave, she drove away.

"Okay. That takes care of that." Natasha strode back inside and to her bedroom, then pulled a large duffel bag from her closet.

"What are you doing?" I resisted the urge to shake her and ask what the fuck she was thinking.

"Plotting mayhem." She unzipped the bag and I gasped at the sight of its contents.

"Holy shit."

Smiling faintly, she pulled a sawed-off shotgun from her bag, along with several throwing knives, boxes of ammunition, and two semiautomatic pistols. After handing me one of the pistols and a box of ammo, she said, "Hope your homeowner's insurance is paid up."

CHAPTER FIFTEEN

NATASHA

"Go ahead. Ask." I loaded the shotgun and set it to the side, then slid the knives into their sheath.

"Ask what?"

"Don't you want to know why I have a Sarah O'Connor stash of weapons and money?"

"I'm sure you had your reasons, but I am curious about the C4."

"It was on sale."

"My sister looks for Kate Spade and Chanel," he murmured. "My wife looks for military-grade explosives. It's sexy."

I rolled my eyes but didn't reply.

He flushed and cleared his throat. "Sorry. Do you have a plan?"

"Yes."

When I didn't elaborate, he sighed heavily. "Natasha, you asked me to give you my trust, and I did, even though I would rather die than give you up to George and his friends."

"Keep that thought. I'm planning to use you as a meat shield." I smirked, then added, "Those divorce papers haven't been filed, and as your wife, I'd inherit everything if I let you and Saoirse die."

I wished I believed my lies. Even after everything he'd done, I couldn't let Lachlan lose his sister, and I didn't want to lose him either.

"Would you stop?" he snapped. "For fuck's sake, woman. Forget how much you hate me and tell me what's going through that crazy fucking head of yours because I am losing my shit here. My sister—"

"He won't get to keep either of us," I interrupted, keeping my voice calm. "See, I'm fucking tired of assholes who think it's okay to hurt innocent people because someone they're related to pissed them off. I'm stopping it. Now."

To his credit, his cheeks turned ruddy, and he

didn't meet my eyes for several seconds. "And now I understand the mini urban-warfare kit."

"Yeah. I'm not letting anyone hurt me again, and I promise to keep Saoirse safe too."

"How are you going to stop them?" He spun and looked out the window, his tense shoulders stretching the seams of his shirt. "We can't just shoot them. We might hit Saoirse."

"We know some things George doesn't. He doesn't know about the hidden passages and access hallways for the staff."

"How did you find those?"

I shrugged and my cheeks heated. "I used to love Nancy Drew mysteries, and this house is the right era to have a few secrets. I got bored one day and started tapping on walls. He doesn't know I've spent the last six months shooting every one of these firearms until I could pick a single leaf off a tree."

"True, but he's going to have guns too, and we still can't use them until Saoirse is out of their reach."

"Call them my plan B. Anyway, the other thing he doesn't know is how much time I've spent at a mixed martial arts studio. I'm fast and strong, and more importantly, I know how to be quiet because my life depended on it when my father was alive."

A muscle twitched in his cheek, but he nodded. "Okay. What else?"

"George doesn't know I'm not afraid anymore." I slid the pistol into a holster at my waist. "Unfortunately, he's impatient. He's not going to give us two hours, so I need to get into position."

"Okay." Lachlan rubbed his face, then sighed. "I trust you. Tell me what you need."

I checked the window, making sure no cars approached before returning my duffel to the closet. "Here's what we're going to do."

———

LACHLAN

After wiping my damp palms on my pants, I checked my watch for the tenth time in as many minutes. Natasha was already skulking upstairs, waiting for me to send George, Enrique, and Matt looking for her.

I hated her plan.

Unfortunately, I couldn't think of a better one that would allow me to protect both her and my sister. At least Natasha would have advance warning from the security app we'd installed on her phone. The proximity alarm would alert both of us the minute they breached the borders of my property.

Finn would have come up with something, but if George was to be believed, my oldest friend was gone. I'd have to grieve his loss later. Despite my worry, I couldn't help a small smile. Natasha's plan was probably close to what Finn would have done.

"Fuck." In an attempt to relax, I took a few deep breaths and moved my head from side to side to release the tension in my neck.

I'd watched Natasha train with sparring partners a few times, and she rarely lost. If she could win against trained fighters, she'd be deadly against George, who was twice her age and spent more time drinking than he did in the gym. Matt wasn't much better, but Enrique…

He might be a problem, but I had to trust Natasha was ready for him. There wasn't another option.

My phone buzzed a warning, making me flinch with surprise. Cursing, I pulled myself together and sent a quick text to Natasha.

LACHLAN

They're here

NATASHA

I heard. Phones on silent now. You
know what to do.

LACHLAN

I still hate this plan.

NATASHA

I still don't care.

"God, I should spank you," I muttered as I silenced my phone and slid it into my pocket.

Steeling myself, I went to the door and opened it, then waited for a black SUV with tinted windows to park at the head of my driveway.

Christ, could they be more cliché?

I folded my arms across my chest and waited as George got out of the front passenger seat and strode toward me—without my sister.

"Where's Saoirse?"

"Where's Tasha?" he countered, smirking at me.

He was clean-shaven, with light brown hair and watery blue eyes, and reminded me of an elementary school bully who forgot he wasn't ten anymore. And like most bullies, he needed just one person to make him stop.

I was self-aware enough to include myself in

that description. Natasha had been the one to stop me.

"You'll see her when I see my sister."

"Stupid bastard." He pulled out a gun, making me arch a brow.

"I should remind you that Finn wasn't the only member of my staff who would like nothing more than to bury you in a shallow grave. Don't think that will end if you shoot me."

"You'll still be dead."

"And you'll still be charged with murder. You were stupid enough to pick my own house to make the exchange, and there are cameras everywhere. Aside from that, once I...convinced Natasha to behave, she gave me all the evidence I need to put you away for a very long time."

I took a few steps toward him but stopped when I smelled body odor mixed with the sour reek of cheap bourbon. "Once you give me my sister, you can take Natasha off my hands, and I destroy all that evidence. Do we have an agreement?"

"Fine, asshole." He glowered at me, then turned toward the SUV and shouted, "Bring the girl here."

Matt and Enrique dragged Saoirse from the vehicle, and, holding her upright between them, brought her to George.

Fuck. She looked barely conscious, and I had to force myself to remain still when I spotted the bruises on her arms and legs. I recognized the floral print sundress as one of her favorites, but it was torn and spotted with blood.

"Gentlemen, I understand that a woman occasionally needs chastisement, but if you touched her inappropriately, the deal is off." I cocked my head at Enrique, then smiled. "Of course, Enrique there is young enough. Guess I could marry her off."

"No." George sneered at me. "Your bitch of a sister is fine. We're saving ourselves for your wife."

"She won't be my wife for much longer. I got what I wanted, so I don't give a shit what happens to her." I shrugged and pretended I believed my own words when every atom of my body screamed in denial. "I already have signed divorce papers. There might be a few spots of her blood on them, but my lawyer won't care."

"Where's Tasha?" George pushed past me, then spun and pointed his gun at me. "If you're trying to double-cross us—"

"Please." I led them into the living room and poured myself a glass of scotch. "You're doing me a favor. My sister got taught some manners, and I'll be rid of my unwanted wife. Drop Saoirse in a corner somewhere."

When Matt and Enrique let her fall to the floor, I crouched next to her and carefully touched her cheek to make her look at me. She opened her swollen eyes and blinked. Careful of my movements, I shook my head almost imperceptibly and whispered, "Shh."

"And? Where is she?" Enrique asked, his brown eyes glittering with avarice.

"Up the stairs, turn right. Last door at the end of the hall." I stood and tossed him a key ring. "She's in a cage under the bed."

As Enrique trotted up the stairs, George laughed and slapped me on the back, forcing me to unclench my hands before I ripped his throat out. "Perfect place for that little cunt."

"I thought so."

I offered George a drink, which he, of course, accepted. Five minutes became ten, then fifteen as I kept up my end of the conversation and tried not to imagine what Enrique would do to my beautiful Natasha if her plan didn't work.

Then again, if it hadn't worked, Enrique would have brought her downstairs already.

Frowning, George glanced at the clock over the mantle. "What's taking him so long?"

After taking a sip of my drink, I shrugged. "Well, she was naked. Guess he's getting the party started, but I'd prefer he not fuck her in my bed. Get her out of my house before you have fun with her."

"Damn him. I told him to wait." Glaring at Matt, George added, "Go upstairs and tell Enrique to put his dick away. It's time to go."

CHAPTER SIXTEEN

NATASHA

"Poor Enrique," I murmured as blood spilled from the deep slice across his neck. He blinked once as I let him slide to the sheet of plastic under our feet. "You have only yourself to blame."

I'd honestly thought Enrique would give me the most trouble, but he hadn't even checked the room before walking into my knife.

Dumbass.

His lips parted as if he wanted to say something, then his eyes closed forever.

Knowing I didn't have much time, I wrapped his body in the plastic, then dragged him into the bathroom and shut the door to hide my handiwork. Either Matt or George would be next, and I wasn't sure which one I'd prefer.

Not that it mattered much. They were both going to die.

Working quickly, I spread out another sheet of plastic. Just in time too. I barely made it into the shadows of the secret alcove next to the bed before Matt walked in.

"Enrique?" Frowning, he glanced at the plastic, then shrugged and moved close enough to look under the bed. He straightened, then turned to face the exit.

Before he could move, I slapped a gloved hand over his mouth and slit his throat, exactly as I'd done for Enrique. Air whistled through the hole in his windpipe as I lowered him to the plastic.

"Again, you have only yourself to blame," I whispered as he died.

I tried to feel bad about what I was doing. Maybe some small bit of me was screaming at the wrongness, but it was more wrong to let them live. All I had to do was imagine them getting their slimy hands on another little girl. Maybe they wouldn't stop with emotional and physical abuse either. Maybe...

My guilt faded as I wrapped him in plastic and dragged him into the bathroom with Enrique.

"One to go." I moved faster as I laid out fresh plastic. George wouldn't wait as long this time.

As I crept into my hiding place, I heard heavy footsteps on the stairs. The thickly carpeted hallway muffled the sound, but I could hear their conversation.

"Damn it," George said, puffing slightly as he walked into Lachlan's bedroom, dragging Saoirse behind him. "I should have done this myself."

He yanked Saoirse's arm, and I grimaced when I saw her face. She looked almost as bad as I usually did after one of my father's visits, but I hadn't counted her into my plans. As long as he let her go before he got into position, everything would be fine, but I hated the thought of traumatizing her.

"Good help is so hard to find," Lachlan replied, his voice warming me from the inside. "I'm billing them for a new bed."

"You assholes!" George shouted as he stomped close enough to let me smell his stench. Frowning, he looked at the neatly made bed, which had not a single spot of blood on it, thank you very much. "Where are they?"

"Maybe they're in the cage with her," Lachlan

replied. "There might be room enough for three if they're friendly."

"And what's with the plastic?" George moved almost within reach, and I tightened my hand around my knife hilt.

"Be serious. That carpet is almost six hundred per square foot. Do you honestly expect me to let a filthy pet on it?"

I grinned at Lachlan's response, but he had a point—and good taste in decorating.

Finally, thankfully, George dropped Saoirse's arm and moved within reach. The minute he turned to face Lachlan, I slid from my hiding place.

This time, I didn't bother to cover my victim's mouth as I set my knife to his throat. There was no one left to rescue him.

"Hey, Georgie Porgy! Didja miss me?"

"What the—"

He didn't get to finish his sentence.

———

LACHLAN

"Hey." Natasha knelt next to Saoirse but didn't touch her. "You're safe now. They're all gone."

"Gone?" Saoirse tried to open both eyes, but the left was too swollen to allow it. "No. I don't see them. They'll come back for me. I—"

The tears thickening my sister's voice broke my heart. My thirst for vengeance already cost me my wife, and I almost lost my sister too.

"Shh. It's okay." Natasha rocked back on her heels. "Will you let Lachlan help you so you can see for yourself?"

"Do you think you're too good to touch me?" Saoirse snapped before struggling to her feet. "I don't need anyone's fucking help."

"No. I don't think I'm too good for anything," Natasha replied quietly. "But I know I scare you, so I figured Lachlan was the better choice."

"Fine." Saoirse brought her hand to her lower lip to wipe at a trickle of blood. "What do you want me to see?"

"In the bathroom." Natasha opened the door to reveal two bodies neatly wrapped in plastic. "Dead guy burritos. Matt is on the left. The other is Enrique."

"Dead guy burritos. Christ." Saoirse laughed, the sound jarring and discordant. "Why?"

"I promised your brother I'd keep you safe." After closing the door to hide the bodies, Natasha shrugged. "I wouldn't wish George on my worst enemy."

Without waiting for a reply, she picked up the edge of the plastic and wrapped George as neatly as she'd done to Matt and Enrique. When she finished, she stood on a clean sheet of plastic before stripping down to her underwear.

I averted my gaze, but... Damn, she was gorgeous. I tried not to miss her softly rounded curves, gone because of me.

Fuck. She already knew how to keep a murder scene clean. My chest ached, and I resisted the urge to wrap her in my arms. No innocent should ever be forced to learn how to kill.

I grabbed George's feet and hauled him into the bathroom with his friends, then returned for her things. I'd already sent a coded text to a very good, very discreet cleaner. The bodies would be gone before sundown, along with their SUV and every last trace of their existence. The cleaner's services were more than worth the six-figure fee.

"Thank you. I'm going to clean up and get packed." Her gaze rested on Saoirse. "Take a tepid bath with Epsom salt. Witch hazel everywhere you can reach, then arnica gel. After that, take some acetaminophen, then pretend you're a dish of caviar and pack yourself in ice."

Her words made me wish I could bring her abusers back to life so I could kill them again. The advice was too detailed to have come from anything but experience.

"Wait. Are you leaving?" Saoirse asked. "Just like that?"

"I think I've overstayed my welcome. Don't you?"

"Let me get this straight." Saoirse got in Natasha's face and put her hands on her hips. "You're going to save my life and get rid of the last of your stupid father's guards, then give advice on soothing my bruises without even staying for supper?"

"Pretty much, yeah. I need to pick up my babies and find a hotel for the night." Natasha smiled briefly. "There's a pan of frozen enchiladas in the freezer. The heating instructions are on the label."

"Babies?" Saoirse spun to face me and punched me in the stomach. "She has children, and you—"

"She means Dante and his kitten." Thankfully, my sister didn't know how to throw a punch—unlike my wife. For a single misguided moment, I wished Natasha would stick around long enough to teach her.

"Children are definitely not on my bingo card." Sighing heavily, Natasha picked up her weapons and handed them to me. "These should probably go with the bodies."

"Are you sure?" I asked.

"Yeah. There's no point in leaving evidence, and I can replace them." After making sure the bottoms of her feet were clean, she strode to the door. "Don't forget to file those divorce papers."

Without waiting for a reply, she walked out.

"I've never seen you look at a woman that way," Saoirse said.

"What way?"

"Like she farts rainbows and pisses glitter. It's disturbing." Saoirse shuddered, then asked, "Do you love her?"

Am I that transparent?

"Yes. That's why I'm letting her go."

"Wow. When did you decide to turn into a pussy? Go get her back."

"Well, considering she doesn't want to stay, and you're scared of her..." I shrugged, then added, "What else am I supposed to do?"

She laughed softly and shook her head. "Oh, she

is terrifying, but you caged her once. I'll help you do it again."

"That won't end well for either of us." I cocked my head toward the closed bathroom door. "You saw what she did to her father and his men."

"You handled it all wrong, and I told you that on your wedding day." She smiled and grabbed a T-shirt from my dresser, then slipped it over her torn dress. "You didn't consider trying to figure out how to make her like it."

PART TWO

CHAPTER SEVENTEEN

NATASHA

"Forgive me, Father, for I have sinned. It's been..." I tried to come up with a date, then added, "I don't know. Maybe a month since my last confession."

The confessional was dark and comforting like the closet I used to hide in when my father was on one of his rampages. These days, I did my best work in the shadows, and I sure as fuck wasn't hiding anymore.

These days, people hid from me because I was the thing that went bump in the night.

I heard the priest sigh from the other side of the confessional as the cloying scent of wax and incense filled my lungs. I imagined him squirming on his hard, wooden seat as he listened to the sins of his parishioners.

Adultery, cheating on taxes…

Little white lies and bigger, blacker ones…

For a moment, I considered asking him to share their sins. He wouldn't, any more than he'd share mine, and I wasn't his confessor.

Hell, I didn't even know why I was here. I wasn't sure I believed in God in the first place, and I didn't want or need absolution. I should have counted myself lucky the holy water didn't start boiling when I walked in.

Maybe I just needed someone to listen. Therapists had to report crimes. My priest… Well, he and I had an understanding.

"Thirty-eight days," he supplied. "How many since the last time, child?"

His faint Afrikaans accent teased, and not for the first time, I was almost curious enough to ask about it. I wouldn't, of course. Personal details weren't part of our relationship.

"Three." I didn't bother asking what he'd meant.

"And?"

"Do you really want to know?"

If people weren't in such a hurry to take advantage of innocents, maybe they wouldn't end up, you know, dead. Totally not my fault. Honestly, I was performing a community service. Or maybe I was cleaning out the gene pool.

Potato, potahto.

Of course, there was that one DMV employee who didn't seem to understand that no meant fucking no. After catching him slipping something into a woman's drink at a bar, I was happy to educate him—and help him continue his quest toward becoming an incel.

Permanently.

I wasn't a complete bitch though. The men who saw me into a cab when I tried to honeytrap them got to keep breathing. Strangely, I liked it when I could let them walk away. It gave me a sense of hope.

One man dared to yell at me, and it took everything I had to keep my laughter inside when he said, "Honey, you need to be careful. With all the misogynistic bullshit men are saying these days, it just isn't safe for a woman to be vulnerable."

Yeah, it was a touch infantilizing, but he wasn't wrong, and his lecture came from a place of deep concern I wished more men possessed.

He even gave me a card for the Caroline Foundation in Arizona, plus one for what my initial research told me was an honest-to-god bondage club called Club Apocalypse, with instructions to call if I needed help. Sadly, the Four Horsemen of Club Apocalypse were all in committed relationships, but if that was where decent men were being bred, maybe I needed to schedule a visit.

If I'd been in the market for a Daddy Dom, Sean Franklin would be at the top of my list. With his golden-brown complexion and muscles on his muscles, he was divine. He was also married to a woman I'd be stupid to cross. The minute my team of hackers and investigators heard his name, they peaced out on me because his wife, one Dr. Gabrielle Knox, was a woman with whom one did not fuck.

Of course, after doing a little research on the good doctor, I was girl-crushing on her hard and totally wanted to be her when I grew up. For a very brief moment, I reconsidered applying for one of her Sirens of STEM scholarships, then shook it off. I wouldn't take a scholarship from someone who actually needed it, and college wasn't on my agenda anymore.

And thus, the women's shelter—which to my surprise was supported in large part by the adult resort—got a great big anonymous donation as a reward for Sean's good behavior.

Well, I assume they did. On the back of the card, I wrote, "Don't disappoint me," then sent it to Lachlan. We weren't married anymore, but that didn't stop me from extorting donations to various worthy causes in lieu of him ending up wrapped in plastic like George, Enrique, and Matt.

Considering I'd gotten the name of his cleaner; I was sure he had some inkling he might end up in their care if he pissed me off.

"No, I suppose not," the priest finally said, dragging me from my thoughts. He pushed a rolled-up piece of paper through the grate separating us. "Call the number."

"No genuflection to the teenaged mother of a tortured prophet?"

He laughed softly. "That's an interesting and not entirely inaccurate description of Mary, but no."

I unfolded the paper and frowned at the number. It wasn't American, but I couldn't place the country code. "Who are they?"

"Call them, Spider."

"Spider?" I asked. "I can't decide if I should be insulted or not."

"Isn't that what you are? You weave a web to trap unwary prey."

I considered the idea and decided I liked it. It wasn't every day a woman got a cool supervillain nickname. Sadly, I couldn't afford a volcanic island lair. Then again, a private island probably wasn't much more expensive than living in Santa Cruz County.

"No, thanks." I crumpled the paper into a ball and tucked it in my purse. I didn't want it, but I wasn't one to leave evidence behind that might have my DNA or fingerprints on it. "I'm not calling an international number that I don't know."

"They have use for your unique skills and can provide resources you only dream of."

"I have my own."

"Not like the assets my friends can give you," he murmured. "Things like protection and a team behind you. They would very much like to meet you, and I—"

"I said no." I rose and gathered Dante's leash.

He sighed, then said, "I'll see you next month."

I didn't reply. Although the priest would indeed see me soon, it wouldn't be in a confessional.

After getting into my car, naturally with Dante in the back seat, his head hanging over my shoulder in a silent plea for chicken nuggies on the way home, I took a few minutes to look up the country code for the number the priest gave me.

"Italy?" I laughed and shook my head, then tucked the paper into my purse for later. "Guess the priest thought I'd be a good mafioso type person."

Dante woofed softly and cocked his head. I swear that dog understood English better than most people I knew.

"Yeah, you're right. Not everyone in Italy is a mobster, and it was rude of me to stereotype. Maybe he thinks I should be confessing to someone at the Vatican."

Knowing Dante's level of anxiety would match mine; I kept my humor and positive attitude the whole way home and even smiled at the young drive-thru attendant who gave Dante an extra nugget for being handsome. Once he was curled up in his bed asleep with his kitty, Angel, I crept silently into my office.

Without wasting time, I opened my computer and messaged one of my hacker contacts. As the priest and his friends would soon learn, there were consequences for fucking with me.

———

LACHLAN

"I've heard of this place," Saoirse said when I handed her the card bearing Natasha's terse instruction. "The Caroline was built on an old cult compound and is named after a woman who died there. It's supposed to be one of the safest women's shelters in the world."

I didn't mention how much I wished Natasha could have gone there. Instead, I asked, "How much do you think I should give?"

She handed the card back and shrugged. "At least a million. Natasha won't be happy with anything less."

"Five hundred grand," I countered. "I'm a bit strapped for cash these days."

"Really?" She sat on the couch across from me and folded her legs under her. "How much has she hit you for?"

"Ten million." I grimaced when the elderly toy poodle Natasha coerced me into adopting tottered to Saoirse and begged to be picked up. The poor thing was deaf, mostly blind, had incontinence issues, and sported a disconcerting underbite that made him look like he should join the Uruk Hai.

Naturally, although the name didn't fit his sweet temperament, the shelter named him Orc.

As hard as I tried not to let it happen, Orc was growing on me. It happened every fucking time too. The poodle was the sixth geriatric animal Natasha decided I should adopt. All came from kill shelters, and my job was to give them a good home for their remaining time, which was just long enough to get attached to them.

Not that it took much.

I could almost hate her for it, but at least I still had Marmite, the ancient Shetland pony who liked to lay his head in my lap for as long as I'd let him. I kept telling myself we had plenty of time, and sometimes I even believed my lie.

Marmite was only forty, and the record for the oldest pony was Sugar Puff, who passed at fifty-six. Not that I researched how long a pony lived or anything.

Maybe Natasha was trying to teach me empathy in the most brutal way possible, but it was surprisingly satisfying to give animals a comfortable home for whatever time they had left. Didn't mean it didn't hurt when I had to let them go, but I also knew the ones I'd already taken were a mere drop in the bucket of unadoptable pets.

Not for the first time, I wondered if I should start canvassing the kill shelters on my own. I had plenty of space and could easily take more than one at a time. After all, now that my vengeance against Steve Ashland was complete, I needed a hobby.

"Yikes." Saoirse plucked the dog from the floor and settled him on her lap. "Guess she's counting it the alimony you should have paid her."

"Piss off," I muttered. "You know perfectly well I tried."

"Or maybe she's still rocking sociopathy. Who knows?" Saoirse scritched the poodle's ears, making him groan with delight. "Natasha isn't really the sharing type."

"No, she isn't. I—"

My phone chimed with an incoming call from an unknown number. Hoping it was Natasha, who used a different number every time she texted me, I accepted the call.

"Hello?"

"Mr. O'Donnell," a woman said. "We have business to discuss."

"Who am I speaking to?" Saoirse frowned and gestured to me to put the phone on speaker. "And how did you get my number?"

"I'm the OG deus ex machina, baby," the woman

replied. "I know all the things, but what I do not know is what your wife has done with my general."

"I'm afraid you have the wrong person," I said. "I'm no longer married."

"And yet you still dance to Natasha's tune," she taunted, making me straighten in my chair. "I'm estimating at least ten million in donations."

"Who the fuck are you?"

"My friends call me Ella. You can call me The Goat."

My blood iced, then heated until I felt like my brain was about to boil. The Goat was not someone to cross. She was powerful and absolutely brutal, but I would take her ass down if she laid a hand on Natasha. "If you touch her... I don't give a fuck who you are. I will—"

"Here's the deal. Find your wife and discover what she's done with Daniel Petersen."

"Or what?"

"I'll start sending you pieces of Finn O'Connor. When I run out of Finn bits, you'll start getting Jerome Marshall's. Then Chelsea Duncan's, then maybe you'd like your pretty sister's fingers and toes. Too bad about Chelsea. I hear she's a great cook."

Her hands shaking, Saoirse paled and pressed

her lips together. Without a sound, I moved to stand behind her and massaged her tense shoulders. As much as I wanted to comfort her verbally and tell her I'd never let anything happen to her, I couldn't let The Goat know she'd gotten to me.

"I don't believe you. Finn was killed by—"

"That's where you're going with this?" Ella asked. "We captured Finn because he was stepping on my toes with Steve Ashland's guards. So far, I've given him a pass because he was following orders, and Natasha cleaned up the three we weren't able to reach. It's your turn to follow orders now."

"I don't follow orders from anyone," I snapped. "Least of all from someone who wants to harm Natasha."

"I didn't say I would harm her." Ella sighed audibly. "Look. I should be pissed beyond reason at her, but—"

"Why are you angry with her?"

"She cost me almost a million dollars when she killed Steve Ashland, but it was too fucking brilliant."

"You were after him too?"

"Have been for months," she replied. "But I suppose it wasn't as long as your twelve years."

"Or Natasha's lifetime," I muttered under my

breath, although I didn't question how she knew about my history with my brother's murderer. Finn might have told her, but it wasn't a great secret.

Softening my touch on Saoirse's shoulders, I relaxed and let out a breath of relief. I might not want Natasha anywhere near Ella or Italy, but The Goat was known for truthfulness. If she said someone was on her *list*, they were already dead and didn't know it. The opposite was also true.

"Yeah, that too," she said, letting me know she'd heard my comment. "Anyway, I've changed my mind about Natasha."

I heard male laughter in the background, then Ella said, "Shut it, Moretti."

"Changed your mind?" I asked.

"Yeah. Because of Natasha's absolute badassery using your own dog to kill her literal cunt of a father, plus certain other activities, I've decided to give her a job."

"An offer she can't refuse?"

"Haha, funny, but also sort of yes. Do you know what your wife is doing these days?"

I found it interesting that Ella referred to Natasha as my wife, as if she knew I still thought of her that way.

"Aside from extorting charitable donations from

me, I assume she's walking her dog and adding to her Tae Kwon Do belt collection."

"Yeah." Ella chuckled. "In fact, I'll match whatever you give to the Caroline. It's a great cause."

"How did you know?"

"OG deus ex machina, remember? Anyway, not sure you've watched the news, but little Natasha has been a busy girl."

"How so?"

"She's been adding to her collection of bodies," Ella replied. "In the last year, she's taken out sixteen men who have assaulted women and children, and one couple who were pimping out their underage foster daughter."

Saoirse gasped and put a hand over her mouth. Hoping Ella hadn't heard her, I said, "Holy shit."

"Right? Anyway, the police haven't connected the dots and come up with serial killer yet, but it's only a matter of time before it happens. I would prefer to have her on my payroll where I can protect her."

"I see." I hesitated, wondering if I really wanted to know, but asked, "Why do you care what happens to her?"

"Because she's a bloody brilliant assassin," Ella replied. "She's clean, careful, and does her research.

At first, she was leaving evidence with the bodies, but it's just missing persons reports now. I don't just want her on my payroll, Lachlan. I need her."

"And if she refuses? I won't force her to accept your offer."

Ella paused and I heard a baby whimper. "Sorry. Nursing the crotch fruit."

"No problem," I said, trying to wrap my head around the idea of someone like The Goat breast-feeding an infant. Then again, like many working mothers, she was probably an expert multitasker.

"Anyway, I don't expect you to. As long as she returns Daniel Petersen in the same condition she found him, I'll accept her refusal, but I also won't step in when she's finally caught. Considering she's crossed state lines into jurisdictions that have the death penalty, it's in neither of our best interest to let that happen."

"I agree. Have you tried to contact her yourself?"

Ella hissed out a curse. "Yeah. I sent Daniel, and she took out the messenger. I need you to call her and pass along the message. She might believe it if it comes from you."

"And what about Finn?"

"He'll be returned when I get Daniel back."

"Fair enough." Although I was still concerned

about my best friend, I trusted Ella to keep her word. "What about the rest of my staff and my sister?"

"I won't harm any of them as long as you don't push me."

"All right. I'll see what I can do."

"Good boy." The call dropped, and Saoirse let out a shuddering breath.

"I can try," she murmured. "Maybe Natasha will listen to me."

"No." I brought up the number Natasha had used most recently and typed out a text.

LACHLAN

> Do you still protect Saoirse?

To my surprise, she answered quickly.

NATASHA

> I shouldn't, but yes.

LACHLAN

> Good. The Goat will come for her if you don't return Daniel Petersen unharmed.

I watched three dots skate across the phone screen while she typed her reply.

NATASHA

Fine. Tell Ella I want her autograph.

Autograph?

And how had she known Ella's name?

Deciding I didn't want to know, I texted a screenshot of the conversation to Ella, then scowled as I read her reply.

ELLA

I want you in Elba tomorrow. Call me when you hit Marina di Campo. Bring Saoirse.

CHAPTER EIGHTEEN

NATASHA

"Well, looks like you get a stay of execution."

Daniel didn't answer. Not that he could have, what with the ball gag shoved in his mouth over the bloodstained priest's collar he still wore. Didn't stop his poisonous glare at me when I showed him Lachlan's texts.

Knowing the last-minute booking was going to cost a fortune, which I fully intended to bill Lachlan for, I scheduled a charter flight to Elba, then gently cleaned Daniel's face with a damp washcloth. Ella had mentioned unharmed, so it probably wasn't a good idea to let her see blood on him. Who knew a notorious mercenary would have a glass jaw?

Alive was good enough for government work, so I took a quick photo of him and sent it to Lachlan, assuming he'd send Ella proof of life.

Truly, I was excited to meet her. With all the bullshit floating around from dumbass men about *your body, my choice* these days, it was nice to see a woman tell them to fuck off before she put a bullet into their useless heads.

Besides, Dante and I were absolute addicts for *Ellavate Your Destination*, her travel show. Maybe if I begged hard enough, she'd let me go with her for her next Shark Week special.

I liked sharks. They were excellent at removing… evidence.

Leaving Daniel tied to the bed, I went to my closet and dragged out a suitcase. "What do you think I should wear to meet The Goat?" I asked, holding up a dove gray Chanel suit in one hand, and a sumptuous cream cashmere sweater dress in the other.

I didn't miss the humor in Daniel's eyes as he jerked his head toward the suit, so I added it to the suitcase, along with a few casual outfits, shoes, undergarments, and toiletries. I'd wear the dress for traveling.

"I guess I should have just called that number," I continued, "but who knew you were working for someone I actually want to meet?"

He grunted behind the gag, so I took pity on him and unbuckled the strap.

I tossed the gag aside but didn't untie him. "Maybe we could become besties. Bitches who slay together stay together, am I right?"

"A match made in hell. The world will never be the same." Daniel swallowed and worked his jaw. "In the interest of my continued ability to hear, will you please turn off the music? I confess, Taylor's 'No Body No Crime' is disturbing, given my current circumstances."

"Spoilsport. Don't diss my Tay Tay." I lowered the volume on *Misandry But Make It Country*, my favorite playlist, but he winced when I started belting the chorus to Wanda Jackson's "My Big Iron Skillet."

What can I say? It's my theme song.

"Were you lying about her wanting to offer me a job?" I asked once the song ended.

With someone like Ella Rose Moretti, AKA The Goat, and La Signora to anyone too afraid to say her name out loud, it was best to confirm first. I wasn't about to walk blindly into my own murder.

"I only lie when it gains me something."

"Lying would gain you your life and my execution."

"Touché, Spider." He wiped the side of his face on his arm, and I used a tissue to clean up the remaining drool. After thanking me, he said, "You impressed her before you managed to capture me. Lying about it would gain me nothing when she already knows I was bested by a little girl barely out of pigtails."

"Like capturing you was hard?" I snorted, then added, "For a mercenary general, you just aren't that observant."

"Nobody expects a fuzzy dart shot into one's backside," he murmured. "Clever girl. Will you untie me now? I'm afraid I must use the facilities."

"You should have been expecting it." I met his gaze and didn't blink. "Exposing me without antici-pating payback wasn't your brightest move."

"Again, touché."

I palmed a short dagger and sliced through the zip ties securing him to the bed. "In the interest of your continued ability to breathe, I suggest you behave yourself."

"Of course." He rose to his feet and stretched. "Excuse me."

After finishing his business, Daniel returned to sit on the bed. "When does our flight leave?"

"Four hours."

"Will you return my phone?"

"No." I zipped my suitcase, then got his passport from my purse and tossed it to him. "I can't have you spoiling the surprise."

He blinked at the passport, then scowled. "You broke into my apartment?"

"Breaking in implies I couldn't steal your key." I threw a travel sized jewelry case into my suitcase, then zipped it shut. "While you were taking your little nap, I packed for you and canceled your lease. The month to month made it so easy to erase you."

Although I made sure he understood my original intention, he laughed softly as Dante laid his head in his lap. "I confess, I rather hope you'll accept her offer. I look forward to working with a trained professional."

I preened inwardly. Fuck Lachlan and the praise kink he gave me, but I still got off on hearing people say I was good at something. Besides, Dante obviously trusted Daniel, which cranked my anxiety down a notch.

"Would I be working with you?"

"Unfortunately, no. At least, not directly." He sobered and scratched my dog's ears. "I am too well known. Your value is in your anonymity, Spider. I will be leading your backup team, but you'll work alone."

"Not gonna lie." I packed my favorite weapons into a carryon, including the sweet Beretta I'd nicked from Lachlan's gun cabinet on my way out. "Love the supervillain nickname and love the idea of a personal team. Do you think Ella will pay me enough for a volcanic island lair?"

Also, wasn't gonna lie. I loved the idea of getting a regular paycheck for my little hobby. Killing was expensive.

Well, killing was cheap. Getting rid of the evidence was pricey. If I worked for someone like The Goat, I could...

I shivered with almost sexual pleasure. Being able to kill without worrying about cleanup was incredibly enticing, not to mention having access to her intelligence resources, which far surpassed mine.

He chuckled softly and the skin around his green eyes creased with humor. "Well, Elba exists because of past volcanic activity, and Vesuvius is a short helicopter ride away. I'm sure Ella would love to have you as a neighbor."

"Close enough, I suppose." I hesitated and swallowed hard, hating myself for caring. "Do you think she'll like me?"

He stood and rested his hands on my shoulders, offering the comfort I hadn't realized I needed. "I know she will, little one. Don't worry."

———

LACHLAN

I repositioned Ella's baby in my arms, disconcerted but also pleased she trusted me enough to hold her child. Although I didn't say it out loud, I considered it a test.

At least Saoirse had been allowed to stay in her room, and although I didn't like being separated from her, it was probably for the best.

I had Ella's baby. She had my sister. I held no illusions that Saoirse would suffer if the infant in my arms let out even the slightest sound of distress. Fuck if I knew how to hold a baby in the first place, but little Lelia seemed happy enough to be held like I cradled Orc.

Holding Lelia's teething toy for her, I wished things could be different. I could have been holding Natasha's baby if I wasn't so fucking stupid.

You could have been her husband. I could have been her friend.

Coulda, shoulda, woulda. And now, my sweetly innocent wife had a body count surpassing my own.

What I wouldn't give to have a do-over, starting with not drugging the French toast and sausages she cooked for me the morning after our wedding. I wouldn't change the haste of our wedding though. After learning what her father had done to her, I was thankful to have gotten her out.

From his place in front of a computer, one of Ella's guards turned to face her. "The Spider has arrived with General Petersen, Signora. They're waiting at the gate. Shall we let them in?"

Spider?

"Does Daniel appear to be unharmed?" she asked.

"Yes, Signora. He has some bruising on his jaw but seems in good health otherwise."

Ella tossed a burp cloth over her shoulder and took Lelia from me. At almost six feet tall, with brilliant purple hair shaved on both sides to leave a long tail, and full-sleeve tattoos, Ella was the opposite of what I'd expected from such a notorious individual. It was hard to picture a nursing mother dressed in saggy leggings and a stained white T-shirt issuing kill orders. Strangely, I felt as if I'd seen her before, but I couldn't remember where.

"Perfect. Call down to the kitchen for snacks and drinks and put them in the yellow sitting room. Oh, and have someone tell Finn he's free to go. He's probably in the kitchen with Sofia."

Ella had already let me speak with Finn, who didn't seem in any hurry to leave. His guest suite was nicer than his apartment, and in exchange for not attempting escape, he'd been allowed to train with Ella's mercenaries. Privately, I thought Finn's willingness to stay with Ella had less to do with the accommodations and more to do with her lovely chef. If he chose to stay, I'd wish him well.

"Who's The Spider?" I asked as she settled Lelia against her shoulder.

"Your wife." Ella laughed softly, then added, "Daniel gave her the totally badass nickname, and I'm gonna make it stick."

"The Spider and The Goat," her husband Cristian muttered as he retrieved a thick manila folder from the desk. "It's a biblical plague of homicidal women."

"Kindly kiss my entire ass, lover," Ella retorted.

"You say that like it's a hardship." He rose to his feet and stalked to her, then swept her into his arms. "As always, I will do as you bid."

Too desperate to see Natasha, I turned my back on their torrid kiss and strode from the office. Before I could reach the stairs, Ella caught my arm to stop me.

"I know you're excited to see her, but I want you to hold back."

As I moved to step around her, Cristian blocked my path, sending my irritation soaring. "Tell me why."

Ella's blue eyes softened, and she sighed. "Because if she sees you, she'll shoot first and won't bother asking questions. You have to know this, so I'm asking you to let me talk to her before you come in."

I grunted, unwilling to admit that Ella was probably right.

"I have a better idea." Cristian took Lelia from Ella and passed her to me. "Natasha won't risk harming a child, no matter how much she hates Lachlan."

"But—"

"She still protects Lachlan's sister," he interrupted before kissing her forehead. "You should also recall what she did to that couple who were pimping out their foster daughter. Lelia will be safe as houses with her."

"Fine." Ella shot me a glare, then added, "You better be right, Moretti."

"You know I am." He swept her long tail of purple hair over her shoulder and kissed her again. "In fact, I daresay Natasha will be an excellent protector for our daughter."

"She'll just wait until I put Lelia down." Lelia blew a spit bubble, and I wiped it away before it reached my suit jacket. "Then she'll shoot me."

"Well, let's hope we can finish our business before Lelia's next feeding, but hold off on joining us until I signal for you. I'll leave the door cracked open so you can listen." Without another word, Ella swept down the stairs, Cristian close on her heels.

Shaking my head, I followed with their baby in my arms to a door on the main level of their expansive villa. The windows were open, and a sultry Mediterranean breeze billowed the sheer silk curtains. I smelled the sea, along with olives and lemons from a nearby orchard. Inhaling, I allowed the pleasant fragrances to fill my lungs, forcing myself into calmness I didn't truly feel.

Although I deserved it, I wasn't looking forward to seeing the hate in Natasha's eyes. Then again, indifference would be worse.

Ella laid her hand on the knob, but didn't open the door. "Are you ready?"

"Yes." I adjusted my hold on Lelia, praying Cristian's observations were correct, and that Natasha would hold her fire.

CHAPTER NINETEEN

"Yay! You're finally here!" Ella Rose herself exclaimed as she threw open the door. "And this handsome boy must be Dante."

Clearly having no sense of self-preservation, she knelt and cooed at Dante, who glanced at me and moved to block her approach. Although his shoulders tensed, he remained calm.

I moved my fingers away from the Beretta tucked in the outside pocket of my purse before standing to shake her hand. She towered over me by almost a foot, and I forced my inner fangirl down when she pulled me into a tight hug smelling of lemon soap and freshly baked bread. Her casual clothes and disheveled appearance made me wish I hadn't worn a suit, but what else did one wear to an interview with the world's most notorious criminal mastermind?

"And with your general, as requested."

"You catching him being careless was the icing on the sweet cake of your curriculum vitae."

"I'm right here, you know," Daniel murmured. He kissed Ella's cheeks, European style. "But you said unharmed, and she punched me in the face."

"Not seeing any blood or a protruding bone," she retorted. Taking my hand, she led me to a comfortable couch and sat next to me, but didn't loosen her grip on my fingers. "So, Spider. Can I call you Spider? I love your supervillain name, by the way."

"Um…sure?" Honestly, Ella reminded me of a somewhat hyperactive teenager—definitely not the Signora of a brutal Italian mob family. "But maybe it should wait until I have a volcanic island lair."

"Elba is sort of volcanic."

"I told her already." Daniel lifted his chin in greeting when another man joined us. "Hello, Moretti."

"And that's Cristian, my husband," Ella said. "Say hello, Cristian."

"Hello, Cristian."

"Smartass."

"You wound me, Cicci," he replied, a faint smile curving his generous mouth. "I was simply following my Signora's command."

Although his dark eyes reminded me of black holes surrounded by thick lashes, I caught the faintest tinge of humor in the fathomless depths of his gaze. Tall, with a prominent Roman nose, thick eyebrows, and a shadow beard I doubted any commercial razor could touch, he was gorgeous.

If you want to get over a man, get under an Italian.

Well, a different Italian, naturally. I wasn't one to poach—not that I'd taken a lover since...

I forced myself to focus. My ex wasn't important, nor was he here.

"It's a pleasure to meet you, Signore Moretti."

"Cristian, please." He sat next to Ella and laid a hand on her knee. "We're delighted to welcome you and Dante to our home."

A maid bustled in with a coffee service and a large cart loaded with snacks. Nonplussed, I watched Ella pile food on a plate as the maid set a crystal bowl of water on the floor for Dante.

"Help yourself," she said, her mouth full. "Definitely try the spanakopita. It's my chef's specialty."

"You should," Daniel advised. "And quickly, before you learn the reason Ella is called The Goat."

"Well…" I selected a piece of crisply toasted bruschetta laden with chopped tomato and basil, along with a small serving of spanakopita. "It does seem to be a strange nickname."

"She eats everything that isn't nailed down, and I wouldn't be surprised if she ate the nails too," Daniel replied.

"Remind me why I wanted you back," Ella muttered. "Should have let The Spider keep you."

Enjoying their banter, I hid a smile behind a bite of bruschetta. It was almost as if they were a family, but I had no relevant experience to base that assumption on.

Maybe they were somewhere between *The Sopranos* and *The Simpsons*. And maybe I was just jonesing for something I'd never have.

As I was trying to decide how to get the conversation turned toward business, Ella said, "I'm sure you're wondering if the job I instructed Daniel to offer you is legitimate."

"Yes, that did cross my mind." I didn't mention thinking she planned to execute me, as that option didn't seem to be on the table anymore.

"It is." She offered me a thick manila folder.

"Inside, you'll find an employment contract, plus payroll and insurance forms. We'll also set you up for Fondo Pensione Integrativo with ten percent matching contributions."

"Is that like a 401k?" I asked, trying to hide my surprise. In what universe did serial killers get retirement benefits?

"Yeah, and we have an accounting team if you don't want to mess with filing your own tax forms. The IRS is a pain even if you aren't working overseas." Ella ate another piece of bruschetta. "The Tomas and Lelia Lupo Foundation will sponsor your employment visa unless you want to get Italian citizenship, which we'll also sponsor."

There was an idea. I could move to Italy and never have to worry about crossing paths with Lachlan again—just as I'd imagined when I walked out of our marriage. Well, not specifically Italy, but somewhere not in the United States.

"And will the job pay enough to cover my... expenses?" I asked, careful not to mention anything that might incriminate me.

"More than," she promised, following my lead. "Besides, TLL will be covering the costs you're talking about."

"Sounds too good to be true," I murmured. "What's the catch?"

"Smart woman." Ella stood and crossed the room, then beckoned to someone waiting in the hallway. "Allow me to present your new partner."

I frowned and shook my head. "Daniel said I would be working alone."

"Daniel isn't the boss here." Her blue eyes hardened into chips of ice, letting me catch a glimpse of what made her so terrifying. "I am. And if I say you're working with a partner, you better get used to having company."

Except I didn't bend for anyone. Not anymore—not even for The Goat. I was scary enough all by my lonesome. "As I said, I work alone."

"And you will—after your first assignment is complete." She tapped her bare foot impatiently, then added, "Oh, and take your hand away from the pistol in your purse. I'll be pissed if you pull a gun on your new partner."

———

LACHLAN

What. The. Fuck.

Although Ella could only have been referring to me, I scanned the hallway for someone else. Did she truly expect Natasha to agree?

Most importantly, what was I about to sign up for?

Not that it mattered. I'd do almost anything for a chance to be with Natasha again, even temporarily —and knowing I had no hope of fulfilling my fondest dream of having her kneel willingly for me. After so many months apart, I still wanted her to look at me like she had on our wedding night, as if I was her knight protector, and not just as bad or worse than her father.

"Well, come on," Ella said, stepping aside to clear the doorway. "I don't have all day."

"This was not part of our deal," I whispered, careful to keep my voice down so Natasha didn't hear me. "I didn't agree—"

"Here's me not caring. Now, move it."

Still holding baby Lelia, I sighed and trudged past her to finally gaze upon my wife for the first time in months. She reached for her purse, then scowled when Cristian took it away from her. Dante growled softly and she laid her hand on his back to calm him.

Her lips pressed into a tight line and a muscle twitched in her cheek. "You better tell me that baby's mother isn't in your filthy kennel, Lachlan. And don't you dare lie. I'll find out."

The comment stung, but I couldn't protest. I hadn't given her any reason to think better of me.

"Lelia is mine," Ella said as she took the baby from me. "And Lachlan doesn't have anything but a litter of Cane Corso puppies in there."

"Fair enough." Her rage palpable, Natasha tossed a thick folder on the couch and stood. "Thanks for the job offer, but I'm out."

"Spider—"

"No, Ella." She grabbed her purse from Cristian and scowled when Daniel blocked the exit. "I won't work with a partner, least of all him."

"Not even for a chance to go after Ronan Doherty?" Ella collected the papers that had fallen from the folder and tucked them back inside, smirking as Natasha's face reddened with fury. "I know you recognize the name, and my intelligence team tells me you're still looking for a way into his compound."

I recognized the name too, but I couldn't figure

out why my old college friend would be on Ella's radar, much less Natasha's. Of course, we'd lost touch years before, so maybe he wasn't the man I remembered—assuming they were the same person.

I couldn't exactly throw stones, considering what I'd done to Natasha, but if Ronan was into the same shit as Steve had been, he needed to be put down.

"My father's partner." Natasha's hands tightened into fists. "Where is he?"

"Same place he was when you found him," Ella replied. "Locked in a manor house on the southeastern coast of Ireland. And as you've already learned, you won't be getting in there without help."

She tilted her head toward me, then added, "Lachlan knows him, and can get you close enough to take out the trash, if you get my drift."

I grabbed a cup from the coffee service and filled it, more to hide my reaction at the confirmation of Ronan's identity than anything else. I remembered his house well after spending more than a few weekends there while we were in college.

Natasha snorted and sent me a poisonous glare. "Of course. Stupid of me not to expect my useless ex to be associated with Ronan."

"I'm not," I murmured. "I haven't seen him in over a decade. Apparently, I'm the only one who's surprised he was in bed with your father. Ella didn't tell me either."

"No, I didn't," she chirped. "I love a good surprise, don't you?"

"Goat, shut the fuck up." As Ella sputtered with laughter, Natasha asked, "And why should I believe you, Lachlan?"

"I did awful things to you that I will regret until my dying day, but I've never lied to you." Taking a risk, I approached her slowly, thankful Dante held his position, then took her hand. Squeezing it gently, I said, "If you want him gone, let me help you. Let me do what I should have done when I married you and keep you safe."

"Now, that's the way to apologize for being a dick. Way better than the weekly roses Natasha donates to a nursing home." When Lelia whimpered and nuzzled her shoulder, Ella lifted her shirt and put her baby to her breast. "Like all women of quality, Natasha prefers bathing in the blood of her enemies over flowers."

"Why are you still talking?" Natasha jerked her hand free and crossed her arms, then glared at both of us. "I'll figure out a way to take him out by myself, so shove your contract up your—"

"Spider, you already know he's guarded by an army almost as big as Ella's in an impenetrable compound," Daniel said softly. "You're good, but nobody is that good."

"Why don't you just take your little army and kill him yourself?" Natasha asked.

"Because it would start a war we don't want," Cristian replied. "If we keep things quiet, we can track down his suppliers without giving them advance warning and stop the auctions at their source."

"And we all know he'd already be dead if you'd found a way in," Ella said. "I'm offering it, and the opportunity to rescue over a dozen women and children he's holding in his cellar for his next auction."

"You also possess a skill no one else has," Cristian added. "Along with being a gifted assassin, you're a fully trained slave, known to belong to Lachlan."

"No." Natasha's shoulders stiffened, but I caught her shudder. "If Ronan has been keeping tabs on me, he probably also knows we're divorced."

"That's why we've been circulating gossip about your reconciliation," Ella replied, surprising me.

I hadn't heard the rumors, and Natasha probably wouldn't care that I no longer associated with anyone from my old life. I doubted anything I did would make her come back to me, but I wanted to be better for her.

Yes, damn it. I still wanted her to kneel for me, but this time, her collar would be the finest platinum instead of steel, and I'd never leash her again. She'd come to me willingly, or not at all.

"The rumors also help conceal your activities. As long as you're Lachlan's slave, no one will associate you with all those unsolved murders." Daniel said. "Ronan is many things, but above all, he's plagued with curiosity. He'll want to know everything—especially since Steve refused to give you to him."

"Wait. Ronan wanted me? How do you know that?"

"It's not important," she replied, shooting Cristian a poisonous glare. "With your leash in Lachlan's hand, you'll have free access to him. Get him alone and—"

Ella drew a finger across her throat and sent Natasha an evil smile. "Invite him into your parlor, Spider."

CHAPTER TWENTY

NATASHA

Ella was offering me the one thing I truly wanted above all others, but the cost...

I rubbed my forehead to ease a growing headache, then reached for Dante. Leaning against my legs, he whined and licked my hand as memories of Ronan Doherty intruded into my head. With ginger hair, warm brown eyes, and an infectious smile, he was everything a young girl swooned over. And stupid fourteen-year-old past me had a crush on him before I knew what he truly was.

In comparison, Lachlan was a fucking saint.

Although he'd never touched me, even the memory of Ronan's gaze on me made me feel like I was covered in slime. I didn't dare allow myself to think about what would have happened if he'd managed to convince my sperm donor to let him have me.

Things were different now though. I wasn't an abused little girl anymore. I had choices and skills Ronan would never dream a woman could have.

And all I needed was a way in.

"Here," Lachlan said softly as he curled my fingers around a steaming cup of coffee. "Nobody will force you to do anything you don't want to, Natasha."

Fuck my life. He was as handsome as ever, and I would have sworn my ovaries started pushing out eggs at the sight of him holding a baby. Worse, he was right. He twisted words, but he'd never lied to me. When he told me I wouldn't regret marrying him for a single moment, he was right. I regretted marrying him for all the moments.

He said we'd have an al fresco lunch when I asked if we could walk on the beach. There were several outdoor meals—overlooking the sheer cliff face leading down to the ocean. I knelt in the grass while he ate from a china plate.

The things he promised to have delivered when

he showed me the dressing room were my collar and tail.

Although the personal cost had been high, marriage to him got me Dante and my father dead. I supposed I owed him for that. If nothing else, I should probably thank him for teaching me not to be so damned trusting.

"No, but I'm not above bribery," Ella said. "You haven't read your contract, but it stipulates you'll receive sixty percent of the assets belonging to confirmed kills. Ronan's estimated net worth is close to a billion Euros."

"Tempting." I considered it for a moment, then shook my head. "But I don't care about the money."

Then again, that kind of wealth would set me up as one of Ella's competitors. The idea wasn't entirely displeasing, but considering we were after pretty much the same thing, we wouldn't actually be in competition. Besides, it was more efficient to work together.

Or... I could retire and buy that volcanic island.

Still didn't mean I wanted to partner with Lachlan.

"Then donate it." She shrugged and moved her baby to her other breast. "Or give it to his victims. Seem to recall Lachlan giving you Steve's."

"Why are you even still talking, Goat?"

"Because you haven't said yes, Spider." Smirking, she laid her baby on her shoulder and patted her back, making the infant let out a prodigious belch. "You know you wanna."

I rolled my eyes and hid a smile, unwilling to encourage her. Ella aggravated the fuck out of me, but despite myself, I liked her.

"You're actually getting off lightly," Daniel said as he encouraged me to sit and laid my barely touched plate on the table in front of me. "She threatened to steal my entire army out from under me unless I agreed to work for her."

"And now you're rich, happily married to the love of your life, and have another baby on the way. Stop whining." Softening her tone, she smiled at me. "As much as you hate the idea, Lachlan is your best shot at getting to Ronan. I want him almost as much as you do, and you're the only chance we have."

"Please, Natasha," Cristian murmured. "We wouldn't ask if we didn't think you were our best hope of eliminating Ronan."

"What else can we give you?" Ella asked. "What would make you say yes?"

I sipped my coffee, then ate a bite of spanakopita,

which was indeed as delicious as Ella claimed. After considering my answer for a few moments, I said, "I want a guarantee from you that I can kill Lachlan if he decides to be stupid and tries to cage me again."

"Done," Cristian replied. "In fact, I'll do it myself."

"I'm not finished. I also want Italian citizenship and a house of my choosing as close to the Swiss border as I can get."

"Done and done. To sweeten the pot, I'll keep Lachlan's sister as insurance for his good behavior." Ignoring Lachlan's growl of displeasure, which made me shiver with trepidation, Ella pulled her phone from her pocket and tapped the screen to put her call on speaker.

The call was answered by a woman with a thick Scottish brogue and I almost choked on my food when I realized who I was about to talk to. "Oy, dairy goat! Give Lelia many kisses from Auntie Gabby."

"All the kisses." Ella chuckled, her blue eyes sparkling with humor. "Guess who I have in my house right this very minute."

"The more important question is whether your guest is still breathing, mo chridhe."

"Definitely still breathing, but you have to guess first."

"Well, you couldn't have caught Natasha Ashland. I can't even find the naughty girl, and I've looked. Even Sean couldn't track her down after she gave him the slip in Phoenix."

Grinning impishly, Ella winked at me. "Say hello, Natasha."

My face heated until I was sure I looked like a tomato, but I smiled. "Hello, Natasha."

"Bloody hell!" Dr. Knox exclaimed. "You caught her! How many mercs did you lose? Oh, my goodness, this is brilliant! Wait until I tell Zandy. She'll scream. Put Natasha on video because I need to see!"

Warmth blossomed in my chest at her infectious exuberance. Never, not once in my life, had so many people been happy to see me, and I'd never been told I was the one person who could do a job. It was...

Hell. I didn't know how I felt. Part of me said I should be happy, but the wiser, more distrustful part said there was a catch.

Then again, I already knew the catch, and he never stopped looking at me. I guess the real question was whether I trusted Ella enough to let me kill Lachlan if he decided to play nasty again. Unfortunately, I didn't have an answer, but I didn't need one. Whether she agreed or not, I'd end him if he dared try anything I didn't want.

Maybe it was more that I didn't trust myself not to willingly kneel for him. God help me, I wanted to. I wanted to put the piercings back in my tongue and suck his cock just to listen to his pleasured groans. I wanted his hands in my hair and his dick in my pussy, and...

I shut the thoughts down and locked them into the mental box with the rest of my bad memories.

Ella turned her phone to face me, pulling me from my uncomfortable thoughts. "See? Natasha Ashland, live and in color, but don't tell Zandy yet."

Dr. Knox looked just like the pictures I'd seen, with rainbow-streaked hair, several facial piercings, and colorful tattoos covering both arms. Sean, her husband and the man who gave me the Caroline's card, stood behind her and gave me a warm smile.

"Aww. Why not?"

"She'll tell Nicky, and Nicky will tell everyone. Besides, I haven't managed to coax Natasha out of the bushes yet."

"Well, I'm sure Ella offered you scads of money to complete our project, so what else do you want, Natasha?"

I repeated my wish list, then added, "And I want signed copies of all your games, plus Ella's autograph."

To my shock, Ella grabbed a pen, then lifted up my skirt and scrawled her name across my thigh. "There. Autograph accomplished."

"And you can expect a pressie overnighted from me," Dr. Knox promised.

I glanced at Lachlan and smirked. "One last thing. I'll need a disposal crew for Lachlan after I kill Ronan Doherty. Oh, and someone needs to get Dante's cat from my house in Santa Cruz. He misses her."

———

LACHLAN

Natasha was a beautiful woman by anyone's standards, but I'd never seen her truly happy.

She simply...blossomed under the praise.

The sight of her soft, slightly embarrassed smile nearly stopped my heart. It was the same expression she offered me on our wedding day, and fuck me, but I wanted it back. More than that, I wanted to have never lost it in the first place.

I'd complimented her, of course, but *you suck my cock so well* didn't compare to *you are the only one who can help us.*

Knowing what I was about to say would probably end with my execution, I caught Ella's gaze and shook my head. "No."

"No to the cleanup crew?" she asked. "Or no to partnering with Natasha?"

"I'm saying no. I won't allow you to put Natasha at risk. I'll take care of Ronan."

"Allow?" Ella murmured. "You might want to rephrase in a manner that doesn't end up with you fertilizing my rosebushes. I don't think you understand who you're dealing with."

I knew exactly who I was dealing with, and I didn't fucking care. "I'll take being plant food over putting my wife in danger."

"Goodness, but that's a bloody decent declaration of undying devotion," Dr. Knox said as Natasha blinked in shock. "I'll be trotting off now, but we'll meet in a few days to discuss logistics."

The call dropped and Ella rolled her eyes. "Did they teach you drama in high school? It's wasted on me. Can you guarantee your ability to get Ronan alone?"

"I—"

"Do you have the resources to obtain blueprints for his house? Or make the kill without his guards hearing it, then get out without being caught?"

I gritted my teeth and glared at her, trying to stop myself from throttling her. "And you're asking me to assume my wife can? You want to send her into a dangerous situation as a slave, without an exit plan. How am I supposed to think any of that shit is okay?"

"Yes, Lachlan, I can, and I truly don't care what you think." Natasha rose from her seat and stood between me and Ella. "I already have the blueprints, and paid a fortune for his security system schematics, including the locations of his cameras. All I need is a way inside and enough time to make him believe I'm helpless."

"You *will* be helpless, Natasha."

"Oooh," Ella murmured. "I'm just gonna hide behind this couch before the blood spray starts."

Paying no attention to her words, I took Natasha's shoulders and shook her gently but let go when she backed out of reach. "You'll be barely dressed and shackled."

"I don't need clothes or a weapon to kill a man." She smiled, baring teeth. "I could always demonstrate if you don't believe me."

Closing my eyes, I prayed for patience before I gave in to the urge to turn her over my knee. "Are you seriously telling me you're considering this?"

"For a chance to kill a man responsible for selling hundreds of people into slavery *and* get paid enough to buy a private island? You bet your ass I am." She returned to her seat and finished the last of her food before opening the thick folder on the couch next to her. "If you all will excuse me, I'll need a few hours to look over my new contract."

What the hell did she want with a private island? "Natasha, we're not done."

She slammed the folder on the table and glared at me. "Why do you even care? Is it the money? Fine. I'll split the payout with you. Happy?"

"Christ, woman!" I scraped my hands through my hair, ignoring Ella's amused gaze on us as she mimed eating popcorn. "I don't give a fuck about the money. It's you I care about. I can't even think about letting you get hurt. Not when I can stop it."

"Aww." I heard a soft thump followed by a male grunt. "Why don't you say stuff like that to me, Cristian?"

"Let's leave them alone, Cicci."

"Oh, yeah, I forgot I just got thrown out of my own house. Come find us on the pool deck when you're finished with your..." Ella smirked. "Discussion."

She, Cristian, and Daniel left us, closing the door behind them.

I didn't bother asking permission and sat next to her. Dante growled softly, but Natasha's hand on his head stopped him from lunging for my throat. He very much did not like anyone close to her, but I felt the same and didn't fault him for it.

"I haven't needed protection in months, Lachlan." She sighed and got more snacks from the cart, then returned to sit next to me. "If nothing else, you taught me not to expect it from anyone, least of all from you."

"I've never wanted to give it to anyone." Taking a risk, I tucked a silky brown curl behind her ear. Her hair almost reached her shoulders, and I wondered if she was letting it grow out. "Just you."

Giving me a delicate snort, she ate a bite of phyllo-wrapped pastry. "Then why didn't you protect me in the first place?"

"In a way, I did," I murmured. "How many of your ribs did I break?"

She opened her mouth, then shut it with an audible snap and glared at me. "Asshole. That was low, even for you."

"I didn't expect you to take it well." I turned to face her and took her hands. "I'm not justifying my behavior, Natasha. I know I fucked up, but I need you to know that it wasn't personal. I didn't…"

I let the words trail off and released my hold on her hands. Personal or not, I should have gotten the truth before I married her, but all I could see was my own need for revenge.

"You didn't…what?" she asked.

"I never expected how much you'd come to mean to me, or how much hurting you would consume my soul." I gazed into her brown eyes and decided to throw my chips on the table. "Please, give me another chance. Let me do what I should have done in the first place and keep you safe."

CHAPTER TWENTY-ONE

NATASHA

Of all the things Lachlan could have said to make me consider tossing around the idea of not killing him...

What the fuck was I supposed to do with *that*?

I'd spent so much time hating him, maybe I was blinded. I never questioned the weekly roses, not to mention the millions in donations he paid without argument just because I asked him to. I didn't even question his quiet acceptance of the shelter pets I made him adopt.

Laying a hand on my suddenly queasy belly, I remembered how many of those animals he'd already lost—just because I was in a snit and wanted him to hurt.

Which made me no better than him or my father. Fuck.

Hello, empathy.

It was a damned bitter pill to swallow. I choked it down, but didn't delude myself into thinking we'd end up with some bullshit storybook happy ending. I would forever remind him of the man who killed his brother, and I'd never forget him forcing me to piss on his lawn.

"Fine," I finally said as I set my unwanted food aside. "I guess the first thing I need protecting from is that contract. Read it and give me the too long, didn't read version."

I'd read it myself before I signed it, just in case he was bullshitting me.

He stole the last of my spanakopita before opening the folder. His warmth caressed my skin as he settled his large body next to me. "First paragraph, Natasha Ashland, TLL Foundation, et cetera, employment at will, meaning you can quit or be fired with two weeks' notice."

"That sounds fair. What else?"

He read further, until I held up a hand. "What does that mean?"

Patiently, he flipped the page back. "It says you will accept assignments at the discretion of TLL Foundation, to be completed under their oversight, and—"

"Cross that out. I choose my own assignments, and there will be no oversight."

"Good girl," he murmured as he drew lines through the passage. "Ella might fight over it, but I agree with you."

I squeezed my thighs together and resisted the urge to punch him. Stupid praise kink. Even coming from Lachlan—maybe especially coming from Lachlan—hearing someone say I was a good girl made my pussy drip.

"Let her. She's in no position to negotiate if she wants me that bad."

"May I suggest rephrasing?" He turned the page over to the blank side and looked at me expectantly. "I have an idea that might suit both of you."

"Go ahead."

He scribbled furiously for several seconds, then read, "Natasha Ashland will be offered right of first refusal on all assignments, without obligation to accept. She may also request supporting services, provided by TLL Foundation, if she so desires, but at no point will such services be a requirement. She retains the right to suggest additional assignments based on her own research, which TLL Foundation is under no obligation to accept. She also retains the right to complete those assignments with her own resources, without approval from TLL Foundation."

"I like it." I forced my next words through tight lips. "Thank you."

He glanced at me and flipped to the next page. "We're going to try to keep that last line, but I'm not sure Ella will accept it."

Why did *we* sound so good? Gah.

"It's worth a shot, and I can work around it if she refuses. What's next?"

"The sixty percent payout for completed assignments Ella already mentioned, plus a fixed stipend of three hundred thousand Euros per year. Definitely keep this part."

"Why?"

"Because it states your payout is based on gross assets recovered, not net, and your stipend is independent of the number of projects you complete. Ella's expenses come out of her share."

"Well, that's...generous?"

"With someone like Ronan, I expect her expenses will be a tiny percentage. I don't see her going after low-value targets unless it's necessary."

Lachlan didn't call me out in so many words, but he was right to do so. Instead of targeting true monsters like Ronan, I'd been limiting myself to people I could snare easily. It wasn't because I was scared, but more because I didn't recognize I could do more.

"Shit." I got up and refilled my coffee. "I hate myself a little."

"Why?" He set the contract aside and gazed at me steadily, making me want to squirm.

"I could have been going after predators like Ronan all along, which would have meant saving more people."

He shook his head. After taking my coffee from my hands, he pulled me down to sit next to him. "Consider your last targets as training missions. You weren't born a killer, honey, and going after someone like Ronan has become wouldn't end well for you if you were inexperienced."

"Yeah, but—"

"You were an innocent, Natasha." He brushed a thumb over my cheekbone. "You had to learn by yourself and gain the experience to be what you are now. Don't be ashamed for following your learning curve."

Double damn him for being right. "How do you know all that?"

"How else?" He cocked his head and winked. "You're not dead or in prison."

"There is that," I said once I thought I could keep the butterflies in my stomach calmed down. "We'll go with Ella's desire for profit."

"I don't know if her decisions are solely for financial gain." He shrugged. "It's possible she wanted to get your father out of the way, so she could take out Ronan, but she said she spent almost a million dollars on a mission you stole from her when you killed him. After I bought up Steve's debts, he had barely half that."

"Neither of you looked in his safe. He had offshore bank accounts, plus cash and jewelry." Amongst other things I didn't want to talk about.

"Maybe don't tell Ella that, but I'm proud of you, sweetheart." He bumped my shoulder and grinned, making his laugh lines crinkle and another surge of wetness dampen my panties, damn him. "I've been wondering how you were supporting yourself."

The question fell out before I could stop it. "Why are you just now being the husband I needed all those months ago?"

LACHLAN

"Because for the first time, I finally get you," I murmured. "I get your motivations, your wishes, desires, and what makes you tick. I get why you're the way you are, and I know it's my fault, but fuck."

This time, Dante didn't growl when I laid my hand on her knee. "You'll probably cut me for saying it, but seeing you become the antithesis of what your father and I tried to make you is sexy, and I will forever regret not working with you to take him down."

I never thought I'd see it again, but she blushed.

"I *get* you, Natasha." I cupped her cheek, but she jerked out of reach.

"You don't know shit about me."

"I know every one of your targets harmed someone," I replied, keeping my voice soft. "I know everyone you executed deserved it. I also know you did it to protect their victims and prevent them from hurting anyone else. That's what drives you, baby, and I'm so fucking honored to have seen your first kills."

"I—"

"Does it worry me sick thinking about the danger you court every time you go hunting? Fuck, yes, it does. It was bad enough with George, Enrique, and Matt." I resisted the urge to pull her close. "But I know it's what you need to do. All I ask is that you let me be the support you'll refuse from Ella."

Her expression hardened as she tapped her thigh to call Dante to her side. "I'll think about it. Let's finish the contract and meet with Ella."

Knowing better than to push her, I moved to the next section. Despite her lack of formal education, Natasha was astute and careful. She didn't give a damned inch on Ella's contract, and I couldn't help but wonder if Ella would be pissed or impressed.

Probably both. If they could manage to get along without trying to kill each other, Ella and Natasha would be unstoppable.

"All right." I returned the edited contract to the folder, rose to my feet, and held out my hand. "Shall we adjourn to the pool deck?"

To my surprise, she let me help her up and lead her from the sitting room. As we followed Ella's guard down the corridor, she said, "Tell me about Ronan. What do you remember?"

I considered her question for a moment. "We

were roommates at Trinity. He always threw the best parties, and I liked him, but he struck me as somewhat nihilistic. I lost touch with him after graduation."

"That's a lukewarm description," she murmured. "Besides, I thought college students were supposed to be nihilistic."

"Have you met him?"

"Yeah, formally when I was a teenager, but I knew who he was."

"And?" I asked when she didn't clarify.

"Past me was stupid and had a crush on him because he gave me a stupid doll for my tenth birthday. Then I heard him ask my sperm donor to sell me to him as a slave, but he wasn't willing to pay what the old man wanted." She shuddered, making me wish she would accept comfort from me. "I've been trying to figure out a way to get to him for months, but didn't think I had a chance until Ella."

"How old were you?"

"Fourteen, but he'd been friends with my father for as long as I can remember."

Meaning Ronan might have been involved with Darragh's murder. I'd probably never know how I'd missed what had been going on under the surface when we were in college. For all I knew, he didn't start his criminal enterprises until after we graduated, but it didn't matter. Ronan was a dead man, if only for the crime of thinking to take my wife.

"He's not going to touch you, because you're not going after him."

She planted her feet, making me turn to face her. "Don't promise that, and don't even think you're going to stop me because that is exactly what I have to do."

"No."

"Yes, Lachlan." She hauled in a deep breath. "I don't give a fuck what you think, but I have to present myself as a slave. Whether it's you, Daniel, or someone else holding the leash, it's the only way I'll get close enough to kill him without ending up dead."

Without thinking, I pushed her against the wall and circled my fingers around her throat. "Not with someone else, little girl. I will put you back into a kennel if you even think of doing this without me."

She gave me an impish smile, and I heard a soft click a split second before the tip of a dagger pressed against my throat. "Don't, Lachlan. Just...don't."

I leaned against her knife and felt a trickle of blood seep under the collar of my shirt. "Then don't fucking test me, baby. I will lock your ass up and risk you killing me if it means you're safe."

Natasha blinked and her eyes dilated. She licked her upper lip as her warm breath feathered over my face. "Wow. I—"

Snaking my hand into her hair, I tilted her head up and kissed her hard—brutally hard. I wanted to swallow her air, her whimpers, her very heartbeat. I needed to make her remember how she came for me, even when she didn't want to, but mostly I wanted her to remember the promise of our wedding night when she gave me her innocence and her trust without reservation.

Her dagger clattered to the marble beneath our feet, and she dug her nails into my shoulders, sending pinpricks of pain mixed with pleasure into my groin. After yanking her skirt up, I shoved my thigh between her legs.

"Smell the blood you drew, Spider," I hissed the name that fit her better than anything else as the heat of her core scorched me. "Does it make you hot? Do you want me to bleed for you while you ride my thigh until you come for me?"

Her head fell back against the wall, and shuddering, she rocked against me. "Fuck off, O'Donnell."

"I'd rather fuck you, little slave. Ride me and give me your pleasure."

I heard a throat clearing behind me. Paying it no heed, I tried to kiss Natasha again, but she twisted her body and jerked an arm free. A split second later, I heard a thud, followed by a male grunt of pain.

Cursing my inability to keep my hands off my wife until we had privacy, I spun around, then blinked.

Ella's guard scowled and fingered his bleeding ear as a dagger quivered in the wall a scant inch from his head. "Was that truly necessary?" he asked.

"Now that you mention it..." Natasha's sweetly charming smile didn't come close to reaching her eyes. "Yes."

CHAPTER TWENTY-TWO

"No fair." I sighed and handed Daniel the dagger from my bra. "I haven't killed anyone all day."

I wondered if I ought to be handing over my weapons while positioned on an outside deck overlooking the Mediterranean Sea on the northern coast of Elba, but Ella, Cristian, and Daniel were determined to disarm me—not that I blamed them.

"The one from your hip too," he replied evenly. "Also, the one under your sleeve, and—"

"Fine." I pouted but couldn't help smiling inwardly at Lachlan's shocked face as I passed

Daniel more knives. "Meanie. And your guard is a tattletale."

The guard in question smirked at me and I stuck my tongue out at him.

"Indeed." He waited with his hand out until I grimaced and gave him the one from the small of my back, but not the last one he hadn't found. "You'll get them back when you learn to control yourself, little one."

Ella snickered, then laughed outright when I blew her a raspberry.

"To be fair," she said, "I'm kind of attached to my staff, and blood is so hard to get out of the upholstery."

"I find it rather amusing," Cristian replied. "Is there any question about why we want Natasha on our payroll?"

To Daniel, he added, "Oh, and please check her purse. I'd hate to have another...accident."

"And that leads us to the next order of business." Daniel pocketed my Beretta, along with my last two throwing stars, including the short push dagger concealed in the silk lining, damn him. "Our pretty little sociopath could use some additional training."

"I am not a sociopath," I replied. "I absolutely do

know right from wrong, and I also care about the rights and feelings of others."

"As long as they're pets and not human," Lachlan countered.

"Or the victims of real animals," Ella said. "Like Ronan Doherty."

"Yes, exactly." I smirked at Daniel and sat, folding my legs under me. "Not a sociopath."

"Whatever." Ella sat next to me, pinning me with a hard, emotionless stare. "I don't give two shits about your clinical diagnosis. That's between you and your therapist, but I'm not sending you in there until you learn some impulse control."

"Hey!"

I did have control. I could hide, be quiet, clean up my mess without anyone catching me, and knew my targets better than their families did. But she had a point. Before I reached Elba and met people who welcomed my specific talents, I'd have never dreamed I could show them off.

And I absolutely was showing off. Mostly because I could, but also because I wanted Lachlan to see what he'd created.

Naturally, it had nothing to do with the orgasm the guard interrupted. Because of course it didn't.

Liar.

"You were saying?" Daniel asked when I stopped protesting.

Flushing, I lowered my head and sighed. "You're right. I was making a spectacle of myself, and I'm sorry."

"This is a safe space, Spider." Ella took my hand and squeezed gently. "But you'll be going up against one of the most prolific, violent slavers in the world. I can't in good conscience send you in there without some assurance that you can stay focused."

"I can," I promised, hoping it was true. "I'll be good."

Why the fuck did *that* come out of my mouth? I'd never gained anything from trying to be good. I usually ended up bleeding for the attempt.

Or trapped in a marriage with someone who hurt me to get back at a man we both hated.

"Being good is overrated." Ella stood and filled a plate from yet another cart loaded with food, then returned to sit next to me.

Seriously. I was beginning to understand why people called her The Goat. The woman hadn't stopped eating since I arrived.

"Be smart, and most importantly, stay alive," she added, her mouth full of pizza. She chased it with a sip from a frosty mug of ginger beer, then went after a third roast beef slider. "I don't even want you to be good. I want you to be careful."

"And to that end," Daniel said. "We're putting you back into slave training."

"No," I said, surprisingly echoing Lachlan's denial.

"Hear us out." Cristian sat across from me and rested his elbows on his knees. "You've already had training, and—"

"I know that." I glanced at Lachlan, noting the tic in his jaw. "What's your point?"

"Being a slave isn't in your head anymore, and honestly, I don't believe it was there in the first place. You put on an act to achieve a desired outcome." Cristian reached toward me and laid a callused fingertip on my breastbone. "Little one, in here, where it counts, you bow to no one. We need to change that because even the tiniest mistake could mean your life, not to mention that of the people you seek to protect."

Well, shit. Was I that transparent? I didn't want to admit it, but Cristian was right, damn him. Even when I was pissing on the ground at the end of Lachlan's leash, I'd never thought of myself as a slave, and I never stopped looking for an out.

"And this time, it can't be an act," Daniel said softly. "It has to be real."

"No." Lachlan pulled me to my feet and positioned me behind him. "I won't allow anyone to enslave her again. Find another way."

It was cliché, but my life passed before my eyes. Not because I was dying, but because I was too shocked to breathe.

Had my ex-husband been replaced by a clone, or what?

Instead of jumping on the chance to make me kneel for him, he was...

Nope. Wrong reality. Reverse and rewind.

As I was trying to put my brain back where it belonged, Cristian got a laptop from a shelf behind the open bar to the left of the infinity pool. After opening it, he turned it to face Lachlan. "Before you refuse, you need to watch something."

"Cristian, no."

"I wish I knew a better way to make them understand, Cicci. I'm sorry." Ignoring Ella's protests, he tapped a button on the laptop.

I scooted around Lachlan to watch as a video played, revealing my father and Ronan in the office I'd had gutted and turned into a library before selling my father's house.

"The business with Darragh O'Donnell is completed," Ronan said before sipping something from a highball glass. "There was an inconsequential addition to the plan, who was also dealt with."

"And?"

"Murder suicide is always so painful." Ronan stood and laid a dramatic hand on his chest. "He shot his lover, then himself. Honestly, it was easier than finding Cherise when she tried to run."

I stilled as my mother's name echoed from the tinny speakers. Both men laughed.

"I should have killed the bitch when I beat her for disobedience." My father snorted and lifted his glass in a toast. "Is she still alive?"

"Don't know, don't care. I still can't believe you didn't sell Natasha at the same time. Infant girls command a good price." Ronan replied.

For the first time, I willingly reached for Lachlan's hand. He enclosed my nerveless fingers in his warm grip, then wrapped his free arm around my chest as if he was trying to keep me from flying apart.

My father shrugged, dragging my attention back to the video. "I figured I'd get more from the stupid bitch if she wasn't hauling around a baby. The flab and stretch marks knocked at least thirty percent off her sale price as it was."

"True." Ronan touched his glass to my father's. "Anyway, I haven't seen Cherise up on the auction block, so I'm assuming she's dead or with her original buyer. Haven't seen him in ages either."

"What about Lachlan?"

"What about him?" Ronan asked, his ginger hair falling into his eyes as he gave my father a roguish wink. "He's too busy with his own life to bother digging, especially with having to take over the family business after the tragic loss of his brother."

"And I assume you want Natasha."

"Didn't I just give her a pretty dolly for her tenth birthday?" Ronan asked, his lips curling with derisive amusement. "I prefer my slaves a bit older, but she'd be worth a fortune to the right buyer if you want to get rid of her."

"Soon. She isn't quite obedient enough yet."

"We'll revisit the idea in a few years." Ronan replied. "After she grows some tits."

Lachlan seemed frozen, and I didn't blame him. Slowly, trying to hold the contents of my stomach in place, I closed the laptop, wishing I could erase Ronan's filthy words from my head.

Lachlan's brother.

My mother. I didn't know whether to hope she was dead, or pray she was alive. Hope was too dangerous, and something I couldn't afford to let myself feel.

A lifetime of bruises and broken promises to match my broken bones.

Fucking all of it was because of two men who thought having a dick meant they could take away a woman's freedom. My father was already dead, but I would see Ronan gasping out his last breaths, knowing I was his executioner.

He would beg for mercy before I let him die choking on his own blood.

———

LACHLAN

I squeezed my hands into fists and tried to focus. How had I missed so much? Why had I never even suspected Steve was a cat's paw for someone else.

Someone I once counted as a friend.

And fuck. The hell I'd put my wife through...

"I'm sorry, Lachlan," Ella whispered as she pressed a mostly full glass of brown liquor into my hand. "I didn't want to show you that video."

I drank it down, but the burn of bourbon didn't erase the ice lodged in my chest. "How long?"

"How long have we known?" She sighed and seemed to shrink, falling in on herself until her shoulders bowed as Cristian pulled her against his chest. "Just over a year. Gabby found the footage in Steve's old security files. I really, really didn't want you or Natasha to see it."

"I need a priest," Natasha said as she took off her suit jacket. "Or anyone you can find who will perform a wedding today. Not picky on the faith or lack thereof as long as Lachlan and I are legally married."

"That will take some time, and we'll probably have to—"

Her hands moved to the buttons on her blouse. "I said now, Ella. Things will end badly for you if I have to ask twice. Also, spread the news, and make sure there's a marriage certificate on file some- where. We want Ronan to have hard evidence that I've gone back to Lachlan."

"I—" Ella blinked and seemed to struggle with a reply. "What the fuck, Spider?"

"Did I stutter?" Natasha bent to take off her shoes, then straightened and twirled a double- edged dagger between her fingers. "Move it."

"Bloody hell." Daniel grabbed her wrist and twisted, making her drop the knife into his hand. "In your fucking shoe?"

To my surprise, and probably everyone else's, she smirked and gave up the blade without protest —and most importantly, without killing anyone. "Never, ever believe I'm unarmed or helpless. Might save your life one day."

As Cristian hustled Ella out of reach, I shook off my stupor and tried to close her blouse, but she knocked my hands away and shrugged it off her shoulders.

After taking several steps away from me, she finished undressing and with precise grace, lowered herself until her knees met sun-warmed concrete.

"I will say this one time, after which I will be silent unless my Master commands me to speak," she murmured. "I will execute Ronan Doherty, and ensure his body isn't found for at least twenty-four hours unless you prefer him to disappear entirely. Further, I will ensure the safety of everyone he holds against their will. I will also provide almost two thousand pages of documentation on his known associates."

I gaped at her, but didn't miss the telling gaze Daniel shared with Ella. I also didn't miss her not specifying a safe exit for herself. Natasha might think herself expendable, but I was more than willing to disabuse her of that notion with my belt on her ass.

"And I will be the perfect slave for my husband and Master, Lachlan O'Donnell without going 'Vigilante Shit' on his ass." She spread her thighs and rested her upturned hands on her knees, revealing her pussy. "But first, he needs to close his fucking mouth, wake up, and be a goddamned Master so I can nuke Ronan and his organization from orbit."

Unable to do anything else, I laughed softly, wishing it could be as easy as Natasha made it sound. "Saoirse told me I needed to cage you and make you like it if I wanted you back."

"I found something I'm willing to be caged for…" She arched her back and lifted her chin, but kept her eyes lowered. "Master."

Having Natasha go her knees willingly…

Justice for her mother.

The man who orchestrated my brother's murder dead at my feet.

I could have everything I ever wanted. Unfortunately, I didn't know if I was willing to pay the price.

Then again…

There was a reason Natasha was named Spider.

She was a killer. It wasn't something I could stop even if I wanted to. I could embrace that part of her…

Or lose her again. Maybe permanently. And that, I wasn't willing to do.

Crouching, I took her hand and pulled her to her feet. After covering her with my jacket, I pressed a finger against her chin, making her lift her head to look at me. "Do you really want a Master, little one?"

Moving my hand to her throat, I turned her to face away from me and inhaled the rich floral scent of her shampoo. "Or are you pretending?"

"I—"

"Are you taking the path of least resistance to your goal because Cristian and Ella said it was the only way?" I lowered my head and nipped her ear, ignoring our audience as they went inside on silent footsteps. "Are you a slave to your need to kill?"

"Lachlan…" She swallowed and took a deep breath. "I mean, Master—"

"You remind me of a bloodstock racehorse." I stroked her cheek with my free hand. "Undisciplined but poised at the starting gate with the thrill of competition coursing through your veins. All grace and power in such a diminutive package, but you require a firm hand on the reins to perform to your fullest potential."

"Christ." She tried to wriggle free but stilled when I wrapped my arm around her.

"But not the whip." I petted the curve of her hip, feeling the brand I'd given her under my fingertips. "You give your best when rewarded with pleasure."

"Stop, please." She wriggled in my arms, but didn't move when I relaxed my hold on her waist.

"My pretty slave needs blood on her hands," I purred, tightening my grip on her throat. "My exquisite Spider needs to watch her victims use their last breaths begging for mercy they don't deserve."

"Please..." She relaxed in my arms and ground her ass against my thickening cock. "Yes."

"Ask me, Spider." I circled her clit with a gentle fingertip, easing my touch when she bucked her hips against my hand. "Ask me to let you cover your beautiful body with their heart's blood. Fucking beg me to let you hear their dying pleas."

She eased herself from my arms and faced me before lowering herself to her knees once more. "I will kill with your permission, Master, but I won't insult you with begging. I will obey my Master's wishes."

CHAPTER TWENTY-THREE

NATASHA

"We have to try this place," Ella said, turning her phone to face me as our charter flight circled into the pattern over the Las Vegas airport. "They have pancakes as big as my head!"

"That's fine." I looked out the window, wishing we had time to do the touristy shit Vegas was famous for. I'd never seen the Grand Canyon, and the closest I was likely to get to Hoover Dam was a flyover of Lake Mead. Although I traveled frequently to take out my marks, I'd never gone on a vacation.

"There is a tapas bar down the street from our

hotel," Cristian replied as he scanned his phone. "It appears they serve brunch."

I tuned them out. My stomach was in too many knots to enjoy a meal, and Ella's constant chatter was exhausting.

Even the sumptuous private jet, complete with cream leather upholstery and a full bar, couldn't stop my second thoughts. Was remarrying Lachlan the only option open to me? He wouldn't hurt me again; first because I truly didn't believe he wanted to, and secondly because I could stop him if he tried to be an asshole again. Maybe I was overthinking things. The quickie Vegas wedding was my idea in the first place, and I'd been more than clear about what would happen to Lachlan if he acted up.

"You look lovely," Lachlan murmured, his breath fanning over the sensitive skin under my ear. "But quite pensive. Are Ella's choices of restaurants not to your liking?"

"I'm fine. Just not hungry." The bump under the fuselage as the landing gear dropped matched the turmoil in my stomach. "I just want to get this over with."

"Natasha, we don't have to remarry." He touched my cheek and gently turned me until I was looking at him. "If Ronan asks, I'll simply tell him I haven't bothered."

"You're probably right, but I don't want to give him any reason to question us." I sighed and let my head rest against the comfortable cushion. "Don't worry about getting stuck with me though. I divorced you once, and I can do it again."

"Of course." His jaw tightened, and after a moment, he nodded. "I'd still like to hear what you would have wanted if this wedding was intended to be forever."

"As long as it's legal, I honestly don't care. We just need to share a room for one night, then we can go back to Italy."

Thankfully, he fell silent. I didn't want to risk opening my mouth and having my wish for a real husband fall out. I wanted a do-over on my wedding night too, where I wouldn't be the only one thinking I'd get a happy-ever-after.

"So..." Ella said, interrupting my thoughts. "I booked us an appointment with a stylist for a dress fitting. Do you know what you want to wear, Natasha?"

"Jeans and a T-shirt." When she opened her mouth to protest, I held up my hand. "No dresses, no flowers, and no bullshit. We're putting on a show, remember? It just has to be legal."

"A show would require a couture dress and—"

"If jeans and a T-shirt is what Natasha wants, then she will have it," Lachlan said, interrupting Ella's objections. "Our wedding will be what she desires."

I shot a glance his way, wondering if he'd been replaced by a changeling. In what world did Lachlan O'Donnell care about my wishes?

Ella pouted, then huffed irritably. "What do you think about that drive-through chapel on Las Vegas Boulevard? We could do the Elvis and pink Cadillac package."

"That's more bullshit, not less," I retorted as my lips curled into a wry smile. "But fine. We'll do the Elvis thing."

After a quick pitstop for Ella's pancakes, during which Lachlan forced me to choke down eggs and avocado toast, we got our marriage license and checked into our hotel, then went straight to the chapel. The celebrant had the Elvis impersonation down pat. The ceremony started with me in the passenger seat, Ella and Cristian in the back with Lelia's carrier tucked between them, and Lachlan behind the wheel of a virulently pink Cadillac. Although I answered when prompted, I zoned out, lulled by the sounds of the city and the desert heat, until Lachlan spoke.

"I have vows I want to read." When the celebrant nodded, Lachlan brought my hand to his lips and kissed it, then pulled a piece of paper from his pocket.

"What are you doing?" I stage-whispered.

"This will be the second time Natasha has turned my life upside down." Still holding my hand, he kissed my cheek. "She won't believe me, but she's made me a better person."

"Lachlan…" I blinked to chase away a few tears. This wasn't real. We were putting on a show for the audience, but part of me still wanted it to be true.

"She made me question everything I once believed and forced me to see the destructive path I'd chosen for what it was." His touch on my cheek was like gossamer. Soft, barely there, and fucking heartbreaking. "She made me want to be better for her, but also for myself."

He slid a ring onto my finger, then kissed my forehead. I glanced down to see a platinum band encrusted with channel-set diamonds. "Like my wife, this ring is elegant and timelessly beautiful. It's the ring she should have had all along, and to her, I vow to be the man she deserves."

"Lovely," the celebrant said. "Natasha, do you have a ring for your husband?"

Since when were we exchanging rings? For that matter, how had he arranged mine in so little time? "I—"

"Right here," Ella pressed a black velvet box into my hand. "The matron of honor always holds the groom's ring."

I opened it to reveal a thick wedding band resting on a cushion of white silk. Its only adornment was a tiny spider picked out in diamond chips. Was it Ella's idea, or Lachlan's?

"Mine," Lachlan murmured, letting me know I'd asked the question out loud. "I thought it fitting."

My fingers shaking, I slid the ring onto Lachlan's left ring finger, then looked up into his compelling blue eyes. I wasn't sure what I expected to find when I studied his face, but the kind smile filled with hope wasn't it.

Fuck me. Had he convinced himself this was real?

"By the power vested in me by the State of

Nevada, I now pronounce you husband and wife. Lachlan, you may kiss your bride."

LACHLAN

Unwilling to give Natasha the kiss she deserved in front of an audience, I brushed my lips over hers, praying I communicated the hopes I had for our future. She might not believe our wedding was real, but I did.

Life didn't offer second chances very often. This time, I wanted it to be forever.

I got out of the Cadillac and jogged around the expansive hood to open Natasha's door and help her out. "Do you want supper before we go to the hotel?"

"Yes, please! I'm starving!" Ella said.

Cristian shushed her and extricated baby Lelia's carrier from the back seat of the Cadillac. "We'll leave you to enjoy your evening. I've arranged a separate car for you, and we'll meet at the airport at nine tomorrow morning."

Natasha looked down at the ring decorating her

left hand, then straightened her shoulders. "Yeah, that works. I guess."

Was she regretting her demand that we share a room? Despite her insistence that we needed to continue with the charade, I wouldn't force her. In an effort to relieve her palpable tension, I cupped her elbow and escorted her to the waiting town car.

"We could stop somewhere if you're hungry," I said.

"Thanks, but I'm fine." Her spine rigid, she climbed into the back seat and scooted over before I could get in. "Let's just go."

"Liar."

"Excuse me?" Ignoring our driver, she pinned me with an angry glare. "What are you talking about?"

"You're not fine." I took her hand and stroked her newly callused palm. "Even I know better than to believe a woman when she says that."

"I'll be fine once Ronan is dead," she retorted. "Nothing else matters."

"I beg to differ." I hesitated for a moment, then said, "You matter. Your happiness matters."

"To whom?" She snorted out a bitter laugh. "You?"

I saw our hotel in the distance, and knowing I had a single chance to soften her, I said, "Yes. You matter to me. Let us have the wedding night you should have had the first time."

She shook her head but chuckled softly. "Actually, that night was pretty decent."

"Only decent?"

"Don't push your luck. And don't expect me to cook breakfast." She sighed heavily, then added, "Why do you even care, Lachlan? I don't understand your game."

"Is it so hard to believe the vow I spoke?"

"You promised me forever last time," she shot back. "We both know how that turned out, so why do you think I'd believe you now?"

"A day will never pass that I don't regret what I did to you, and I still hate myself for it." I brushed a kiss over the callus on the side of her thumb, but didn't ask where it came from. "I know I don't have the right to ask, but I want a second chance."

"Lachlan, I..." She closed her eyes and rested her head against the seat. "Yeah, that's a lot to ask."

"You deserve better than decent, and I hope you'll let me give it to you."

She pressed her lips together and turned away. Knowing I had just a scant window of opportunity, I added, "Please. Let me regain your trust I should have never thrown away."

A faint, ghostly smile illuminated her gorgeous face. "Okay, fine. I'll most likely kill you in the morning."

I let out a surprised laugh. "I didn't take you for a *Princess Bride* fan. You're a bit young for it."

"Who isn't?" Our car stopped in front of the valet stand, and when the door opened, she accepted a hand to help her out. "That movie is as old as dirt, just like you."

Still laughing, I followed her out, then wrapped her hand around my elbow to escort her to our suite. Once we were locked inside, I led her into the bedroom and cupped her cheeks, then gave her the kiss I'd wanted to give her after our wedding. Her squeak of surprise turned into a whimper as I plundered her mouth, and her hands tightened on my shoulders.

She relaxed into my embrace, her body pressing against mine. My cock thickened against her taut belly, but I didn't dare push too fast, no matter how much I wanted to be inside her.

Pulling away, she blinked at me, her swollen lips parted. "You never kissed me like that."

"Like what?" Hoping to gentle her, I stroked her back, once again feeling the knobs of her spine.

"Like you actually meant it." Natasha took a step

back, still looking at me as if I was a mystery to be unraveled. "I don't know. It's different."

"We can stop right now," I said, although I kicked myself for every word. "I'll sleep on the couch, and you can have the bed."

"No." Slowly, she eased her T-shirt over her head and tossed it on the floor. "Make me understand."

CHAPTER TWENTY-FOUR

NATASHA

I didn't know what to believe.

This Lachlan was not the same man I married the first time. Worse, he was making me feel things I had no business feeling—like maybe there was more to life than eliminating people who didn't deserve to exist.

And yes, it was like a really stupid romance novel plot, but I could tell the difference in his kiss. Comparatively, the kisses he gave me on our wedding night were technically perfect. The one he laid on me just now was... not.

He trembled in my arms as if he was holding himself back. As if I was the only person in the world who could give him succor. I felt for a brief, brilliant moment that I held his soul in my hands.

That didn't mean I was willing to trust him again, but I decided to see where he was going with this completely uncharacteristic behavior.

His touch reverent, he slid his hands down my ribs as he lowered himself to his knees. "Let me make love to you like I should have."

I caught the words before they came out, but I really wanted to remind him that making love didn't fit us. We were not—and never would be—in love. Then again, he rocked my world the first time, and I was willing to see if he could deliver on his promises.

A woman had needs, right? Who was I to stop him from scratching my itch? As long as I didn't catch feels for him, everything would be golden. And instead of busting my ass cooking breakfast for the ungrateful jerk, I'd leave him sleeping in the wet spot and wouldn't bother with a wave goodbye.

I nodded my agreement, but he shook his head. "I need the words from you, Natasha. Tell me you want this."

Since when did Lachlan give a shit about consent?

"I... Yes." The words tasted like ash, but I said them anyway. "Make love to me."

"Your wish..." He unbuttoned my jeans, and the rasp of my zipper was loud in the quiet room. "My command."

His hand burned like fire as he slid it down my leg and lifted my foot to remove my sneaker, and I held in a gasp when he repeated the process with my other shoe.

"Lachlan—"

"Say it again, Natasha."

"What?"

"Tell me you want this."

God help me, I did. My skin felt too tight for my body, and I shivered as he rose to his feet. Even knowing what he was... Knowing he was the definition of danger and duplicity...

I wanted him.

"Tell me." He sank his hand into my curls and tugged gently, forcing my chin up. "Tell me you want more pleasure than you ever dreamed. Tell me you want me to fuck you until you scream with passion."

It was definitely past time to peace out, but I couldn't. I was probably about to make the biggest mistake of my life, but...

The words wouldn't come.

"Fuck me, Lachlan." I hauled in a breath, praying I wouldn't end up on the evening news as yet another dead woman chewed up and spat back out as fodder for true crime podcasts. "Fuck me and leave bruises."

"No." He gentled his touch on my hair and kissed my forehead. "I would give you everything I have, but not that."

"Sorry, what?"

"Bruises, sweetheart. You don't get to ask me to give you pain." He kissed the tip of my nose and shook his head. "You don't get to ask me to give you another reason to hate me."

Smiling sadly, he picked up my T-shirt and gently eased it over my head before zipping up my jeans. "Decide what you truly want, Natasha. When your head is straight, I'll be on the couch."

Stalling the protest I still couldn't vocalize, he trailed his fingers across my jaw. "I'll see you in the morning."

Without another word, he walked out, leaving me confused and fuming as he shut the door behind him. Biting back a vicious curse, I picked up my shoe and threw it against the window. The stupid thing got caught in the sheer drapes and slid to the floor with a soft plop, making me want to scream.

"What the fuck just happened?" I asked, although no one was around to answer. "Seriously, is he for real?"

I wished Dante was with me so I could unload my crazy into his understanding ear, but he was probably hanging out in Ella's kitchen waiting for treats. Cursing myself again, I tossed my other shoe at the window, then paced the room.

Had I screwed up with Lachlan? He'd never once come after me following our divorce and had silently obeyed every one of my spiteful edicts for months. It hurt a little, knowing he thought I was looking for ammunition against him.

I wasn't. Not really, and definitely not right fucking now while my core was still pulsing with desire. Besides, I hadn't given him a single reason to think otherwise.

Yeah, no. I didn't trust him—not yet, and probably not ever—but it might be time to change the game.

———

LACHLAN

It took less time than I'd expected for the door separating the bedroom from the rest of the suite to open. Natasha wasn't one to leave a challenge unanswered, especially now that she'd grabbed her power with both hands.

She probably wouldn't believe me, but I meant what I said. Perhaps we'd get to the point where we could make love with the bite of pain I knew she craved, but it wouldn't be tonight.

This was our second chance, and I refused to squander it.

Silvery moonlight made her gleam as she glided to the center of the room and lowered herself to her knees. She looked like a goddess, gloriously nude, with defined muscles tracing lines across her body. Her piercings were gone, but I didn't miss them.

They were our past, and we were well rid of the degrading marks of subjugation she never deserved.

"You're awake," she murmured.

"Yes." I rose to my feet, then crossed the room to help her up. "And The Spider kneels for no one unless she desires it."

"What are you doing to me, Lachlan?"

I wanted to turn on the light to see her face but

decided to let her hide in the shadows. They were her home, more now than ever before.

"Nothing you don't ask for. Nothing that would cause you pain." I moved behind her and kissed a path up her shoulder to her tender throat. "And nothing that doesn't bring you to the heights of joy."

"I think I'm broken." She lowered her head, letting her curls conceal her face. "I don't know what to ask, or how I should feel about anything."

My heart stuttered and missed a beat at her painful admission. Because of me and her father, she had no idea what a healthy relationship looked like, but I'd fix my mistakes if it killed me.

"You're not broken." I petted her silky skin until she relaxed under my touch. "Let me show you."

Slowly, I kissed her spine, following the trail of vertebrae until I reached the swell of her beautiful ass. She shivered under my touch, but I didn't think it was because she was chilled. She was out of her comfort zone.

"Good?" I knelt and skimmed my hands up her legs before turning her to face me. I inhaled the scent of her, thick and sweet with flowers and her unique perfume.

"Yes."

"You'll tell me if it's not." Before she could reply,

I kissed the top of her mound. "May I touch you here?"

"I..." She tightened her hands into fists, then relaxed and spread her feet a scant few inches further apart. "I want more."

"Good girl." I circled her clit with the tip of my tongue, then eased a finger toward her opening. "How much more?"

Without warning she stiffened and pushed me away. "I need you to stop teasing me. Your days of edging me are over, so fuck me or get out."

"Natasha—"

"You heard me." She lifted her chin and glared at me. "Which is it going to be? And by the way, you don't get to kiss me again."

"All right." I invaded her space and yanked her into my arms, concealing my satisfaction at getting a secret she hadn't meant to share.

My young bride was terrified. Despite her attempts to hide her fear behind bravado, I saw it in her face. Natasha held herself stiffly, her hands clenched into fists at her sides. Her eyes darted to me, then to the door leading from our suite, and a rapid pulse pounded in her graceful neck. She wouldn't purposely show how much she longed for intimacy, and I was betting she hated the idea of being vulnerable to anyone, least of all me.

Without giving her a chance to protest, I carried her into the bedroom, then tossed her on the bed before freeing my throbbing erection.

"Lachlan!"

"Shh." Instead of kissing her, I laid a finger over her lips as I settled between her spread thighs, letting her wet core scald me with its heat. "I've decided to give you what you asked for, unless you've changed your mind."

For now, at least. My beautiful Spider would soon learn I wasn't about to give up on her or our future together.

"I haven't." She met my gaze and wrapped her fingers around my shaft, lining me up with her entrance. "But if you try to kiss me, I'll make you regret it."

"I have no doubt of that."

I slammed into her, relishing her pleasured cries as I fucked her hard. For a moment, I worried I'd hurt her, but she wrapped her legs around my hips and lifted herself to meet my thrusts.

"So...fucking...tight." I wanted to punish her, make her realize what she was missing. But I couldn't. Not without risking everything. The stakes were too high.

"Yes!"

Her nails scored my back, the sting forcing me to redouble my efforts. I wanted to take my time, but I wouldn't last much longer. Needing to make her come before I did, I slid my hand between our bodies and pinched her clit.

She cried out wordlessly and tightened around me, her inner walls squeezing rhythmically with the force of her climax. The base of my spine tingled in warning, and with a shouted curse, I pulled out and fisted my cock. My cum sprayed her chest and abdomen, marking her with pearly liquid.

Before she could speak, I leaned down, close enough to hear her soft, gasping breaths, and put my lips to her ear. "You'll get my cum when I get a kiss from you."

A brilliant smile lit up her face as she cupped the back of my head and pressed her lips to mine in a scorching, but too brief kiss. When I tried to coax her into more, she twisted her hips under me and did something with her arms that sent me flying. I landed on the floor with a bone-jarring thump, thankfully missing the edge of the dresser with my forehead.

Unhurriedly, she rose, letting my seed drip down her torso. "I'm going to shower. Make sure you're not in my bed when I get back."

She sauntered into the bathroom, shutting and locking the door behind her. I chuckled then rose to my feet. Natasha didn't know it yet, but she'd given me everything I needed.

CHAPTER TWENTY-FIVE

NATASHA

These days, things weren't much different than they were during my first go-around with Lachlan, but at least I got to use a toilet. Privately, I thought it was more because Ella and Cristian didn't want me to pee in their backyard —not that I blamed them, because...gross.

My piercings were back too, along with wrist and ankle cuffs I actually liked.

Gifted to me by Ella and her James Bond crew of highly skilled artisans, the smooth, polished steel hid special treats. All I had to do was touch a hidden trigger on any of the four cuffs to release deadly sharp blades. They weren't long enough to reach a man's heart but were more than capable of severing arteries or tendons.

Even the matching collar had a little something special added to it. Concealed behind the clasp rested a tiny plastic ampoule containing a poison Ella said could kill within seconds. Wearing it made me want to pretend I was Lucrezia Borgia.

I didn't want to think about it, but the poison might be my own exit plan if things went south. Knowing Ella, I wouldn't be surprised if that was what she intended it for.

"Open, Spider," Lachlan murmured as I knelt under a brilliant azure sky decorated with puffy clouds.

I ignored the milling guards, who pretended they were watching my debasement, and let the fragrance of lemons and olives consume my senses.

Of course, it wasn't debasement if I consented, now, was it?

Maybe it was, and I just didn't care as long as it got me close enough to Ronan to kill him. I parted my lips to reveal my tongue, studded with four small platinum balls. Barely a month after I remarried my husband, I'd fallen into automatic obedience, just like old times.

Well, it wasn't quite like old times.

Instead of being washed with a garden hose, I soaked in a gigantic tub surrounded by orchids, while I indulged in bubbles, candles, and wine. The sensory deprivation chamber was gone, as was the unseasoned ground chicken and chopped vegetables I ate from a dog bowl. My kennel was a tastefully sumptuous suite with French doors leading to a balcony overlooking the sea.

I ate kneeling at Lachlan's feet on a thick cushion, while he fed me high-protein, nutritionally dense delicacies Ella's chef and my trainer put on my menu. My nights were spent wrapped securely in his arms after hours of making me come until I fell unconscious.

Maybe it wasn't so surprising that I let him fuck me. I'd kept up with my birth control, and a woman had needs, after all. Thankfully, he hadn't tried to kiss me since our second wedding night, but stupid me wanted him to. God, I'd almost given in and let him. Talk about too stupid to live.

The truly astonishing part was that Lachlan swore he hadn't taken a lover either, and I seriously didn't know how to feel about the fact that I let him sleep with me every night.

Lachlan was many things, but he wasn't a liar.

That wasn't the only thing I was beginning to believe about him either. I still couldn't get over the vows he'd spoken, and absurd ideas like *forever* were intruding into my head like the most annoying earworm ever.

Gotta say, I liked my second wedding better than my first, but yeah, no.

Thankfully, I didn't have a lot of time to ruminate over that particular folly. After eight-hour days divided between slave practice and a truly sadistic personal trainer who took honing my body and reflexes as his raison d'être...

Let's just say it didn't take Lachlan long to send me to dreamland. Hell, I didn't even dream. It was as if my nightmares knew I was too tired to pay attention, so they decided not to show up.

Seriously, a girl could get used to it. I was in the best shape of my life.

I missed my soft, voluptuous curves though. Despite my father's constant jabs about my weight, I thought I looked like one of those gorgeous models in a Rubens painting. I wished there was some way to keep my formerly generous ass and still be able to wriggle through the air ducts my trainer set up as part of my daily obstacle course practice.

Once Ronan was dead, I'd bake. There would be

scones with crème fraîche, cookies, brioche with tender golden crusts and sweetly dense crumb, cakes with homemade buttercream and jam filling... Victoria sponge, pear tarts with candied ginger...

And homemade pasta. *All* the pasta. I'd make sage-infused brown butter sauce on butternut ravioli. Or linguini with Puttanesca rich with fragrant olive oil and anchovies... The Parmigiano Reggiano would be measured with my heart—never a scale or spoon—and fuck anyone who dared give measurements for cheese in recipes. It was a crime more heinous than using a cellphone in the theatre.

I swallowed a mouthful of drool and tried to focus. As much as I wanted my beautiful, lush body back, I wouldn't stop training—not when I knew Ronan wasn't the only person out there who sold humans for fun and profit.

To my disappointment, Lachlan didn't give me his cock. Of course, I hadn't expected him to. He used toys on occasion but wouldn't touch me in public. And he never let me come.

Damn him.

Instead, he knelt and made the bell hanging from my clit hood chime as he pushed a diabolically effective vibrator into my pussy. As the toy sang the song of its people, Daniel strolled to me and sank a fist into my hair before pulling my head back.

I had hair to pull this time. I really wanted it gone before we went after Ronan, but Daniel disagreed unless I was willing to shave my head. I was. Lachlan was very much not in agreement.

The exercise was necessary, no matter how much I hated it. Daniel, Ella, and even Cristian were all trying to accustom me to letting people other than Lachlan touch my hair without going all murder-y on them.

Somehow, they'd all figured out it was a trigger for me, although I never told them how my father used it to drag me down the stairs, across gravel, or pretty much anywhere it would hurt.

"Don't call her Spider." Daniel pushed his finger into my mouth and tapped the back of my throat, making me swallow before I gagged. "We've discussed this."

"*You've* discussed it." Lachlan turned up the vibe and I relaxed into the sensation, focusing on the conversation as I'd been taught. "My wife is named Natasha O'Donnell. Spider is my slave."

"Wrong. Spider is an assassin who strikes fear into men's hearts," Daniel replied as he used a wipe to clean his hands. "Natasha is a slave, and you need to address her as such to make this work."

"Master—" I swallowed a gasp as Lachlan twisted the vibe to hit yet another sweet spot inside me. "May I speak?"

"Yes."

The evil toy stopped its work, and instead of sighing with relief, I kept my voice evenly modulated. "If it pleases you, Master, you could call me Arachne. Tell Ronan you didn't like my name and changed it. He'll be dead before anyone makes the connection."

I didn't give a shit what Lachlan called me, but he needed to pull himself together and focus if he expected me to kill Ronan without both of us ending up dead.

"Beautiful weaver," he murmured as he petted my hair. "But you weave death instead of cloth, don't you?"

Ooh, I liked that. I stifled a shudder of pleasure, hanging on to my slave persona with both hands before I gushed over the compliment.

"Or you could call me Slave. If Ronan asks, tell him I don't have a name anymore." As much as I wanted to meet his beautiful blue eyes, I kept my gaze lowered. "If it pleases you, Master."

"Oh, good job, little one. That will keep your Master on track," Daniel murmured. Turning away from me, he snapped his fingers. "Justin, do you want this very obedient slave to suck your cock?"

Lachlan growled like a fucking dog and bared his teeth in a legit snarl, despite knowing poor Justin was happily married and wouldn't touch me. Rolling my eyes, I got to my feet. At least he'd stopped chewing on Daniel when we worked to desensitize me to touch, but he still couldn't grasp the finer points of slave ownership.

"Fuck's sake, O'Donnell." I got in his face and stabbed my finger into his chest. "What part of you Master, me slave do you fail to comprehend?"

"And we've lost her again." Daniel rubbed his forehead and sighed. "Lachlan, she's got it. She's bloody perfect when you're not being an ass. I'm beginning to think she's not the one who needs the training."

"Piss off," Lachlan muttered. "I will never permit her to be touched by anyone."

"Then leash me," I countered. "A leashed slave is untouchable unless their Master gives permission."

"That will *never* happen, Natasha."

"Ahhh!"

The guards scattered like pigeons before a hawk

as I strode across the lawn to the cliff overlooking the sea. Lachlan chased after me, either in an attempt to fuel my irritation, or because he wanted to convince me to accept his bullshit.

"Natasha, stop!" he called.

I spun to face him and put my hands on my hips, uncaring that everyone was watching a naked slave prepare to throw down with her Master. "Listen to me, Lachlan, because I will say this only once. I have worked my ass off to get ready for this assignment, but you can't even get my name right."

He lifted his gaze heavenward, then sighed and nodded. "I know that, but you're so damned beautiful when you kneel for me. All I want is my wife, safe and happy, and fuck you if you think this is easy for me."

Aw, dammit. If I wasn't careful, Lachlan might just possibly make me fall in love with him. I couldn't keep listening to that shit without wondering if it was true. No woman could. And that, I couldn't afford.

"Yeah, whatever." He was too lost in his own anger to look at me. Besides, willingly subjecting myself to slavery wasn't exactly a walk in the park for me either—especially with so much at stake. "Do you know why Ronan isn't already dead? Ask yourself why we missed his last auction and lost over a dozen people into the slave trade. Three guesses, and the first two don't count."

"God damn it, Natasha!" He grabbed my shoulders and shook me. "Do you think I don't know that? You're asking me to do the two things I swore I would never do."

"Lachlan—"

He slumped and rested his forehead against mine. "You're asking me to leash you, baby. You want me to let other men touch you. I can't do it."

"Not even if leashing me saves my life?" I stepped out of reach and lifted my head to meet his tortured gaze. "Think about it, but don't speak to me until you have a good answer."

Without another word, I walked away, grabbing my silk bathrobe before I entered the house. He'd either figure it out, or I'd find another way into Ronan's compound.

It hurt, but I was done caring. Ronan was going to die—with or without Lachlan on the dumb end of my leash.

————

LACHLAN

"You have three choices, my friend." Cristian clipped his cigar, passing me the cutter before he lit up. Strangely, he turned to glance at the expansive garage to the left of the house and several dozen yards away, then checked the time on a slim cellphone.

"Forget Ronan and take my wife home," I muttered.

"That would make four choices, but Natasha will never agree." He took a drag from his cigar and exhaled. "You can leash her as she's asked you on multiple occasions, thus alleviating your aversion to physical contact from strangers. You could forgo the leash and allow the touch you so vehemently oppose."

"None of the above. What's your third?"

"Allow her to select a different Master, which would set us back at least a year while the new candidate ingratiates himself with her target." He grimaced and swirled his scotch before taking a sip. "Not that we actually have another candidate."

"Also unacceptable." I lit my cigar and gazed over the edge of the infinity pool. "She's mine."

Except... Natasha gave me the one argument I couldn't dispute. What if leashing her saved her life?

"The Spider belongs to no one," Cristian murmured before sipping calmly from his glass of scotch. "She is much like my Ella. Such a woman might consent to submit, but one must bend before one is broken under her stilettos." Laughing softly, he added, "Although with my wife, I can safely assume stiletto refers to her shoes, and not to the knives Natasha carries."

"Not helpful."

"No, I suppose not, considering one of Natasha's confirmed kills was performed with such a shoe. She drove the heel into her victim's eye. Ella just *had* to buy the same ones."

"Really not helpful," I muttered, making Cristian laugh. "Sexy as fuck, but not helpful."

"Indeed. Natasha will kneel for you, but never forget she has her own agenda, independent of yours."

"Agenda..." I stilled as my mind latched onto the worst thing Natasha could do. "Do you think she'll try to infiltrate his compound by herself?"

"I do." He glanced at the time and his jaw tightened almost imperceptibly. "She left for the airport about an hour ago. She has chosen to refuse both an escort and a backup team."

"And you let her go?" I grabbed Cristian's collar and hauled him to his feet. "Why didn't you tell me sooner?"

"I was asked to withhold that information by someone who wouldn't lose a minute's sleep over making me a widower." He gazed at me steadily, without trying to get away. "I won't make the mistake of doubting her. Neither should you."

I relaxed my hand on his collar and let him go, knowing I'd do the same if someone like Natasha threatened my family. "Fine. What do you suggest?"

"You seek to prevent her from achieving her goal, Mr. O'Donnell. She knows this and has made the only choice she could. Without you, she might have a slim, very improbable chance. Unless..."

Cristian's lips quirked into a faint smile, and I resisted the urge to strangle him. "Unless what?"

"Her chances increase to possible if you can remember she is a slave." He touched his chest. "And as I told both of you weeks ago, you must believe it inside."

"I..."

That was the big problem. I didn't see her as a slave anymore. She was a powerful, brilliant young woman. Even when I had her locked in a dog kennel, she never lost the quiet dignity and pride that kept her spine straight—no matter what I did to her. Her bearing had incensed me at the time, but looking back, my anger was a disguise for reluctant admiration.

"What would you do to save her life?" Cristian asked before I could formulate a reply. "Would you do the thing you most detest if it means she comes home to you?"

"I already gave up my vengeance."

It wasn't even a lie. Ronan was going to die because he needed to be put down—exactly as I should have done with Steve—and without involving innocent people.

"Sometimes that's the easiest thing to let go of." His eyes went distant, and he smiled as he gazed at something in the distance. "Natasha and Ella are very much alike, but so too are you and I."

"What does that mean?" As much as I wanted to punch him until he told me where my wife was, I forced myself to listen instead.

"I coerced Ella into marriage for revenge. I thought giving it up would make her stay." He refilled his glass from the bottle on the table and took a sip. "But what I had to give up was the idea that she would change herself to conform to what I thought she should be, when I should have accepted her as she was."

Cristian met my eyes, then added, "A close friend once told me to ask myself if I loved the woman I wanted her to be, or the woman she actually is."

"Damn you." I scraped my hands through my hair. "I have to try."

"That's all any of us can do." "He returned to his chair and picked up the cigar he'd dropped. "Natasha took my wife's Veyron, which happens to be a thirsty bitch with a nearly empty petrol tank. Perhaps you should hurry, as she's probably stranded by the side of the road."

"Thanks." I caught the fob he tossed at me, then gave him an unwilling smirk. "You gave her that vehicle on purpose."

"Of course. You'll be driving the fully fueled black BMW sedan parked in the garage to the left of the Porsche. I've also instructed the pilot to wait for you if she managed to make it to the airport. I'll send someone for the Veyron later." He reached into his pocket for a hand-printed card, and after passing it to me, he added, "That's the name and address of the hotel we've reserved for you and Natasha. You'll find a car and driver waiting at the Cork airport. You'll be receiving some packages at the hotel as well."

I nodded and accepted the card, but before I could reply, he added, "Oh, and Lachlan?"

"What?"

"Ronan's next auction is in less than forty-eight hours, but we have not been able to arrange an invitation. Contact him. You must convince him you have a slave you wish to sell."

"Damn it." I gritted my teeth as my phone chimed with an incoming text containing Ronan's phone number. "I hate this."

"You'll hate yourself more if you let her go without you." Pointing at my phone, he added, "That's Ronan's public number. He won't question how you got it, but your call will probably pass through a secretary or two before he gets the message."

"Thanks." I spun on my heel and hurried to the suite I shared with Natasha, then threw our training equipment into a suitcase, including a sheer black dress, her leash, and lastly, a dragon tail whip. As I packed clothes for myself, my anger grew.

"What the fuck is she thinking?" I tossed a set of her throwing stars into the bag, but didn't find any of her daggers or her pistols. "Did she consider the danger? Or even make sure the car she took had enough fuel?"

For the first time since I let her go all those months ago, I thought I could indeed become the Master I needed to be.

And Natasha's ass would learn that lesson soon.

CHAPTER TWENTY-SIX

NATASHA

Still cursing my idiocy, I traipsed back to Ella's car lugging a gas can. The Veyron was a sweet ride, but damn, it sucked fuel like an unsupervised eight-year-old with a bag of Halloween candy.

Yeah, I could have called for a rescue, but that would have meant admitting failure. Besides, it was a beautiful day, and perfect for the two-mile walk to a gas station.

Well, the weather was nice when I started. A chilly breeze whipped up as threatening gray clouds accumulated in the sky. As the cold drizzle dampened my face, I shivered and broke into a jog, trying my best not to jostle the gas can too much.

With luck, Cristian kept his mouth shut, meaning I might have enough time to get to the airport without Lachlan catching me. Of course, I'd only asked for an hour, which was yet more evidence of terminal dumbassery.

Thankfully, the Veyron was in sight, but as I approached, a black sedan pulled to a slow stop behind it. His face hard and as implacable as I'd ever seen it, Lachlan stepped from the sedan. Leaning against the fender, he crossed his arms over his chest.

And naturally, the clouds decided to open up, drenching me in seconds. Lachlan opened an umbrella and smirked at me.

Fucking perfect.

Deciding I was as soaked as I was going to get, I slowed my pace to a walk. After reaching the Veyron, I dumped the gas into the tank and tossed the empty can into the trunk.

He held the umbrella over me, and I felt his heat against my back before he spoke. "I've caught a naughty slave."

Shivering with a mix of cold and trepidation, I didn't object when he draped his coat over my shoulders and gently pushed my arms into the sleeves, somehow managing to keep the umbrella steady at the same time. "Um...sorry?"

"After you crawl to the BMW, you will kneel on the floor in the back seat, where a slave belongs."

"But—" He circled my throat, his long fingers tightening until I struggled for air. The umbrella tumbled away, driven by the strong wind.

"You may either obey now, or I will administer your punishment on the side of the road." Leaning close to whisper in my ear, he added, "You will strip naked and bend over the hood. I will then whip you until I decide your chastisement is complete. I will also remind you how much more a whipping hurts when the weather is cold. Do you understand?"

"Wow. You finally got your Master act together. Nice work." I knocked his hand away and tried to brush past him, but he caught me and twisted my arm, forcing me to bend until my face touched the wet steel of the Veyron's hood. He didn't hurt me, but the position would definitely become painful if I tried to move. "Lachlan—"

"I did not allow you to speak, much less call me by name," he interrupted as he stroked my upturned ass. "When I let you go, you will say nothing. You will do as I ordered and count yourself fortunate that I'll delay the whipping you've earned until we're in the air for Ireland. You may nod if you understand."

His tone was different. The spite that used to color everything he said when I lived in the kennel was absent, as were the tentative requests he tried to pretend were commands during training.

Spiteful Lachlan was easy to ignore. I would do the bare minimum to make him shut up and go away. I was beginning to believe he wanted to be the husband I should have had in the first place, but nervous Lachlan was just fucking annoying because he was in my way.

Master Lachlan had a live wire going straight to my pussy.

I swallowed hard and nodded as best I could with my face pressed against the hood of a car.

"Good. Now, stand up." The roughly barked order didn't match his soft touch as he helped me straighten. He looked me up and down, then arched a blond eyebrow. "What would a well-behaved slave do if she wanted to ask her Master for forgiveness?"

"I—"

"Did I say you could speak, slave?"

He pressed gently on my shoulder, erasing my confusion. Slowly, I lowered myself to my knees on the wet asphalt and dropped my chin. My pussy heated, driving the lingering chill from my body, and I stifled a needy whimper as he tangled his hand in my hair.

"Very nice," he murmured. "Now, crawl to the BMW."

I obeyed instantly, even though he used my hair as a leash to direct me to the rear passenger-side door. I definitely should have hated it but didn't. Maybe I'd grown used to people touching my hair. Or maybe it was just Lachlan.

The act of crawling made me remember the butt plug tail I used to wear, but I didn't cringe at the memory anymore. In fact, I kind of wanted it back. I refused to contemplate why.

Although my knees were protected by the fabric of my jeans, the rough asphalt abraded my palms. Holding in a sigh of relief, I crawled into the car and didn't flinch when he slammed the door behind me and got my things from the Veyron before loading them into the BMW.

Leaving me dripping on the floorboards, he said nothing as he drove us to the airport. Unwilling to test his newfound resolve, I kept my trap shut too.

Silence had always been my friend, but my head wasn't remotely quiet. Too many thoughts jostled for supremacy, not the least of which was trying to decide how I felt about giving him control.

Not that I gave it. As we'd been trying to convince him to do for weeks, he took charge of me without asking, finally claiming me as his.

I was proud of him for getting his head out of his ass, but I couldn't figure out why I didn't hate it.

I expected to. I expected his commands to chafe. I expected to despise every moment of my performance, knowing that failure would mean my execution and the loss of more people to Ronan's filthy auctions.

Knowing that if I was lucky, I'd get to die quickly. The chances of getting to Ronan were good. So were the odds of me killing him. Me getting him alone long enough to watch him die, then get rid of the body while evading dozens of guards...

Yeah. Even if I had Lachlan, and our performance was textbook perfect, it didn't look too good for the home team—not that I'd tell him that.

Why then, did my heart race and my body sizzle? Why did prickles of pleasure spiral through my body from his very touch. Why did his orders, delivered in that sexy Irish accent, make me drip?

And why the fuck did I feel like kneeling for him was exactly where I needed to be?

LACHLAN

Thankfully, the storm soon cleared sufficiently to allow our departure. I decided to use the preflight time wisely and, without speaking, led Natasha into the small bedroom in the back of the aircraft, again using her hair as a leash. In too big a hurry to get her warm and dry, I didn't make her crawl.

Her cheeks colored and she dropped her chin before struggling with my jacket as she toed off her sodden sneakers. Even in training, she'd never gifted me with such a true, unguarded reaction. Compared to the woman I married and caged, who obeyed just long enough to plot her escape, or the one who bullied me unmercifully during training if I made the slightest misstep behaving as her Master, this Natasha was relaxed and supple under my touch.

She didn't stiffen or appear to force herself to obey—not even when I held her hair as I made her crawl in the rain across several feet of wet pavement —and the constant tension in her shoulders and neck eased.

I'd long suspected her father had used her hair to physically control her. Judging by the number of times she'd demanded a hair clipper over the last few weeks, I wondered if the tears she cried when I had Jerome shave her head were from relief rather than sadness.

Knowing her wet clothes would make undressing a challenge, I helped her. She moved easily, her limbs soft as I eased her shirt over her head. Her only mistake was to giggle at my irritable curses while I tried to extricate her from her muddy jeans. Unfortunately, her soft laughter cut off too soon, as if she realized her error.

Although I should have corrected her, and she would probably scold me for not doing so, her laughter was too rare to discourage. Instead, I said, "Good girl for undressing without being told."

When she didn't reply, I added, "You may thank me verbally, slave."

"Thank you, Master. And thank you for helping."

"It was my pleasure." I tucked a lock of wet hair behind her ear and nipped her pierced lobe. "There's a bathroom through that door. I require my slaves to be clean, so bathe quickly with very warm water, dry off, and return."

I wanted to erase her shivers and the blue tinge on her lips more than I wanted her clean. She didn't huff and glare at me, so I assumed my request came out as the terse order I'd intended. Of course, she might have been too chilled to bother.

"Yes, Master."

She hurried into the bathroom and, after a beat of hesitation that wouldn't have been caught by anyone who didn't know her, left the door open. She turned the water all the way hot and stepped into the tiny shower before letting out a barely audible groan of pleasure that made me want to join her.

Sadly, there was neither room, nor time. As much as I wanted to take her straight to bed, I couldn't. We had too few hours to ensure our performance was perfect, meaning I'd have to give her the whip marks that would lend credence to her position as a slave.

As if she knew we'd be taking off soon, she hurried through rinsing her hair and turned off the water. After joining her in the bathroom, I handed her a towel.

"Slave, answer my next question freely."

"Of course, Master." She dried her hair roughly, then finger-combed her curls into place.

"When should I whip you?"

Frowning, she cocked her head, but kept her gaze lowered. "I don't understand, Master."

"When should your whipping happen to present the best bruises to Ronan?"

If I hadn't been watching, I'd have missed the split-second flicker of rage in her beautiful brown eyes. It vanished as quickly as it appeared, and she closed her eyes, seeming to relax every muscle in her body one at a time.

For a moment, I wondered if I'd slipped out of character. Natasha rarely let me get away with trying to treat her gently when we were Master and slave though. She would have said something rude if I had.

"Midday tomorrow, Master," she finally said, her tone even and modulated.

"So, a whipping after we take off, then again tomorrow after lunch?"

Keeping her expression neutral, she said, "If it pleases you, Master."

"Good girl." Without offering her fresh clothes, I opened the pocket door leading into the main cabin. "Kneel, then crawl to your seat and fasten your safety belt. We'll do your first whipping after we reach altitude."

"Yes, M—"

"You may not speak."

The flight attendant, an older man with graying

hair and a military bearing, didn't bat an eye at Natasha's nudity as he brought us bottled water and small plates of snacks delicious enough to have come from Ella's kitchen. I refused his offer of wine for both of us. One glass probably wouldn't hurt, but we needed clear heads until we finished our task.

Afterward? I'd dress Natasha in fine couture, then treat her to a steak dinner with the best of wines—including all the lobster she wanted. Perhaps crab instead. She loved steak Oscar, and to my amusement, always asked for the cook to slap the cow's ass and walk it past the fire.

I took a sip of water to hide my smile, but I needed to get my head back in the game. Natasha was depending on me to keep her safe. After everything I'd learned about Ronan, there was no room for anything less than absolute perfection.

And for the first time, I thought I could give it to her.

CHAPTER TWENTY-SEVEN

NATASHA

The plane leveled, making me tense as the flight attendant returned to his seat near the galley. I wasn't looking forward to the whipping Lachlan promised me, but I was interested in seeing if he'd go through with it.

Even when I was trapped in his kennel, he'd never given me more than a pop or two with a riding crop, which I hadn't appreciated as much as I should have. He could have done so much worse. My father certainly had.

Maybe my change of heart had more to do with reviewing all the files Daniel had on Ronan Doherty, which far surpassed mine, and less to do with my six weeks of humiliation at Lachlan's hands.

After my first day in the kennel, I'd have said he and Ronan were the same, but I couldn't have been more wrong. Unlike Ronan, Lachlan wasn't driven by greed and sadistic cruelty. Grief and helpless anger made him do what he did to me, and when he finally learned the truth...

Well, let's just say I was pretty sure I knew how he felt. After all, I'd done the same thing—with a much larger body count. I had to admit to some soul-searching though. It wasn't right to spend so much time blaming him for my problems. Purposely hurting him, both financially with the millions in donations I'd strongarmed him into, or emotionally with the numerous elderly pets I'd forced him to accept so he could watch them die, was cruel, and I'd spent well over six weeks at it.

It took a very special person to rescue an aged shelter animal, knowing they'd leave too soon. And damn him, Lachlan hadn't missed a beat—even for Marmite, the neglected pony who bit everyone who got close to him. I'd managed to keep the little shit for less than a month before the bruises from his bites started matching what my father used to leave on me. At least I got his overgrown hooves dealt with, along with a bath and grooming.

And naturally, because both of them were little shits, he decided Lachlan was his best friend, even going so far as to allow Lachlan to groom him without requiring sedation.

I'd always wished for a pony. If I was ever in a position to get another, it would be a sweet draft horse from one of the many rescues Teresa, my vet, kept sending me—not a Shetland pony risen to plague the earth from the lowest circles of hell.

If he hadn't started chasing me with his teeth bared, I'd have kept Marmite despite his evil temper. I didn't even want to think about Orc, the truly unfortunate-looking poodle whose name matched his disposition. Yeah, according to Teresa, Lachlan got along with that little Uruk Hai reject too.

Yeah, I was a touch jealous, but honestly, I was happy to get Marmite and Orc into a loving home—even if it wasn't with me.

Oh well. At least Dante and Angel liked me. Well, Angel liked Dante. She tolerated me as long as I obeyed her demands for treats, cuddles, and catnip.

After unbuckling his seatbelt, he stood and gazed down at me, his gorgeous blue eyes betraying not the slightest hint of emotion, just as Daniel and I had been trying to teach him.

Heh. I'd spent six weeks learning to be a slave, so he got to spend the same amount of time learning to be a Master. Seemed fair, right?

"Crawl to the bedroom," he ordered softly. "You may not speak."

I unbuckled my seatbelt and sank to my knees, then crawled obediently, listening for the soft sound of his footsteps as he followed me. He slid the door shut behind us, and I heard a soft click. Although I didn't look, I assumed he was locking us in.

Keeping to my slave persona, I rested my weight on my heels and put my hands in position on my spread thighs while I waited for his next instruction. My core clenched and wetness trickled from my exposed sex as the expensive wool of his trousers brushed against my back.

Instead of touching me, he went to his suitcase and retrieved a short whip with a curled lash that ended in a point. I winced inwardly, remembering the dragon tail from my time in his kennel. He hadn't used it often, but it stung like a bitch. Worse, it didn't leave much in the way of marks.

"Red," I said, "or whatever you want for a safeword."

"Slaves don't get safewords." His lips quirked into a faint smile as he drew the lash through his fingers. "But it's cute that you think you would."

"Okay." Refusing to think about why his reply turned me on so much, I breathed through the need gathering strength in my belly. "Let's call it a timeout for technical difficulties. The dragon tail doesn't leave marks like we need. Do you have something else?"

Still smiling, he shook his head. "No. The dragon tail is perfect for my purposes. Now, stand up and bend over the bed. Toes pointed in, please."

Despite knowing whatever Lachlan planned would hurt, I erupted into a full-body hot flash as I stood and lowered my torso to the bed. Gently, he nudged my feet apart, exposing my soaking pussy to the cool breeze from the air vents. As he'd asked, I moved my feet until my toes were the way he wanted, knowing the position wouldn't allow me to clench my muscles against the pain.

With a quiet hiss, the first blow fell, leaving a stripe that burned like all the fires of the sun across the lower curve of my ass. I bit back a yelp and tried not to move as the second and third fell in quick succession.

"Good girl for staying quiet," Lachlan

murmured. Without waiting for me to reply, he delivered several more blows, dividing them between my ass cheeks and upper thighs.

My legs quivered and I locked my knees before I collapsed to the bed. Fuck. Lachlan must have been holding back when I was in his kennel, because... damn.

Maybe he was right. I couldn't imagine not having marks from that nasty whip. Tears of pain welled, scorching my eyes as I blinked them back, although I wondered if he wanted to see them.

After all, my father wouldn't have stopped until I was screaming.

But Lachlan wasn't my father. And even more inexplicably, the panic attack I'd expected never showed up. Instead, the heat in my core grew.

Deciding to take a chance, I let the tears fall, along with a quiet whimper I hoped he didn't hear.

To my shock, he dropped the whip next to me on the bed, then caressed my ass, his touch both soothing and agonizing.

"There's my very good girl."

———

LACHLAN

My cock surged at the sight of her tears, but I forced myself to attend to her instead of taking advantage of the silky, wet promise of her exposed core. After-care wasn't a Master-approved activity, but I had a better idea that would make both of us happy and give her even more protection from Ronan.

Leaving her sprawled on the bed, I went into the restroom and dampened a cloth with cold water. She hissed out a protest, but didn't move when I laid the cold compress on her ass.

"For the next thirty minutes, we're going to discuss what I want to happen. You may move and speak freely during that time, after which you will rest until we land."

She quirked a brow at me, then positioned herself on her side facing me. "Well, the dragon tail hurt like a bitch, so you'll be happy about that, but I'm still not convinced it will leave marks like we want Ronan to see."

"Seeing you control yourself through the pain so well was hot as fuck." I sat next to her and reposi-tioned her body until her head was in my lap, then stroked her side, enjoying the feel of her silky skin. "I do like giving you pain, but only because I suspect you enjoy it."

"Not going there, asshole."

"Are you sure?" I eased my hand between her legs and lifted it to reveal wetness on my fingertips. Under her irritable gaze, I licked her juices away and smirked when she rolled her eyes. "This is what I really like, and I would never yuck your yum."

"Still not going there." She tried to sit up, but I held her still until she gave up and whispered a soft curse. "But fine. What's your brilliant idea?"

"I need to know something first."

"Okay, shoot."

I resisted the urge to laugh at her word choice. "Do you know if Ronan saw you before we got married the first time?"

"Probably, but I tried to make myself scarce whenever he came around." She grimaced, then added, "I liked my body, but I think I got fat in the hope he would lose interest."

"I miss all of those luscious curves," I murmured. "So succulent and soft, and perfect."

Blushing, she sat up and moved to sit next to me. "Thanks, I think, but if I'm going to keep squeezing my ass through the air duct on my obstacle course, it's going to be Ella's version of the Keto diet from hell and four hours of personal training a day until I retire."

"A terrible loss," I murmured as I curled my arm around her shoulders and pulled her close. "From what I remember, and what we saw in the video Ella showed us, he likes to have things no one else does."

"You think he would have wanted me, regardless of my appearance, just because my father told him no?"

"Possibly." I shrugged, then added, "I haven't seen him in years, but it fits what I remember of his personality."

"Excuse me." She scrambled from the bed and dug into her suitcase for a laptop. "I might have some evidence to corroborate that."

She scanned through a directory of files, then opened a photo with typed notes at the bottom of the image. "These girls are twins and were stolen from a market in Pyongyang when they were fifteen. Between the statistically low incidence of twins in Asian populations, and the fact that he had to go into North Korea to get them—"

"You think I'm right."

"For slavers, those girls are priceless, so pretty sure you are." She closed her laptop and set it aside. "Where are you going with this?"

I took her hand and kissed her fingertips, making her bite back a gasp. "I have something just as unique, and just as priceless as those North Korean girls."

Laughing, she shook her head. "Damn, that's cheesy as fuck."

"You'll be my odalisque." I pinched her chin, forcing her to look at me. "Trained, fed, and groomed to my specifications to be my perfect companion. No marks shall ever mar your stunning body because I refuse to have my view spoiled. No one touches what belongs to me, and you will be dressed so that everyone will wish they could see you."

She blinked and her eyes dilated. As if shaking off her arousal, she pulled away and straightened. "Congratulations. You passed Master 101. Do you think Ronan will go for it?"

"You will be the one thing he cannot have," I murmured. "Not for any price. He won't be able to resist the challenge I'll present, but it will require one tiny thing from you."

"Oh? What's that?"

"You have to pretend you love me enough to die for me."

It seemed only fair, since I loved her enough to

sacrifice myself for her safety. Unfortunately, she wouldn't believe me if I told her that.

She burst out laughing, then got up to get clean clothes from her suitcase. After hurriedly dressing in black leggings and a T-shirt which read, "My favorite season is the fall of the patriarchy," she said, "I don't wish you dead anymore, but that's pushing it, Lachlan."

I tugged her hand, encouraging her to sit next to me once more. "Think about it. After I tell Ronan that you killed a man to save my life, and are now my devoted bodyguard with benefits, he'll be foaming at the mouth to get you alone."

"And then I can get stabby, and..." To my shock, she threw her arms around me and kissed my cheek. "Best idea ever."

For a split second, she was the joyous twenty-two-year-old woman she should have been allowed to be, but too soon, her brown eyes went flat and cold.

"Ronan is already dead. He just doesn't know it yet."

CHAPTER TWENTY-EIGHT

NATASHA

Lachlan spent precisely twenty minutes outlining his plan, which would indeed have me fawning at his feet. I didn't like that part, but I really liked the idea of making Ronan so desperate to get something that he got careless.

He would see a willing slave in excellent health. A well-dressed woman, who wanted nothing more than to stay at her Master's side. He would also see a Master who literally changed a slave's body to meet his criteria.

Lachlan's plan would totally work and would alleviate all of the problems we'd had with him during training. He'd be able to turn his aversion to leashing me or allowing other people to touch me into a Master's preference.

Well, damn. Look at me, admiring someone else's Machiavellian idea.

"Do you think you can do it?" Lachlan asked as he draped a cashmere blanket over me.

"Yeah." I plumped the pillow under my head and tugged the blanket to my chin. "Piece of cake that I'll never get to eat."

He laid down behind me, and... Fuck my life, spooned me like we were an actual couple. "Can I tell you a secret?" he asked.

"Sure."

"I've practiced, and can now make stuffed French toast, sausage, and fruit compote without setting any fires. And for supper, you'll have lemon cannelloni."

"God, I miss pasta." I laughed softly. "Is that still in your freezer? I thought I gave the last of it to Teresa for taking care of Dante and Angel while we dealt with my father's guards."

"I found some hidden under your black bean enchiladas, then I learned to make it myself, including the lemon-infused pasta." He settled himself closer and kissed my shoulder. "Saoirse says it's almost as good as yours."

"Impressive." I turned over to face him and made a show of looking for hidden cameras. "Who are you, and what did you do with Lachlan O'Donnell?"

"He's been learning to cook." Lachlan cupped my cheek, his blue eyes softening as he met my gaze. "And learning to give a diabetic cat insulin shots, cleaning up messes left by an incontinent poodle, and—"

"I'm sorry," I burst out. "I shouldn't have forced you to take care of those animals like I did. It was cruel and spiteful."

"Shh." He silenced me with a soft brush of his lips against mine. "I didn't have to say yes. I took them because I thought it might make you think better of me, then figured out I actually enjoy it. Especially Marmite. He's a treat."

Gently, he encouraged me to turn over and wrapped his arm around me, pressing my back against his muscular chest. Some little devil on my shoulder made me rub my still-sore butt against his groin, making him chuckle.

"Behave yourself, slave. As enticing as it sounds to slide my cock into your wet pussy, you need a nap."

"And naturally, you get along with Marmite," I muttered. "Both of you are evil."

"Evil?" He reached over me to dim the bedside lamp. "He's a sweet little guy, always chasing after me for treats or grooming."

"He spent almost a year alone in a paddock when his owner died, and no one would take him because he's vicious," I replied after yawning widely. "I had to have Teresa sedate him before I could groom him. Even then, he bit me, and when he chased me, it certainly wasn't for treats. Don't get me started on what he did when we had to take care of his teeth and hooves."

"So, basically, you did all the hard work on his rehab before I got him. I particularly liked the ribbons you braided into his mane, and the cute little wings on his shoulders you made when you did his body clip."

"Why are you even still talking?"

He kissed the back of my head and chuckled. "Maybe he was missing his owner and lashed out at the one person he knew would be kind, no matter what he did."

"Stop trying to make me feel better." I yawned again, then tucked my face under the blanket. "And if you're not going to fuck me, shut up and let me sleep."

"Oh, little slave…" He reached under my shirt and pinched my nipple until I squeaked. "Fucking is for animals. You're not getting my cock until you beg me to make love to you."

"Don't hold your breath." I pressed my thumb against a pressure point in his wrist, forcing him to let go of my breast. "Or, you know, do hold your breath. It will save me the trouble of killing you later."

When he laughed, I jabbed my elbow into his ribs but couldn't help thinking about how he managed to change the narrative on me. Instead of sending him a mean-ass pony to torment him, he'd turned it around to make me sound like I possessed benevolence and altruism.

Ugh.

I mean really. How very dare he?

"Sweetheart, as several people have mentioned, if you truly wanted to kill me, I'd already be dead."

"Lachlan?" I asked, pouring every drop of saccharine sweetness I could muster into his name.

"Yes, love?"

"Jump off a bridge."

LACHLAN

Natasha relaxed and her breathing slowed as she drifted off. Although I wanted to join her, I stayed awake to watch her sleep. She usually slept deeply enough to not remember them, but she was plagued with nightmares. I was sure at least some of them came from her father, but didn't delude myself into thinking she didn't dream about the time she'd spent in my kennel. For all I knew, she dreamed about Ronan and all the people she hadn't been able to save.

In order to soothe her through them, I didn't sleep until I absolutely had to. Maybe someone who bought a person as a punching bag slash sex toy wouldn't give a moment's thought to their slave's distress, but that wasn't me—not anymore.

Yes, I'd hated her at first. I hated what she represented, and her tie to the person who murdered my brother. But all of that had changed.

And yes, I was desperate to have her go to her knees willingly for me, but I wouldn't force it, and I no longer wanted her to be a permanent twenty-four seven slave.

Well, not unless she chose it for herself.

I swallowed a dry laugh, knowing she wouldn't.

After making sure Natasha was deeply asleep, I eased myself from the bed, grabbed my phone, and after sliding the door shut behind me, returned to my seat.

Once I was seated, I made a few arrangements I hoped Natasha would enjoy, then pulled up Ella's contact and tapped it. To my surprise, she answered on the first ring, as if she'd been waiting for my call.

"I assume you're halfway to Ireland by now," she murmured. "Where's Natasha?"

"We're less than two hours out. Natasha is sleeping," I replied, keeping my voice down. "I need a favor."

"Another one?" Giggling softly, she added, "Your second is threatening to steal my chef and take her to California, and your wife traumatized my general. I also sent your sister to a safe house in Zurich."

"Zurich? Why?"

"I was going to send her home, but decided she'd be a target if things don't go as planned with Ronan."

"You have my deepest appreciation, Ella. Thank you."

"De nada. So, what else can I do for you?"

"The favor is a small one I think you'll be happy to do."

"Okay. Let's hear it."

"I want you to find Cherise Ashland. If she's already dead, try to find her body so Natasha can give her a proper burial. If she's alive, kill her owner and get her out."

Ella coughed, then cleared her throat. "Well, there might be a teensy problem with that."

"Which part?"

"Um…the killing her owner part."

"Does that mean you've already found her?"

"She's in Finland."

"And?" I kept myself firmly in my seat, even though I wanted to wake Natasha to tell her the news. "What's the problem with killing her owner?"

"They're sort of married. She refused to leave him."

"What?" I forced myself to keep my voice lowered. "Are you fucking kidding me?"

"I know, right? Anyway, yeah. According to multiple members of the team I sent, Cherise literally climbed the dude like a monkey to keep them from shooting him, and he kept turning to put himself between them and her like they were actually a couple instead of Master and slave. Fucking disturbing, if you ask me."

"Was she drugged or under duress?"

"That's the weirdest part. He asked if they were from Ronan. When they told him I sent them, he said he didn't care if they killed him as long as I personally guaranteed Cherise's safety." She took an audible breath, then added, "So, yeah, no. I can't authorize a hit on her Master, but I have their address if you want to take Natasha to visit after you deal with Ronan. Pretty sure you need to see that fuckery for yourself."

My phone buzzed with an incoming text, and I glanced at the mapped address in suburban Helsinki.

"Unbelievable. That's just—"

"Fucked up, right? Anyway, I sent a counselor in with the team, and she said Cherise's Master encouraged her to talk to the counselor privately. Then he just... God, Lachlan, I can't even make this shit up."

"You can't make what up?"

"I went personally with a different counselor. They didn't know I was coming, and I shit you not, but Cherise sat on a stool and bossed her Master around while he cooked a fucking standing rib roast with homemade bread, and a roast vegetable medley of carrots and parsnips, all the while chatting about how great her life was. When we sat down to eat, her Master plopped her on his lap and fed her from his own plate, then regaled us with tales of her getting a PhD in chemistry and how he was trying to talk her into a second one for physics."

Like mother, like daughter. I couldn't help remembering Natasha's wish to study biochemistry.

"Was she under the influence? Did you see any bruises?"

"No to the bruises, and she offered to strip naked to prove it, which was weird as fuck. Neither of them had any, but she served a very nice Burgundy with the meal." She sighed heavily, then laughed. "Fuck me, but I still don't believe it, and I saw it for myself. That leads me to something else."

"What now?"

"Cherise is pregnant, and she gleefully showed me I don't even know how many sonogram photos while her Master rubbed her feet."

"Holy shit."

"Right? He looked at her like she farted rainbows."

I understood Ella's confusion, as it matched

mine. To know Natasha's mother had been safe and presumably happy all these years...

"Why haven't they reached out to Natasha?"

"This is the part that actually does sound plausible," Ella replied. "After he bought Cherise, he changed their names and went into hiding with her to keep Steve and Ronan from finding them. They knew Steve was dead, but Cherise's Master didn't want to risk drawing Ronan's attention to her or Natasha, especially not with Cherise pregnant. The baby is due in six weeks."

When I didn't immediately reply, she added, "Fuck, I can't even call him her Master. He dotes on her like a damned fool. Kind of like you do with Natasha, if you want my opinion."

Even though she was right, I said, "I didn't ask for it."

"Too bad. Anyway, Cherise loves her daughter. After all these years, she still tries to keep Natasha safe, and I..." She sniffled, then I heard her blow her nose. "Fucking emotional shit making my eyeballs leak like I'm a goddamned faucet. Consider your favor granted and let us never speak of this again."

CHAPTER TWENTY-NINE

NATASHA

My hand over my mouth, I backed away from the door until I reached the bed. My knees buckled and I sat hard.

Holy. Fuck. Was it true?

I hadn't heard Ella's side of the conversation, so I couldn't be sure, but Lachlan made it sound like she'd found my mother.

Part of me wanted to rush into the main cabin and make him tell me the truth, but another part wanted to wait and see if he told me himself. Before I could decide, the pocket door slid open, landing in its mounting with an audible bang.

"Natasha! I'm so glad you're awake! I have a surprise for you." He grinned excitedly as he sat next to me. Taking my hand, he said, "I really should keep this a secret, so I don't distract you, but I can't wait to see your face when I tell you."

"Well? What's your secret?"

"Ella found your mother."

My heart thudded at the confirmation of what I thought I'd overheard. "Is she safe in Elba yet?"

His face colored and he shrugged. "She's safe, according to Ella. She lives with her Master near Helsinki and—"

"What?" When he hesitated, I grabbed his arm. "Why Finland? Do not even tell me she's still enslaved."

"She and her Master are in hiding." He shrugged and gave me a wry smile. "Ella couldn't believe it either, but apparently, they're very much in love. Cherise refused to leave him."

"After all these years... Unbelievable."

"That's what I said." He took my hand and brought it to his lips. "Ella says Cherise misses you very much."

I tried to parse through my feelings of delight mixed with anger, mixed with sadness. It all whirled in my head until I had no idea which would come out on top. "Let me guess. They're in hiding because of Ronan."

"Yes." He wrapped an arm around my shoulders and pulled me close, then dabbed my face with a handkerchief that smelled of laundry detergent mixed with his cologne.

When did I start crying?

"Shh, love. It's okay." He wiped a few more tears away and hugged me tight. "But I have another secret that might make you feel better."

For that matter, when did I become his love?

I rubbed my eyes and nodded. "Okay?"

"She's pregnant. You're going to be a big sister."

Wondering if I'd gone temporarily deaf, I stuck a finger in my ear. "I'm sorry, what?"

"The news surprised me too." He looked down at his hands. "Was she young when she had you?"

"She was barely nineteen," I whispered, feeling faint. "I found her birth certificate and an old passport in my father's safe."

She'd been so young, and so very beautiful, with a bright, open smile and a cute little gap between her front teeth. I'd had one too, before my sperm donor sent me to the orthodontist.

Hell, I didn't even know why Steve kept her documents or how he'd gotten them in the first place, but it was yet another thing to hate him for. Had he bought her? Stolen her from a family that might still miss her? Not for the first time, I wished I'd killed him with my own hands instead of using Dante.

"I promise you. The minute Ronan is dead, I'm taking you to meet her."

To my disgust, I burst into noisy, yet surprisingly cathartic sobs. I hadn't cried in... Hell, I couldn't remember, but Lachlan didn't stop whispering endearments as he rocked me until I managed to stop bawling.

"Blow." He held his handkerchief to my nose until I obeyed, then wiped my face with a clean one. "All better?"

I pulled myself together and tried to get my emotions under control. "Let us never speak of this again."

Shocking the hell out of me, he burst into laughter. "That's exactly what Ella said when she cried over your mother's story."

"Will you tell me?"

"Of course."

He repeated the parts of their conversation I

hadn't overheard, but I held up a hand to stop him. "Wait. Say that again. I don't think I heard you properly."

Chuckling softly, he brushed hair out of my eyes and kissed my forehead. "Not only did he let her boss him around while he cooked supper, but he fed her from his own plate while she sat on his lap."

"Unbelievable." There just wasn't another word to describe the situation, but I was...

Happy? Hurting because we'd lost over twenty years? I decided I was feeling both, but mostly I was glad she'd found someone who loved and protected her.

"Indeed. Ella also sent Saoirse to a safe house in Switzerland. She'll be protected until we deal with Ronan." After encouraging me to lie down, he covered me with the blanket. "Rest now, love. We'll be landing soon."

Lachlan didn't know I'd overheard part of the conversation. He could have kept the news to himself instead of telling me. I'd have even understood if he hadn't said I was about to be a big sister, because fuck, if *that* wasn't distracting. But he told me anyway.

For once in my life, a man did something for no other reason than to make me happy. Belatedly, I remembered Jerome giving me Angel. Although it had been a nice gesture, it wasn't the same.

Telling me about my mother had been a risk. I might lose focus or drop the mission to kill Ronan altogether in favor of rushing to see her. I might even get careless and put myself and Lachlan in danger. Or worse, my mother and unborn sibling.

He'd considered those possibilities and told me anyway. Hell, the jerk had wiped my tears and held a freaking silk handkerchief for me to blow my nose.

Something shifted in my chest, making me short of breath. All these months... He'd been trying to be the man I needed—even when I made it difficult. I inhaled deeply and let it out, feeling lighter and...

Free.

Slowly, I rose to my feet and his eyes widened when I undressed and lowered myself to my knees. "Please, make love to me, Master."

———

LACHLAN

Natasha's words clicked within me, and I realized I could have everything I'd ever wished for—even if part of me didn't think I deserved it after what I'd done to her.

I cleared my throat, and thankfully, my voice remained steady. "Are you sure, love? Is this what you want?" Before she could reply, I stood and circled her, letting my hands brush against her muscular shoulders. "Do you kneel for me because you think you should, or because you want to?"

She sat on her heels and rested her upturned hands on her spread thighs, as she'd been taught, but lifted her chin to meet my eyes. "The days of me doing anything I don't want to are over. I'm on my knees because I want to be."

"Such a good girl," I murmured as I unfastened my trousers. "Open your mouth. I want to feel those pretty tongue piercings slide against my dick."

More quickly than I thought she would, Natasha parted her lips and stretched her neck as if anticipating my cock. I couldn't help enjoying the way she focused on my thickening shaft.

Leaning close, she swirled her tongue around the crown, making me swallow a groan of pleasure. Keeping her eyes on my face, she took me deeper until I bumped the back of her throat. I felt her swallow an instant before she took all of me. I tried to pull away, knowing I wouldn't last if I had to suffer such delicious torment for much longer.

Without warning, her hand shot up and she tightened her fingers around my balls, her eyes filled with challenge as she forced me to stay still.

"Natasha, fuck!" She hummed around my cock and my knees almost buckled under me when she loosened her grip on my scrotum and rimmed my ass with a wet fingertip.

She increased the suction on my cock, and slowly...painfully slowly...she released me from her mouth.

"You were saying?" she asked.

"Bad girl." I tried to clear the spots from my eyes and hauled her to her feet. "Very bad girl."

"Ooh, is Master going to spank me?" Her brown eyes lightened almost to gold, and she unbuttoned the top few buttons on my shirt. After delivering a gentle bite to my nipple, she added, "I might as well earn that spanking."

She giggled and didn't stop me when I spun her around and pushed her shoulders until she bent over the bed with her luscious ass exposed. Instead of answering, I brought my hand down in a hard slap, leaving a pink handprint. She squeaked and tried to wriggle free as I kept spanking her until her bottom was red and hot to the touch.

I could have kept spanking her forever—especially when she lifted her hips for her punishment—but I wanted to hear her pleasure even more. Deciding turnabout was fair play, I flipped her to her back and dropped to my knees between her splayed thighs.

"Do you still hate edging?" I asked.

Her expression turned pensive. "I don't know. Maybe?"

Although disappointed by her answer, it didn't surprise me, and I wouldn't push. If I didn't manage to fuck things up with her again, we'd have plenty of time to explore each other.

"Then I won't, but you'll be a good girl and give me at least two orgasms before I make love to you." I didn't wait for her reply before burying my face between her legs.

I sucked her clit into my mouth and lashed it with my tongue as I slid two fingers into her wet channel. Crying out, she bucked her hips and sank her hands into my hair. I found the sweet spot inside her and rubbed hard, making her scream my name as a gush of fluid bathed my face.

I lapped at the honey and salt of her spend,

drawing her sweet scent deep into my body as I slowly drove her to another climax.

"God! Lachlan!" Her short nails dug into my scalp, sending a shivery sting coursing down my spine.

Her passionate cries were like the sweetest music, and although my cock ached with the need to be inside her, I redoubled my efforts. Using my free hand, I pinched her nipple, dragging another scream from her as she convulsed with another climax.

"There's my very good girl," I murmured as I kissed her inner thigh before scattering more kisses on her taut belly. Slowly, I pressed my lips to every inch of her, relishing her labored breaths as I finally reached her lips.

"Please, please, make love to me?" Her whisper lifted at the end in question instead of demand.

Doing my best to keep kissing her, I tore off my clothes. This was how it should have been between us—like our first night together, but better.

So much better. My anger and disgust at both her and at myself were gone.

"Yes." She reached between our bodies and gripped my erection, positioning me at her entrance. "I'm ready."

"I think I've been ready all my life." Slowly, with

my eyes fixed on her beautiful face, I eased inside her, feeling as if I'd finally come home.

"God, yes." She wrapped her calves around my hips and surged upward to take me deeper. "Perfect, but I'm not going to last long."

"Then you'll come twice." Praying I could keep my own climax in check, I lowered my head and rasped the scruff of my beard against her neck as I kissed the tender skin under her ear.

Her legs tightened around me, and she dug her nails into my shoulders. The sting drove me like a goad, and I took her mouth in a searing kiss as her inner walls clamped down on my cock. My lower back tingled, and I gritted my teeth, trying to hold on. I moved my hand to her luscious breast and teased her nipple, making her gasp and cry out as her inner walls massaged my dick.

"Fuck, yes," I hissed. "You feel so good, love. Give me one more."

"I..." Her face reddened with exertion, and she panted like she was running a race. "I can't."

"Oh, I beg to differ." I slipped my hand between our bodies, then rubbed the barbell in her clit hood against the sensitive bundle of nerves in a way I knew would send her into orbit.

"Lachlan!"

I smiled at her shrill scream of pleasure and, still working her clit, I fucked her hard, increasing the tempo until sweat beaded on my body and my head ached from the force of holding myself back.

"God, yes!" She sank her hands in my hair and pulled. "Kiss me, please!"

I was lost the minute I tasted her sweet lips. Never—not even on either of our wedding nights—had Natasha begged for a kiss.

CHAPTER THIRTY

NATASHA

Oh, god. What have I done?

Clearly, my brain had hung up its *Gone Fishing* sign and was offline from too many orgasms.

Lachlan's kisses were brutal, claiming, dominating things. He took without asking, never giving me a chance to refuse. And I loved it. I loved driving him crazy enough with lust that he'd risk a knife in his belly. But this...

This kiss was tender, reverent, and his gentleness was even more devastating than his cruelty.

He groaned into my mouth and thrust deep, his

body shuddering as he emptied himself into me. It seemed as if I could feel his seed scorching me, trying to find its way past my birth control.

Fuck, I was ridiculous. I blamed Lachlan and his thick cock.

Don't forget his tongue and fingers...

I wasn't sorry though. For the first time since our wedding night, I had a chance to see what our life would look like if we forgave each other. Well, less him and more me. I needed to forgive him for what he did to me, and in this somewhat hard airplane bed, with his scent embedded in my skin and his softening cock still inside me, I thought I might be able to.

My body still limp from his attentions, I didn't protest when he rolled off me and pulled me into his arms, spooning me against his broad chest. I felt like I needed to say something, but my muzzy brain didn't offer any helpful suggestions.

"Are you okay?" He cleared his throat, smoothing the roughness. "Did I hurt you?"

"You didn't hurt me."

"And?" Gently, he rolled me to face him. "Are you okay?"

I nodded hesitantly, then shook my head when I

caught the worry in his steady blue gaze. He deserved to know what I truly felt—even if I wasn't sure about the right words.

"Physically, yes. Mentally..." I laughed softly. "My brain decided to take a vacation, so this might come out weird."

He settled on his back next to me, and after pulling the blanket over us, moved me until my head rested on his chest. "I don't mind weird. I promise I'll listen without judgment."

"I feel like I should despise you, but then you decide to not be an asshole, and I feel like I might start to actually like you." I hauled in a breath. "And then I hate myself because I shouldn't, then you piss me off, and it's all okay, and then you do something to make me think I should forgive you for stuffing me into a dog kennel for six weeks."

He stroked my hair, making me resist the urge to close my eyes and fall asleep. "I hope you do some-day, but I won't ask for it."

"There you go again!" I lifted my head to glare at him and stabbed my finger into his chest. "Christ, Lachlan! Stop being so nice so I can keep hating you."

His chest shook with laughter, and he wiped a

few tears of mirth from his eyes before his gaze hardened. "No. I will not stop caring for you, or being nice, or whatever bullshit you tell yourself. I'm not changing how I treat you out of some sense of obligation or because I want to earn your forgiveness. I'm doing it because I—"

The intercom chimed, cutting him off. Cursing, he helped me sit up as the flight attendant said, "Mr. and Mrs. O'Donnell, we're beginning our final descent into Cork. Please return to your seats and fasten your safety belts."

I couldn't decide whether to be thankful he didn't finish his sentence or wish he had.

"This isn't over, Natasha," Lachlan warned as we hurried to dress. "In the interest of our task, I'll drop the subject for now, but we will be discussing it later."

"Um...okay?"

Before I could slide the door open, he grabbed me and pushed me against the bulkhead, then delivered one of those deliciously brutal kisses to my swollen lips. He tangled his hand in my hair, then whispered, "And don't even think you'll escape that conversation. I will tie you to our bed and spank you until you listen. Do you understand?"

I gulped and my core twitched with renewed arousal. "Yes, Master."

Smiling, he kissed my forehead before letting me go. "That's my very good girl."

Quivering with desire, I didn't protest when he opened the door and escorted me to my seat. It took me two tries to get my seatbelt fastened, and I scowled when I caught his smile of amusement.

Stupid praise kink.

Thankfully, I was more or less coherent and calm by the time we landed. When Lachlan and I finished gathering our things from the stateroom, the flight attendant offered us hooded black sweatshirts.

"Put these on," he ordered. "We have your driver waiting on the tarmac, but Ella prefers your heads be covered until you reach your hotel room."

"No need. I have one."

Lachlan shook his head. "It's still wet from the storm, remember?"

"No, I actually didn't." Keeping my irritation at myself for being brainless in check, I smiled and accepted the hoodie from the flight attendant, then put it on over my T-shirt. "Thanks."

Within moments, we were settled in the back of a steel-gray Mercedes with dark tinted windows. I very nearly knelt on the floorboard at Lachlan's feet but sat on the bench seat next to him instead. I was both disgusted with myself and sad that I hadn't given in to the impulse.

———

LACHLAN

We waited while Ella's driver checked us into our hotel. A soft drizzle obscured the glow from the windows, but I could see people dining in the attached restaurant. I wished I could take Natasha out, but room service would have to do. It was bad enough that we had to cross a crowded lobby to get to our room. I couldn't risk exposing her further.

The driver returned quickly and opened my door. He gave me a pair of keycards, then hurried to help Natasha from the vehicle. After retrieving our luggage, he said, "You have packages waiting in your suite, with Signora Moretti's compliments. She hopes you find everything helpful."

"Everything?" I shouldered Natasha's bag before grabbing my own.

"I wouldn't presume to guess what the boxes contain, sir," he replied, his eyes twinkling as he handed me a business card. "Call that number when you're ready to complete your task. We'll have a team in place to assist with extraction."

"Fair enough." I took the card, then offered my free arm to Natasha. "Shall we?"

"We shall." She grinned impishly and wrapped her hand around my elbow. "Can't wait to see what Ella sent us."

Instead of answering, I hurried her through the front door, waving the attentive bellhop away with a flash of our keycards. She lowered her head and kept up with my rapid pace as we ascended the stairs and found our room. Once the ornate door was shut behind us, I locked it.

With a sigh of relief, she took off her hoodie and tossed it over a chintz-covered chair, then spotted Ella's packages on a gilded occasional table near the window. After crossing the room, she picked up the larger of the two and shook it.

"What do you think she sent?"

"We'll never know unless we open them."

"True." She slid a switchblade from her pocket and sliced the box open, then picked out an enve-lope addressed to both of us. After opening it, she smiled as she read. "Ella says the boxes are my reward for not killing anyone, and that there's a garment bag in the closet with our outfits for Ronan's party."

"Well..." I gestured at the open box. "Let's see what we have."

Nodding, she pushed packing paper out of the way and frowned when she found a slim manila folder. After setting it aside, she extricated four polished steel cuffs and another collar similar to the one she wore during training.

"This is weird. I already have cuffs."

I slid the folder across the table and took a seat to read the contents. "Oh, brilliant," I murmured, offering her the page I was reading.

She scanned it and a wide, delighted smile lit up her face as she tossed packing material to the floor, finally extricating a small jewelry box containing a nose ring with four channel-set diamonds. "This is so freaking cool! I can't even imagine how she managed to put remote triggers for those cuffs in a nose ring, but it means I can activate them even if I'm stupid enough to get tied up."

"Can you reach it with your tongue?"

"I think so, yes. This one is bigger than the one I'm wearing." She stuck out her tongue and managed to touch the smaller ring in her nose. Her face falling, she added, "And it's great as long as I don't get gagged too."

"Let's think positively." I set the nose ring and cuffs aside, careful not to touch any of the diamonds. "What's in the second box?"

She slit the box open and cocked her head at the sight of a thin steel chain about two feet long and decorated with crystals. "My new leash, I presume."

I flipped to the next page contained in the folder and couldn't contain my relief. With this one item, my misgivings faded. Yes, she would be leashed, but with a weapon hidden in plain sight.

"It's actually a garrote. The clasp for the collar is a quick release. Jerk twice in rapid succession and it will come off. The instructions say you'll get about ten uses out of it before it needs to be replaced."

"Oh, damn, my precious." She hugged the chain to herself and grinned. "Lachlan, please. You *have* to let me wear it. Pretty please with a blow job on top?"

Sighing, I rolled my eyes. "Leave it to Ella to produce a leash I can tolerate letting you wear."

"Please, Daddy?" She blinked those huge brown eyes and clasped her hands as if she was praying.

I couldn't help laughing as I shook my head at her antics. "Yes, you may wear your new leash."

"Yay!" She straddled my lap and kissed my face. "Thank you!"

"You're welcome, love." I rolled my eyes, then added, "The last page in the folder was about your shoes."

"My shoes? What about them?"

"Black Louboutins with blades hidden in the toes. I assume they're in the garment bag."

"I think I just came." Her eyes softened and she slid to her knees between my feet. "Now, about that blow job…"

CHAPTER THIRTY-ONE

NATASHA

Instead of ordering room service, we spent all night tasting each other. It was surprisingly satisfying and...

Fuck me, it was fun. We had a freaking pillow fight, for fuck's sake. Never once had I laughed during sex.

Or, you know, had a pillow fight. Or wine from the minibar dripped on my belly so Lachlan could lick it off.

Or... I cut myself off before I hopped on for another ride.

Save a horse, ride... Ride the man who truly gets you.

God help me, but every minute I spent with him

made it that much harder to hold on to my lingering anger. I was in serious danger of falling for him even harder than I had on our first wedding night.

Hell, between Ella's wonderful gifts and marathon sex, I'd barely noticed our gorgeous suite. Furnished with impeccable antiques and decorated with soothing shades of cream and peach, it was the most beautiful hotel room I'd ever seen.

Unfortunately, I was starving, and I was sure Lachlan was in the same condition. Rolling over in his arms, I poked him in the side. "Wakey, wakey, chicken bakey. You hungry?"

Grunting, he rolled over to check the time on his phone. "Mm. We overslept. You have about ten minutes to shower before breakfast arrives."

"Or..." I nibbled the tendon under his ear. "I could shower later and have you for an appetizer. That morning wood looks scrumptious."

"I believe I've created a succubus, but it's time to get to work," he murmured. Before I could stop him, he slid from the bed and put on his trousers, hiding my view of his taut ass. "Go shower with hot water, little slave. Put on street clothes."

"Why?" Hoping to change his mind, I wrapped my arms around his waist and rubbed my aching core against the bulge in his pants.

Without warning, he spun me around and slapped my ass. "Because I said so."

Scowling, I rubbed the sting from my butt, wondering where my *hit first, ask questions never* instincts went. "Fine. I'm going already."

Still grousing, I hurried through my shower and dressed in a pair of jeans and a somewhat rumpled cotton sweater. I smelled the savory perfume of grilled sausage as I opened the door.

My stomach rumbled loudly. Okay, so food first, then jump the hot guy uncovering the steaming plates of breakfast deliciousness.

He held my chair, and I sat, then poked at the strangely pale sausage patty with my fork. "What is this, and why are there baked beans?"

I almost questioned the grilled tomatoes and mushrooms, but they looked too good to worry about whether they should have been served for breakfast.

The beans, on the other hand... I grimaced and considered dumping them on Lachlan's plate.

"White pudding, and one must have proper beans." He lifted a spoonful of beans to his lips and his eyes drifted shut as he chewed. "Try them."

Dubiously, I tried a bite and nearly moaned. Rich with tomato, garlic and onion, the beans practically melted in my mouth. Instead of being sticky with too much sugar, the Irish version was savory and so damned good.

"Good girl," he murmured. "Try a bite of pudding with them. You'll like that."

Focusing on his breakfast, he cut into a fried egg, then swept a triangle of buttered toast through the sunshine orange yolk.

"Note to self." I ate a grilled mushroom, loving the hint of rosemary and butter. "Learn to make white pudding and baked beans that don't make me want to gag."

"And I will eat every bite." He cut a sausage patty into quarters and ate it. "The white pudding is pork sausage with barley and oats."

I attacked the eggs, swirling bites of sausage through the yolks. "Way better than stuffed French toast."

"Do you know why the British call sausages puddings?"

"No clue." I ate a tomato, then wiped a trickle of juice from my chin. "Also, don't care. This is really good."

He chuckled and leaned back in his chair to watch me eat. "It comes from the Middle English word, poding, which refers to a meat-filled animal stomach."

"Lachlan…" I pointed the tines of my fork toward him. "Don't tell people how sausage is made. It's delicious, but nobody really wants to know."

Laughing outright, he checked his phone for the time, then hurriedly finished eating. "Eat up, love. You have an appointment in just a few minutes."

"Appointment?" I devoured the remaining mushrooms, using my last piece of toast to scoop up all the saucy goodness. "What appointment."

"I have a stylist coming." He leaned over to touch my hand. "They will be cutting your hair."

LACHLAN

Natasha's fork fell to her plate with a clatter as her lower lip quivered.

For a moment, I worried that she'd cry, but she launched herself from her chair and landed in my lap. Cupping my face in her warm hands, she kissed me, then pulled away too quickly.

"You're trying to drive me crazy." She rubbed her

eyes like a tired child and sighed. "After all these weeks of begging you for a clipper…"

I touched her chin to make her look at me. "You're not shaving your head, love. The stylist will cut it very short, but I will never permit you to shave it completely."

"And what will Ronan think?"

"I don't care what he thinks. If he asks, I'll simply tell him I let it grow because you're a very good girl."

"But—"

"Your gorgeous hair is a trigger for you, Natasha," I said, my voice quiet, but no less determined. "If you're worrying about it, you won't be focusing on Ronan. I understand that now."

"When did you arrange all this?" She swept her arm toward the room service cart. "Breakfast and a haircut?"

"During our flight while you were sleeping."

Tears, glistening like diamonds, slid down her cheeks. She swiped them away with the back of her hand, then gave me a watery smile. "And suddenly, without warning, the somewhat stabby heroine of our story decides the asshole hero isn't so bad."

"Somewhat stabby?" I slid my hand around her to the small of her back and tugged on the sheathed dagger hidden under her sweater. "Darling, you're *very* stabby, and I love that about you."

Her breath hitched and she swallowed, her throat working as she tried to speak. "I—"

"Shh." I silenced her with a gentle kiss. "You will not say it back until those words are the only ones in your mouth. Don't say it until you feel as if you'll die unless they can be spoken. Do you understand, little slave?"

A soft knock at the door interrupted her before she could reply, and I couldn't decide whether to be furious or thankful my guest was a few minutes early. After gently easing Natasha from my lap, I went to answer it.

"Good morning," A woman with midnight braids and a pink smock smiled at me. "I'm Lindy, the stylist you scheduled."

"Come in, please." I held the door for her, while she bustled inside with a satchel and what looked like a folding director's chair.

She spread a large white sheet on the floor, then set up the chair in the center of the fabric. After laying out scissors and combs, she asked, "Who will be going first?"

Natasha's cheeks pinkened and she gave me a

smile before clambering up to sit in the tall chair. "Me. I need you to shave my head."

Smiling sadly, Lindy wrapped a hairdresser's cape around Natasha's shoulders and fastened it. "A stylist dies a little inside when we have to shave such gorgeous hair. Are you sure?"

Although Natasha's hair was beautiful, if having it cut off made her more confident, then she would wear it short—as long as she wasn't completely bald. I didn't want either of us to have the reminder of our ugly past.

"It grows." As if knowing I'd protest, she added. "Don't shave it completely. It just needs to be short enough that nobody can grab it."

Lindy studied her for a moment, then nodded. "All right. Let's get started."

Lindy worked quickly, and I tried not to look at the soft, brown curls falling to the sheet. In no time, she turned Natasha to face me, revealing a precise fade that highlighted Natasha's chiseled jaw and truly suited her heart-shaped face. Lastly, Lindy groomed her eyebrows.

With her big brown eyes and pointed chin, Natasha reminded me of a wee pixie. Ronan would be entranced.

I scowled at the thought and wished I could

make Natasha wear a veil. I could pass it off as being a Master's wishes, but the obstruction to her vision would handicap her.

Holding a mirror for Natasha, Lindy asked, "Do you like it?"

"It's perfect. And thanks for taming the unibrow."

"It was my pleasure." Lindy gathered her things, and after giving us a friendly nod, left the suite.

Leaving the coffee service for later, I cleaned up the remains of our breakfast and pushed the room service cart into the corridor, then closed the door before engaging the security bolt.

"Yay!" Before I could turn, Natasha threw herself into my arms and went straight for the button on my trousers. "Alone at last."

Wishing we had more time; I pushed her arms to her sides. "Kneel, slave. You may not speak."

The brief flash of hurt crossing her face almost made me relent, but we had barely half a day to perfect our performance. Gentling my tone, I laid my forefinger over her lips. "We have to practice, love. I need to know we can do this together, and most importantly, I have to make sure you're safe."

She graced me with a soft smile, then kissed my cheek before lowering herself to her knees.

CHAPTER THIRTY-TWO

Lachlan was right. It was time to get my head out of the gutter and my hands off his cock.

Boo, hiss.

But I was low-key irritated too. How dare he be so damned amazing that I forgot why we were in Ireland in the first place? We were in Ireland so I could execute a piece of trash human—not to have a fucking honeymoon.

"Good girl." He stroked my new crewcut, the touch surprising me with how sensitive my scalp was. "You will remain kneeling and silent while I call Ronan. I will have the phone on speaker."

Still gazing at me as if he expected me to break position or speak, he returned to his chair and tapped a contact. The phone rang once before it was answered by a woman with a brittle Irish accent.

"Doherty Imports. How may I direct your call?"

"This is Lachlan O'Donnell. Ronan and I are old friends from college. I'm in Cork for a few days and wondered if he'd like to meet up for a pint."

"Of course, Mr. O'Donnell. May I place you on hold?"

"Certainly."

I heard a soft click before faint guitar music emanated from the phone's speaker. Lachlan's face hardened with each passing second, and unsure whether I wanted to comfort him or myself, I tried and failed to resist the urge to crawl to him.

To my surprise, he didn't chide me. Instead, he cupped the back of my neck and encouraged me to rest my head on his thigh.

The phone clicked again, and the sound of Ronan's booming voice made me flinch.

"Lachlan, old boy! It's been an age! How are you?"

"Quite well, thank you," Lachlan replied, his tone smooth and modulated. "I was in town and realized we haven't spoken in much too long. I didn't even know how successful your business has become. I'd love to buy you a pint to celebrate your good fortune."

"Yes. The import business is quite…lucrative these days." Ronan chuckled, and I tried to control my shudder of revulsion. "I heard you married Steve Ashland's daughter. How did that come about?"

"He owed me a significant sum. I took the girl in payment."

"Then had your dog kill him when he tried to kick her in the face. I heard all about it." Laughing hard enough to make himself cough, Ronan added, "Bloody brilliant. You get the girl and whatever's left of his money."

"Indeed." Lachlan's grip tightened, then released almost as quickly. "I do hope you're up for that pint in the next few days."

"I might have something better," Ronan purred. "I could possibly assist you in recouping your loss."

"Oh?"

"Let me ask you something. Are you attached to the girl?"

I risked a glance at Lachlan's face. Did Ronan not know that we divorced? If he did, I could totally see that working in our favor. It took a very determined

Master to return his ex-wife to slavery—at least, that was how Ronan would perceive us.

Lachlan's fingers bit into my throat, nearly cutting off my air. "She's lovely, and we've come to an...understanding regarding her behavior and appearance."

"That's very good," Ronan murmured. "Is she with you?"

"Of course. She's an excellent traveling companion." Lachlan's lips twisted. "And so very obedient."

I swallowed a laugh. That ship had long sailed. I obeyed Lachlan only when I wanted to, but maybe I wanted to more than I should.

"Funny, I remember her father saying she wasn't."

"I'm not her father," Lachlan replied, gazing down at me. "I prefer my possessions unblemished. There are better ways of ensuring proper behavior."

"I couldn't agree more. If you're not particularly attached to her, I could possibly arrange a transaction of sorts that would enable you to regain the loss you suffered."

"All right. Shall we meet for that pint around seven or so?"

"Nothing so Plebian, old chap." Lachlan's phone buzzed with an incoming text. "I'm having a small gathering at my estate this evening. I texted you the address, but you probably remember it from our college days."

"I couldn't have told you the address, but I remember how to get there."

"Smashing." Ronan's laughter sounded like nails on a chalkboard. "And tell me. How is the lovely Saoirse these days?"

My muscles tightened and I barely restrained the urge to leap through the phone and strangle Ronan. When Lachlan's thigh quaked under me, I closed my fingers around his knee in a desperate attempt to keep us both together.

"She's quite well," Lachlan replied, his voice taking on a hard edge. "She's staying with friends in Paris for now, waiting for me to choose an appropriate husband for her."

I couldn't help but note his comment was the first time he'd flat out lied in my presence. Not that I blamed him for sending Ronan several hours southeast of where Saoirse actually was. I held no illusions that Ronan wouldn't look if he thought it would gain him something.

"I know several good candidates," Ronan replied, "if you're interested."

"Thank you. I'll keep that in mind. And thanks for the invitation. What time shall I arrive?"

"I agree with seven. The party starts at nine, so we'll have plenty of time to catch up over supper. Black tie, if you please."

"Have we gotten posh in our old age?" Lachlan asked. "I rather miss the pool parties we used to have."

Funny, but I almost thought Lachlan meant his last comment, and I didn't blame him. Although rare, I missed those too few and too short days when I was left alone with the servants and could pretend they were my family.

"You have the right of it. That damned Goat..."

"Goat?"

"Just an annoyance, old friend." Ronan sighed as if he was tired, then added, "My apologies, but there is no rest for the wicked. I must get back to work."

"Of course." Lachlan petted my head like it was the only thing holding him together. "I look forward to catching up."

When he tapped the phone to end the call, I crawled into his lap and wrapped my arms around him. Disobeying his order of silence, I said, "I'm sorry, Lachlan."

"For what?" He didn't look at me, but that was okay.

"For losing someone who used to be a friend, baby." His tense shoulders relaxed under my touch. "I don't actually have friends, but I'm pretty sure it feels awful."

"It doesn't." He stroked my jaw with a gentle fingertip. "He was once a friend, but the minute he threatened you—"

"Not Saoirse?"

"My sister as well, but mostly you." He pressed a kiss to my forehead, then smiled sadly as he eased me from his lap. "Always you."

———

LACHLAN

I don't actually have friends...

Natasha could have created platonic relationships with people, but I'd stolen the opportunity from her, starting with my sister. It was no surprise that she'd eschewed making friends, given what we'd done to her.

"You're close with Teresa," I murmured, hoping to remind her that she might have one friend. Teresa was her vet, and despite their professional relation-ship, I knew they spent time together.

"Eh." She sat on her heels and placed her upturned hands on her splayed thighs. "Maybe. We do wine tastings and shit."

"Do you enjoy each other's company?"

She lowered her eyes, then nodded. "I guess so."

"Then you have a friend." I cupped her chin and tilted her head up. "Now, the time for talking is over. While I shower, you will go through your morning exercise. I want your body warmed up and ready before I finish."

Giving me a brief nod, she rose gracefully, then moved to the center of the room before flowing into her first Tai Chi position. I tore my gaze away from her beautiful body and hurried into the ensuite to complete my ablutions.

When I returned, she was spinning a wooden staff in her callused palms. The weapon blurred as she whirled and leapt to me. Cursing softly, she jerked the staff aside before it crushed my nose.

I held my ground and decided not to question how she'd managed to hide the weapon in her small suitcase.

The staff dropped and she winced. "Sorry, Master. You surprised me."

"Do that again," I replied. "From the beginning of the form, but I want you to strip first."

"Yes, M—"

"Actually, no." I went to my suitcase and retrieved the sheer black dress I'd packed for her. "Wear this. I want you to practice as you'll be presented. We'll save Ella's dress for the party."

"God!" She rolled her eyes and giggled. "Seriously, who are you, and what did you do with Lachlan O'Donnell?"

"As you and Ella might have mentioned, he pulled his head out of his ass."

She caught the gossamer fabric out of the air. "Too bad. I might enjoy introducing him to pegging."

I caught her staff and pulled it from her hands. "Love, if you come back alive and unharmed, I'll permit your wish."

"Oh, you are so on." She stripped quickly before tugging the dress over her head. After smoothing it into place, she held out her hand for the staff. "With an offer like that, you bet your ass we'll come out alive."

I couldn't resist a smile at her unintended pun, but she didn't appear to notice what she'd said.

"I have no doubt, my love." I pulled her close,

then dipped her as if we were waltzing before kissing her. "Show me everything."

"Um..." She lowered her head and stepped back, leaving me with her staff. "Are you sure?"

"Everything," I repeated. "Show me how deadly you've become, darling."

She caught the staff I threw at her, and bent her head side to side, cracking the joints in her neck. "Yes, Master."

The dress didn't hinder her movements for a single moment. Her dance of incipient violence was sheer poetry of precise, economical motion. Although I wanted to, I'd never ask where she found weapons in that tiny black dress. Throwing stars, push daggers, and the occasional short-barreled handgun all found their way into her performance.

I leaned back in my chair and simply watched her elegant movements. "So fucking beautiful," I murmured.

She straightened and inhaled deeply. "Thank you, Master."

"Kneel for me, darling."

She obeyed, lowering herself to her knees without dropping her gaze from my face. Carefully, she opened her fingers, allowing two throwing knives to fall to the carpet.

"May I speak?" she asked.

"No." I rose from my chair and strode to her, then tugged her nose piercing to make her look at me. "Never drop your blades, slave. Are you not my bodyguard?"

I felt a stream of air pass my face a split second before I heard the thud of one of her blades embedding itself in the wall behind me. She gave me a heartbreakingly sweet smile, then willfully disobeyed me. "Never, ever think I'm unarmed, Master. Might save your life someday."

CHAPTER THIRTY-THREE

NATASHA

"You can't be serious," Lachlan snapped, his blue eyes flaring with anger.

"As a heart attack. Ronan probably won't have a full contingent of guards in place." I held up one finger, then a second. "We won't have to separate him from a crowd of guests."

"I know all that," he interrupted before I could put up a third. "And I agree with your points."

"Then what's the problem?" I finished the last of the pizza we'd ordered for a late lunch, then returned the blueprints and security schematics to their file folder. "Ronan did us a massive favor, and I refuse to waste the opportunity."

"The problem is..." He held up a finger. "Your plan won't work because I won't be leaving you alone with him while I rescue his victims."

"Lachlan, come on. Even without the crowd and his guards, we don't know how much time we'll actually have."

He held up another finger. "Ask yourself if you would blindly obey a strange man after being kidnapped and probably traumatized. Seeing a woman might convince them to follow us out."

I nodded grudgingly. "Yeah, I see your point, but honestly, it's pretty likely that a woman helped trap them."

"Also a very good point, but we'll have to hope for the best." A third finger went up, mirroring my gestures. "And lastly, you will not kill him unless I'm there to watch."

"I..." My cheeks heated and I looked down. The lifetime of abuse I suffered wasn't Ronan's fault—at least, I didn't think so—but he'd taken Lachlan's brother. "I'm sorry. You have more reason to want him dead than I do. Would you like to take the kill shot?"

"No, love." He caressed my cheek and tilted my face up, then kissed me. "I want to watch you do it. I want to watch Ronan die knowing one of his potential victims killed him. We conceal his body, then rescue the people he's holding captive."

"Damn you." I sniffed a few tears back. "Of all the things you could have said…"

"What did I say?" He erased the wetness on my cheek with his thumb.

"You're making me think about catching feels for you."

Hell, I was more than thinking it, and it wasn't just because his plan was better than mine. Dividing our forces might sound more efficient, but we didn't know exactly where we'd find the women waiting for rescue in Ronan's enormous basement. Honestly, it would be easier to get them out if we took care of Ronan first.

It was because instead of lashing out with anger, he treated me like an actual partner—one who occasionally got on her knees for him. It was because he held me tight to his chest when we slept. Or maybe it was the way he fed me from his plate before taking anything for himself.

So what if my feelings were a little prehistoric? The lizard brain wants what it wants, and he'd generously provided food, sex, and comfort. It had nothing to do with how much I was beginning to enjoy his company.

Oh, the lies we tell ourselves.

The laugh lines under his eyes crinkled with humor. "From Natasha O'Donnell, that's as good as a declaration of undying love."

"Very strong not-hate," I muttered.

"I'll take it." After giving me a scorching kiss that left me gasping, he strode to the wardrobe and opened it to reveal a garment bag. "We have about thirty minutes before we need to leave. I've already texted our driver."

"I'll…" I burst out laughing and ran a hand over my head. "I was going to say I'd fix my hair."

"Makeup like you wore to our first wedding." Grimacing, he added, "But not to hide bruises."

"Sweet and innocent, right?" I grabbed my makeup bag from my suitcase. "Twenty-minute face that makes it look like I'm not wearing makeup?"

"Exactly."

I went into the bathroom and got to work. After deciding my eyes were as good as they were going to get, I applied my favorite dark mauve lipstick. "Remind me. It's two heel taps for the blades in my shoes, right?"

"You have it." He straightened my collar, positioning the leash to fall between my breasts. "You know the sequence for your cuffs too."

"I do."

He knelt to slip my feet into the gorgeous, deadly pumps Ella sent in my seriously hot care package. "What is the old saying?"

"What old saying?"

"You are…" He slid his hand up my thigh and tugged the holster containing my favorite short-barrel nine. "Loaded for bear?"

"Yeah, no." I laughed and shook my head. We so didn't have time for me to take him in a wanton manner, but the feel of his palm sliding ever closer to my core made me wish we did. "Ronan's guards are going to confiscate the obvious weapons."

"He won't check," he countered. "You are a slave, my love. I'm his old college friend. He won't see either of us as a threat."

"From your mouth to God's ear. I'd rather be facing a grizzly," I muttered. "We're going to be counting on the garrotes and the knives in my cuffs and shoes. If he does find my stash, tell him you like having Steve's daughter as a bodyguard, but let him take whatever he finds."

Lachlan sighed and straightened my dress. "You're right, of course. I still hate it."

"Same." I checked the clip on my collar and

handed him the free end of my pretty leash. "Shall we?"

My dress was a decadent confection of flowing black, revealing the inner curves of my breasts. The silk was draped and pleated to conceal the important bits, namely, all the toys stashed on my person. If Ronan's guards were inattentive, I could enter his party with six daggers, two pistols, and an additional garrote concealed in a diamond encrusted chain around my waist. Lachlan was also armed, but not as well as I was.

That damned tuxedo that fit him like he'd been sewn into it was dangerous all by itself—at least to me and my raging libido. I couldn't wait to get him out of it.

"One moment, slave."

The address flipped one of my annoying switches, and he caught me before I dropped to my knees.

"Yes, Master?"

He cupped the back of my head and kissed my forehead, nearly making me melt into a puddle.

"You do not kneel for anyone but me, Natasha. If Ronan asks, you look to me for instruction, understand?"

Christ. He was seriously trying to make me fall in... Well, very strong like.

"I understand, Master."

"Good girl." He curled the end of my leash around his hand. "Shall we?"

"We shall." I wrapped my hand around his elbow and allowed him to escort me down the stairs and through the lobby, my head held high.

I wanted to say the dress and shoes made me feel pretty, but it would have been a lie. Being on Lachlan's arm, loaded for bear as he'd mentioned...

I was at the top of my game. Deadly, sexy, and confident. I wasn't just pretty. I was a goddamned goddess.

Lachlan helped me into the same gray Mercedes we'd used for our trip to the hotel, then fastened my seatbelt. I didn't once consider kneeling on the floorboards.

The Spider didn't go to her knees—unless she wanted to.

———

LACHLAN

The driver pulled into traffic and navigated his way through Cork to the M8 heading north. "The team is waiting for your instructions," he said, his voice soft. "I assume you have a plan for your task, but let's talk about your extraction."

Natasha rested her hand on my knee, silently encouraging me while my brain tossed around everything that could go wrong, not the least of which was getting caught.

I had to trust in her skills though. She was talented, deadly, and absolutely determined to kill the man who had my brother murdered. I should have known someone was pulling Steve Ashland's strings. The hit was too careful and precise to have been planned by that abusive idiot.

I also had to do my part and resist the urge to tie her up, put her on a plane, and take her somewhere safe.

"We're looking at the north gate," I replied, focusing on the conversation. "It's concealed by forest on two sides. We'll use the hedge maze for cover."

"That was to be my suggestion as well."

Reaching between the front seats, he passed a small box to me. "These are for you and Natasha."

"What are they?" she asked as I opened the box.

"Voice activated transmitters. Stick them on your skin like a bandage, but fair warning. They hurt like a bitch coming off. When you've completed your task, say *watermelon*."

The devices were tiny and nearly transparent, with a sticky back as the driver described. I passed one to Natasha, and she stuck it on the lower swell of her breast where it would be hidden by her dress.

"Waterproof?" I asked as I affixed my transmitter to my chest under my shirt.

"Of course. Watermelon, said by either of you, will be our cue to move in, retrieve the captives, and..." He chuckled softly. "And then we're blowing up the house. I'm telling Ella it was Natasha's idea. We were just following orders."

"Way to throw me under the bus, but no. As much as I want to torch everything he's touched, the house is worth several million pounds." An evil smirk lit up her face and she giggled. "It has a moat, so I might take it and pretend it's my volcanic island lair."

"Why do you want a volcanic island?" he asked.

"Elba is—"

"Why does everyone want me to move to Elba? Since I have a cool supervillain name, I need an island to match." She laughed softly, then added, "Although Ireland is an island."

"No." I squeezed her knee and tried to hold back my laughter at my incorrigible young bride's antics. I'd been wondering about her desire for an island. "You aren't allowed to take it over."

"Spoilsport."

The driver chuckled as he accelerated to pass a slower vehicle. "In any case, we haven't tested the code Natasha gave us, but we have a specialist if it doesn't work."

"What kind of specialist?" I asked. I'd been too focused on ending Ronan to consider what would happen to his assets, but I liked that Natasha was thinking of the future.

"One for security and electronics. If she can't get the gate open, we have another well-schooled in demolitions. We'll blow the gate off its hinges if we have to."

"Sounds like a plan." Natasha unfastened her seatbelt and slid across the bench seat to cuddle under my arm. "Are we there yet?"

"No."

"Are we there yet?" she asked again.

I felt her shake with silent laughter when the driver cursed under his breath.

"Behave, young lady," I murmured. "Unless you want Daddy to paddle your bottom until it's red."

"No to the behaving. We'll discuss the Daddy dynamic after we're out, and most definitely after you fuck me until I speak in tongues."

"God, Natasha." I coughed, trying not to laugh at her. "Your mouth sometimes."

"Baby, you love what I do with my mouth."

Her riposte sent the driver into paroxysms of laughter, and I rolled my eyes. "Focus, love. We're ten minutes out."

"Got it." She moved to the other side of the bench seat and ran her hands over her body to check her weapons. "We go in. Make nice. You offer Ronan a chance to sample me, I kill him. We say our special word, find his victims, and exit stage left."

CHAPTER THIRTY-FOUR

NATASHA

I tried not to think of the first time Lachlan took me to a party.

This time, the circumstances were completely different. Dante wasn't with me, for one thing, and I walked tall, moving into my role of a valuable, cherished slave. I was dressed to the nines and armed well enough that I didn't need Dante to protect me. My leash was held by a man I trusted.

Well, I mostly trusted him. I was on the fence about whether he would allow me to make the kill or whisk me away if things got the slightest bit sketchy.

One thing was the same though. We were both putting on an act.

This time, I'd be going up against a killer. Although he wasn't known to have combat training, Ronan had history as a street fighter, meaning he'd fight dirty.

That was okay, because I fought dirtier, and I was trained. He'd never expect a slave to have spent six months sparring with a retired Army Ranger who took up mixed martial arts for fun and profit.

Not gonna lie. He kicked my ass on the regular. I made a note to hook him up with Ella.

"Guard at your six," Lachlan murmured into my ear as he helped me from the Mercedes.

"One at the door. Two patrolling the gardens," I whispered when I caught the fiery glint of their cigarettes. "Watch the one at the door. He's paying attention."

Under the direction of the guard manning the door, our driver moved the Mercedes several yards away and parked. Hopefully, I'd have the chance to get his name, but now wasn't the time.

I kept my eyes down but lifted my chin as I followed Lachlan to the open front door. It shut behind us with an ominous click as Ronan strode across an expansive foyer tiled in Travertine marble.

"Welcome!" He slapped Lachlan's shoulder and pulled him into a one-armed hug. "It's good to see you, old man."

Ronan's brown hair had threads of gray at the temples, and a few wrinkles surrounded his eyes, but he was as handsome as ever, which made me furious. People's outsides needed to match their insides.

"You as well." Lachlan dropped my leash and returned the hug. "You've renovated, I see. My compliments to your decorator."

I kept my eyes down and remained perfectly still, hanging on to my control with the tips of my short fingernails. Ronan wasn't paying me any attention, and it would have been so easy to tap the leftmost diamond in my nose ring and slit his throat with the blade in my left wrist cuff.

Unfortunately, there were a few too many eyes watching his and Lachlan's reunion.

"Ah, yes." Ronan waved a dramatic arm to showcase a tastefully decorated foyer I barely noticed. "Cost me a fortune, but definitely worth it."

"A man's home, and all that," Lachlan replied.

"Indeed. But enough about home improvements." He looked me up and down and I resisted the urge to shudder. "Is this truly Natasha?"

"Who?" Lachlan gave him a blank stare that I would have applauded if I dared break our performance. "Oh, yes. I just call her Slave."

Still studying me, Ronan cocked his head. "I didn't think I would, but I prefer her with the baby fat she used to have when she was a teenager."

Lachlan shrugged and snapped his fingers at me to follow as Ronan led us across the foyer to a door opened to reveal a sitting room with a wet bar and a table spread with appetizers.

"I quite enjoyed the challenge of transforming a chubby mess into what I want to see."

Ouch. That might have stung if I hadn't been absolutely positive Lachlan was putting on a show. He'd told me more than once that he missed my curves.

He pinched my chin, forcing me to lift my head. "Is she not exquisite?"

"She is." I held very still while Ronan circled me, and didn't move an inch when he fondled my ass. "Seems very fit too."

"Slave, you may speak. Do you wish Ronan to touch you?" Lachlan asked, without reaching for my leash.

"I will do as my Master commands," I replied, keeping my eyes down.

"Bloody hell, she'd be worth a fortune," Ronan muttered, thankfully letting go of my ass. He'd come too close to one of the push daggers concealed in the folds of my dress.

"Even more when you consider she's been training to become my bodyguard." Lachlan chuckled and pointed at the floor, silently ordering me to kneel. "Steve Ashland abused her horribly, and the smallest bit of kindness earns her undying devotion."

He nudged my knees apart with the toe of his dress shoe, then added, "Isn't that right, slave?"

I nodded, but didn't speak.

Ronan chuckled. "A bodyguard? Since when do you need one?"

"I never did find my brother's murderer," Lachlan replied. "It seemed wise to have one I can bring to social engagements."

"Such a loss with no path to vengeance." Ronan went to the bar and filled two highball glasses with scotch. "I was very sorry when I heard the news."

Lachlan shrugged and took the proffered glass. "I don't actually care. Whoever killed my brother has my thanks, but I'm also not stupid. The killer probably has me in his sights too. Slave is the fourth such bodyguard I've trained, and I daresay she won't be the last."

Yeah, no. I was going to be Lachlan's first, last, and only.

"Hmm." Ronan studied him, his brown eyes cold and speculative. "I have several acquaintances who would love to own Steve Ashland's daughter. How much do you want for her?"

"I haven't decided if I'm willing to sell her."

"Two million?"

Lachlan chuckled and shook his head. "She's worth at least twice that, and you know it."

Aww. I definitely owed Lachlan a blow job for that, even though putting a price on a human life was abhorrent.

Lookin' at you, health insurance companies. And your little shareholders too.

"A high price for a slave who hasn't proven she can please a man or protect him as you say she can."

"And she'll be worth no more than a common slave if you sell her to someone who abuses her because of who sired her." Lachlan countered. "I take the debt Steve owed me out of her body every day, yet she will die to protect me. Is that not worth a princely sum?"

Ronan moved closer to Lachlan, and I stiffened,

my body tensing with the visceral urge to get between them. "Then you won't mind a short demonstration."

———

LACHLAN

Four men dressed in unrelieved black burst into the room at the same moment I felt a cold steel blade slide between my ribs. The pain was all-encompassing, stealing my breath, but not the immediate urge to put myself between Natasha and anything that might threaten her.

Before I could blink, she had two dead. A third tried to grab her wrist, then screamed when she activated the blade in her cuff. His cry of pain cut off when she slit his throat. The fourth, wary of her, pulled a gun, but she shot him before he could do the same to her.

"Oh, brava!" Ronan clapped his hands as I sank to the floor and pressed a hand over my wound. "You truly are exceptional, my dear. And now that I don't have to pay for you..."

He waggled his brows, then ducked, neatly

avoiding the throwing star Natasha aimed at his face.

"Your turn," she murmured, stalking closer.

He lunged for her, catching her collar, then forced her to the floor with his knee in the middle of her back. My head swimming with pain and blood loss, I staggered to my feet but couldn't muster the strength to force my body to move.

"Such a deadly little thing," Ronan crooned. "I don't think I'll sell you. I've always wanted you; did you know that? With your Rubenesque curves, all that hair, and such an innocent face, you were perfectly delectable. Would you like to grow your hair again, precious? Perhaps eat some freshly baked bread and pasta from my hand?"

When she didn't reply, he said, "Goodness, you're a very good girl, aren't you? You may speak."

Without warning, she bucked, sending Ronan off balance. He had time for one shout before she was on him, the blade at her wrist poised over his jugular.

"No, I'm really not a good girl." A sweet smile, reminding me of the innocent young woman she'd once been, ghosted across her face. "And, honestly, I'd rather eat your heart."

He paled and his eyes widened as he reached for

something I couldn't see. "Obey me, slave! Get off me right—"

"And I seriously don't have time for a villain monologue, what with a husband and a dozen of your victims to rescue."

The blade at her wrist sliced cleanly across his neck as a sharp crack of sound echoed. Natasha blinked with surprise and paled, her hand moving to clutch her belly.

"Watermelon!" I stumbled and dropped to my knees, catching her before she fell. Blood gushed from the bullet hole in her abdomen, draining her life before my eyes. "God fucking damn! Watermelon!"

I heard a concussive boom from outside. For a moment, I wondered if it was Ella's crew gaining entry to Ronan's compound, but it didn't matter.

They wouldn't come soon enough.

Forgetting my own injury, I pressed on her stomach in a desperate attempt to stanch the flow of blood.

"So dumb," she whispered, blinking her eyes slowly. "Shoulda known the bastard was packing."

"Shh, love. I need to get the bleeding stopped."

Her hand shaking, she touched my face. "S'ok," she slurred. "I got the bad guy, didn't I?"

"You did, baby." Praying I could keep her focused on survival, I added, "And we agreed that you could peg me if we lived through this."

Fuck, if she lived, I'd let her do whatever she wanted—including caging me in my own kennel.

"Woulda been fun." She closed her eyes, and her face relaxed into the softness I'd once tried to erase. "I'm tired. You can let go now."

"Natasha—"

"Stop." She nestled her head into my chest. "I forgive you, Lachlan. Make a good life for yourself."

I'd dreamt of earning her forgiveness, but not like this.

Never like this.

"Shh." I kissed her, tasting blood. "It's all going to be fine."

"Yeah, not gonna happen, but before I go..." She laughed, then coughed up more blood. "You wormed your way into my heart like a fucking tick, but I love you."

"I fell in love the moment I saw you." I murmured the truth I'd hidden from her and from myself for too long.

"Mmm." A steady trickle of blood leaked from the corner of her mouth as her breathing became labored. "Nice to know, but I think I'm ready to see what's on the other side now."

"Never, slave." I heard the sound of pounding footsteps as I laid down next to her and slowly, painfully, pulled her into my arms. We would go together or not at all. "I'm never letting you go. Obey your Master and live."

CHAPTER THIRTY-FIVE

NATASHA

Note to self... Avoid getting gut-shot.

Or if a gut-shot happens again, have a Master who can successfully order you to live.

Still wasn't sure how *that* came about. It wasn't even a thing except in fairy tales, and I sure as fuck wasn't Sleeping Beauty or Snow White.

But I'd begged Lachlan to stay alive in what I thought were my last few moments—at least mentally. I had no idea if I said it out loud.

I remembered fading, then getting loaded on a stretcher as someone slid a needle into my arm and pressed something hard on my belly that made me give up the struggle for consciousness.

The next thing I knew, I was waking up after surgery, screaming mad because I couldn't find Lachlan. By the time they got me restrained and sedated, I'd torn open most of the surgeon's meticulous work.

Because yeah. Drugged out of her gourd and enraged Natasha was one crazy bitch. Who knew?

When I woke from a second surgery to fix the damage, I was sharing a room with my husband, who was in worse shape than I was. I legit wanted to kill Ronan again for that.

Thankfully, Ronan's captives were safe and recuperating in one of Ella's safe houses. They got the rescue they'd probably been praying for while I was busy bleeding out in his sitting room. I'd never begrudge them that. They were part of the reason I went after Ronan in the first place.

I also had Dante and Angel sharing a cushy memory foam bed under the window on the other side of the room. Although I loved having him with me, I didn't need him to be my anchor keeping me from either killing someone or hiding in the closet with yet another PTSD episode. He could finally just be a beloved lap warmer.

Well, maybe someone else's lap. Mine barely fit his head, much less the rest of him—not that he didn't try it on occasion.

I focused on moving my hand to the controls for my hospital bed and pressed the button to lower my torso. Finding a comfortable position wasn't easy, but I managed it. Gotta love the good drugs that kept me stoned as fuck and feeling very little pain.

Proving all—well, most—was right in my universe, Lachlan was in the bed next to me and had a cannula feeding oxygen into his nose. I wished I had the strength to reach across the scant few feet separating us and touch him.

I'd gotten off lucky. The gunshot had done some soft tissue damage that almost bled me out, but I'd heal. The blood in my mouth that made everyone think I was bleeding internally was from where I accidentally bit down on one of my tongue piercings.

Ronan's knife cost Lachlan his spleen.

And I'd been too slow to stop it. Also, clearly too stupid to suspect Ronan had a weapon in the first place. Some bodyguard I was. I should have known better, but Lachlan and I both assumed he relied too heavily on his guards to bother arming himself.

But my Master would live, albeit with some

dietary restrictions. Not gonna lie, I was kind of looking forward to controlling his diet as much as he'd controlled mine back in the day, but I wouldn't make him eat unseasoned ground chicken.

Because no.

Actually, there probably would be ground chicken or turkey, but I'd make it taste good. My turkey meatloaf wrapped in bacon was fantastic and I could adjust the recipe to better fit his dietary requirements.

"You're awake," he slurred, his words muddled with the same drugs coursing through my body. "Wish you were in bed with me."

I did too. More than anything.

"Yeah, not happening right now, lover." I started to laugh, then winced when the hole in my belly complained. "Because too much owie, but maybe the nurse will push our beds together if we ask nicely."

To my shock, he sat up, then swung his legs over the edge of his hospital bed. Clutching his own wound, he staggered to me.

"Lachlan! What are you—"

"Move over, slave," he ordered, his voice thick with pain. He gripped the edge of my bed, and his knuckles whitened with strain as he struggled to hold himself up.

Hurriedly, and with some difficulty, I turned to my uninjured side and held my blanket open for him. His pained groan hurt my heart as he settled himself next to me.

"Better?" I asked, spooning him as he'd so often done for me. The narrow bed was a tight fit for two people, but it seemed Lachlan intended to stay all up in my space anyway.

Not that I was complaining.

"The best." He laced his fingers with mine. "How could lying next to my wife be anything but perfect?"

Christ. The things he said sometimes...

"Sleep, baby." I kissed the back of his head, ignoring the throb of warning from my gunshot wound.

"You sleep too, slave. I love you."

"Love you more."

"Impossible." His breathing steadied and slowed as he drifted off.

I couldn't—wouldn't—take back what I'd said when I believed I was dying. Despite everything he'd done to me, I did love him. I loved his accented, death-by-sex voice, his kindness to all the unwanted pets I'd sent his way, and his determination to keep me bundled up and safe. I loved the way he kissed me before ordering me to my knees.

Yeah, I was head over heels for the husband I'd been desperate to escape and never wanted in the first place. And I forgave him too—something I should have done ages ago but hadn't because of the malignant bitterness darkening my soul.

But coming *this* close to being an ex-Natasha taught me something.

Forgiveness isn't for the recipient. It's for the giver. It's for clearing the slate, soothing the wounds of the past, and letting go of the hurt before it festers. Maybe the pain I'd inflicted on Lachlan didn't measure up to what he did to me, but he stopped the minute my father was dead.

I hadn't.

Instead of moving on with my life—including the therapy I desperately needed, I let that ball of spite grow and poison my heart. I didn't much like the past me who wanted to see Lachlan hurting. Having been on the receiving end of such cruelty, it sucked ass.

Laughing inwardly, I wondered if Marmite's and Ogre's opinions of me would change now that the tumor of my hate was gone. Animals could be sensitive that way. Hell, for all I knew, that was why Saoirse refused to be in the same room with me.

I was in no hurry to offer the same courtesy to my sperm donor though. Some things were unforgivable. Maybe the rage would fade someday, but until then, I'd channel the emotion into my new career as an assassin.

Most of all, I wanted to be someone my soon-to-be-born sibling admired—not someone too bitter and angry to embrace them and love them unconditionally. I'd be their big sister, but I wanted to be more like the fun auntie who hopped them up on sugar, toys, and cuddles before sending them back to their mother.

Or was that a grandparent's job? Having had neither grandparent, nor fun auntie in my life, I had no idea.

I hadn't met my mom or her husband yet. We'd talked on the phone, and I couldn't wait to see her in person, but she was too pregnant to travel, and I was, you know, too full of holes to go to her. If I thought I could actually do it, I might have tried it on my own. I wouldn't go without Lachlan though, and honestly, neither of us were ready to leave the hospital yet.

I would have to remind myself not to refer to her as Cherise though. Her name was Arja, and her husband was Aatos Korhonen. I didn't know the name he used to have before they went into hiding. At least I had a picture of her. She looked so much like me, with curly brown hair reaching her shoulders and brown eyes. With luck, Lachlan and I would be out of the hospital before she gave birth.

"Little slave, you're thinking too loudly," Lachlan whispered. "You should be sleeping."

"I—" A soft knock interrupted me, and I feigned sleep when our private nurse bustled in.

I heard her sigh deeply, then grumble under her breath about newlyweds as she left on quiet footsteps.

Smiling, I inhaled Lachlan's spicy scent and fell asleep with my husband in my arms.

———

LACHLAN

Natasha looked beautiful. Her brown eyes were almost amber with delight under a black hat trimmed in faux mink, and the matching coat covered a cream cashmere sweater dress she wore with boots and the sexiest over-the-knee socks. A few snowflakes danced around her and landed on her cheeks like diamonds.

"I can't believe I'm going to see my mom tomorrow." Her arms laden with canvas shopping bags containing all manner of fresh produce, low fat dairy products, chicken, fish, and staples she deemed necessary, she bounced on the balls of her feet as I unlocked the door to our new home less than ten kilometers from her mother's. "And thank you for buying us a house close to her, and for having our stuff delivered and unpacked."

I chose not to mention the many hours she and her mother had spent video chatting, or the constant texts flying between them while we recovered from our injuries. After all, they had almost twenty-three years of missed time to make up for.

"It was my pleasure, love." I took off my coat and hung it in the closet, leaving my shoes on the mat as Orc twined around my ankles looking for attention. Marmite was in the barn behind the house. I couldn't wait to see him, but I had other plans for the evening. The teenager next door would have already given him fresh water and food, and according to her father, the girl spent more time with my pony than she did with her family.

Not for the first time, I considered giving him to her. Every pony deserved a little girl, and considering Natasha's history with him, I didn't think it would be her. Then again, Orc would sit in her lap preferentially over mine, despite her tales of how he used to snap at her. Perhaps there was hope for her and Marmite.

Dante and Angel were ensconced in a huge dog bed near the unlit fireplace in the living room. Dante lifted his head and glanced at the gas log as if he expected me to light it. I obliged his wishes.

Although I was still a bit sore, Natasha was much better. I was, of course, delighted she was well, but had to force myself to remember she was fifteen years younger than me, exceptionally fit, and hadn't been injured as badly in the first place. Although she'd been shot at close range, the small-caliber round hadn't been a hollow point, and passed through her body at an angle, thankfully just missing her internal organs.

I was even growing used to my new low carb, low fat diet, which she managed with the determination of a general commanding their troops, much to the irritation of our private nurse. God, I already missed her lemon cannelloni, but it was a small price to pay for the happiness shining in her face. Of course, Natasha was an imaginative cook. I was sure she could come up with a healthier version.

I hadn't told her yet, but I transferred ownership of my house in California to Saoirse. The property held too many memories, and I wanted us to have a fresh start. Finland seemed as good a place as any for that, but I'd also purchased an island in the Caribbean. It didn't have an active volcano as Natasha wished for, but the island would eventually boast a magnificent British colonial mansion built just for her with a gourmet kitchen and plenty of space for our burgeoning collection of pets. At just under four hundred acres, we could even add a few saddle horses.

Or perhaps children, but that would be a conversation for another day.

Whilst her excitement was infectious, it was past time for us to reconnect in the most intimate of ways. Between the endless video conferences spent with Ella gathering information on Ronan's known associates, recovering from our injuries, and absolutely no privacy, we'd barely even kissed.

Thanks to Ella's people, Ronan's body was found burned beyond recognition in an accidental garage fire, and all evidence of our presence was removed from the house and from Ronan's security footage.

The few guards who had seen us had also been elim-
inated. Natasha's targets would be unaware they
were being hunted until she slit their throats.

Ella had already paid her for the hit on Ronan.
Natasha took one look at the nine-figure payout,
covered her eyes, and told me to invest it. Part of it
went to her island, and the rest to a talented broker,
who would make sure she had a generous income
for the rest of her life. I considered liquidating some
assets to pay for the island myself, but I split the
purchase price with her, ensuring she would have a
stake in our future. Naturally, her name was on the
deeds for both the Landbo house and her island.
Later, she could choose a house in Italy near the
Swiss border if she still wanted one.

I followed her into the kitchen. She dropped the
shopping bags on the table, and after giving both
dogs and Dante's cat some attention, returned to
the foyer to take off her boots, coat and hat. When
we finished putting our groceries away, I put my
hands on her shoulders and turned her to face me.

"You may not speak, slave," I said, letting my
voice deepen into a low purr. "Go into the bedroom,
undress, and kneel in the center of the room."

She opened her mouth, then closed it and
cocked her head. Instead of protesting, she tugged

my shirt from the waistband of my trousers and lifted it to reveal the angry red scar on my abdomen.

"Time out for technical difficulties, Master," she murmured.

"I'm fine." After moving her hands to her sides, I turned her toward the bedroom and swatted her succulent backside. "But no acrobatics."

"Yes, Master." She took a step, then turned a cartwheel, her sock-covered feet barely missing the edge of the quartz countertop. "No acrobatics."

Must not laugh...

"Bratting will get you a thorough spanking, little slave."

She giggled and evaded me, her eyes sparkling with joy. "Can't catch me! I'm the gingerbread man!"

Seeing her blossom into the playful, happy person before me sent a pang into my chest, and I resolved to make her smile every day for the rest of our lives.

I lunged and caught her before she could do another cartwheel. Although I considered throwing her over my shoulder, I thought better of it. Despite her apparent wellness, I wouldn't put undue pressure on her bullet wound.

Or worse, drop her. I wasn't in top condition and

wouldn't be for at least another few weeks. Thankfully, we were both done with pain medication.

"First, you're going to get a spanking for refusing to let me carry anything," I warned as I circled her throat with gentle fingers. "Then you'll get another for bratting."

"But if I let you carry all the heavy stuff, you might not have the strength left to make love to me all night, Master."

I refused to admit that she was probably right. We'd had a long day, and I was tired—but not too tired to make love to my beautiful wife.

Tightening my fingers around her throat, I said, "The time for talking is over, slave. You will walk into the bedroom, undress, and kneel in the center of the room facing the picture window."

Her breath hitched in her throat, and she relaxed into gorgeous obedience, lifting her chin, but keeping her eyes down. Crossing her arms behind her back, she walked ahead of me until she stood in the middle of our bedroom. Slowly, giving me a show, she laid her phone, three knives, and a pistol on the dresser, then undressed and carefully folded each piece of clothing before lowering herself to her knees. Finally, she spread her thighs, revealing her pussy glistening with moisture.

I laughed inwardly. She was unarmed when she was naked, but she would never be helpless.

"Such a very good girl." Ignoring the twinge of pain in my ribs, I crouched and dragged a finger through her wetness, then sucked it clean. "And so very sweet."

CHAPTER THIRTY-SIX

NATASHA

My arousal faded when I spotted the lines of pain deepening on Lachlan's face as he crouched to touch my pussy. Fuck me. I should have told him no.

Clearly, he was still feeling a little ouchie. The old, not-stabbed Lachlan would have tossed me over his shoulder like a rag doll and spanked my butt all the way to bed. We'd have to be gentle but I couldn't complain. I was too damned happy to finally have privacy and a whole night to spend debauching each other.

There would be too few of those nights once I finished healing up. Ella was already lining up my hits, beginning in less than a month, and I was looking at twice that long to complete the assignment.

After that? I wasn't sure anymore. Part of me wanted to continue, but it would take years to execute enough slavers to make a sane person think twice before engaging in the skin trade. Frankly, it sounded exhausting.

The other part...

I wanted children someday. Maybe it was different for Ella, but I couldn't see myself letting go of my baby long enough to kill someone who needed to be dead. And what would happen to my kid if I fucked up?

Daddy, Mama got shot again!

Great. My imagined offspring was a tattletale. A story like that would go over *so* well at parent teacher conferences.

If I fucked up really badly, I'd leave Lachlan behind to tell them I was gone. I already knew what growing up without a mother felt like, and although Lachlan would never abuse them, I refused to let my children miss their mom like I had.

Believe it or not, at just a scant few days shy of my twenty-third birthday, I finally realized I wasn't immortal. I know, shocking, right?

Did Ella really need me to take out the trash? Ronan had been a challenging kill because of his inaccessibility and the extent of his business dealings, but the remaining targets lacked the assets necessary for his level of security. I wasn't her only assassin, and I certainly didn't need the money. I'd already gotten a paycheck with a stupidly ginormous number of digits on it.

Hello, volcanic lair...

I definitely did not ask how Ella and Gabby Knox managed to transfer all of Ronan's assets to the TLL Foundation without anyone catching on. I was a decent researcher, but hacking into international banks was not part of my skillset.

Our contract *did* say my employment was at will though. I could give notice after I got rid of Ronan's associates, maybe pinch hit for the really difficult cases, or...

When Lachlan's belt made a hiss of leather against cloth as he pulled it free, I decided to ruminate over my existential angst later.

Much later, because my gorgeous man was about to make me a very happy woman.

We wouldn't have the *fuck me and leave bruises* kind of night like we both enjoyed, but maybe it was better that way. Maybe we needed soft and tender to counteract what we'd survived. The thought wasn't any less enticing.

"You said I could peg you if I killed Ronan and survived." I rose to my feet and slid Lachlan's belt from his hands, then let it fall to the floor.

"So I did," he murmured, his beautiful blue eyes sparkling with banked arousal mixed with humor. "I believe you'll find lube and a strap-on in the bottom drawer of your dresser."

Christ, that man... Who even did shit like that?

Apparently, *my* man did shit like that.

"Yum, but later." Slowly, I unbuttoned his shirt, then stroked my hands over his muscular abdomen to his trousers. They slid down his legs and he kicked them away, along with his socks and shirt.

"Oh?"

"First, we'll free the erection," I murmured, tugging at his boxer briefs until they joined his pants on the floor. Careful not to touch his injury, I pushed on his chest until he reached the bed and sat down. "Lie back, but don't bother thinking of England."

He barked out a surprised laugh as I helped him settle against the pillows. "I told you that on our first wedding night."

Yes, he had. Even though he'd hated me, he

made my first time wonderful. He could have locked me in the kennel that night, wearing a full face of theatrical paint and the tattered remnants of an ugly wedding dress. He might have stolen my virginity on the lawn where I used to pee, or in front of his men while I was bent over a steel sawhorse after being hosed down with cold water and washed with what I still hoped wasn't dog shampoo.

He didn't. Instead, he gave me the perfect wedding night.

I never asked him why, and I wouldn't because it no longer mattered. We were different people, and I was in a place where I could cherish those memories for what they were. I could separate our first night together from everything that came after because I now knew there had always been some part of him that cared.

And tonight, I was calling the shots. I'd make this time just as special for him as he did for me—hopefully without annoying his stab wound.

Didn't mean I wouldn't torment him. Just a little...

"So you did." I went to the drawer he mentioned and found leather cuffs along with the promised strap-on phallus. And hell to the yum, there were even soy candles, some rope, a blindfold, and... Oh, man, we were going to have *fun*. "And payback is a bitch."

———

LACHLAN

Without protest, I let Natasha cuff me to the bed. Less than a month ago, her words might have given me cause for concern. I would have wondered if I was about to be another notch in the bedpost cataloguing her kills.

People would probably say I was crazy for trusting her, but in our shared present, I suspected she planned to tease me to madness instead of drawing a blade across my throat.

I hid a smile as she licked her lips and gazed at me as if she couldn't decide where to start, then carefully helped me turn to my stomach, making sure my wrists weren't twisted in their bonds. I couldn't help but wonder if she'd intentionally left them loose enough for me to escape.

Knowing Natasha, it had indeed been purposeful. For a moment, I wondered if it was a test of my resolve, but the thought skittered away when she touched me.

Instead of lubing me up in preparation for what I'd promised she could have, she straddled my hips. I smelled sweet almond as a slow trickle of warm liquid coursed between my shoulder blades. She smoothed the oil over my skin and began massaging the tension from my muscles.

"Oh, fuck." My eyes drifted closed. In this moment, she wasn't a deadly assassin. She was a woman intent on giving her man pleasure.

"Feel good?" she asked, working at a particularly stubborn knot where my neck met my shoulders.

"Very good." My cock throbbed against the sheets, and I resisted the urge to rub myself against the silky fabric. "You can keep doing that as long as you want."

Forever if she had a mind to.

Laughing softly, she moved to the other side of my neck and pressed her fingers into the tense muscles.

I bit back a gasp of pain but soon melted into a boneless puddle under her careful ministrations. Unfortunately, as good as the massage felt, it didn't ease the ache in my balls, or the need to plunge into her delicious pussy.

"Sorry!" She lifted her hands, and I nearly moaned at the loss. "Are you okay? Did I hurt you?"

"I'm better than okay, and it only hurts when you stop touching me." I lifted my hips, reminding her of what we'd agreed to. Although I'd never done anal and didn't particularly look forward to upholding my end of the bargain, I didn't worry Natasha would purposely harm me. "Do you need help with your strap-on?"

"Someone sounds eager." She plucked the strap-on from the pile of toys and put it on, then slid a pillow under my hips. "Maybe I should blindfold you."

Black silk covered my eyes, but I didn't protest. Payback was indeed a bitch, and this night was for her.

She traced her fingers over my ass in a seemingly random design that sent sparks ricocheting up and down my spine. The snap of a plastic cap opening startled me, and I clenched reflexively as cool liquid dribbled between my ass cheeks.

Slowly, as if she was giving me time to object, Natasha rimmed me, spreading the lube until I felt it drip down my inner thigh. As I'd taught her so long ago, I relaxed and allowed her to push a slick fingertip into me.

"Naughty," she murmured, making me realize I'd clamped down. "I just remembered I bought some ginger root. I wonder if I should carve a plug for you."

Dark pleasure surged as she pushed her finger deeper to brush my prostate, and I bit back a gasp. "As you wish, Mistress."

"Mistress? Does that mean I get to call you slave?" Removing her finger, she laughed softly. I imagined her rolling her eyes as I heard the sound of leather hissing through metal buckles behind me.

She drizzled more lube over my exposed asshole, then something fell to the bed next to me, presumably the bottle. It bounced, and I wondered if Natasha had emptied it completely.

"Nah," she said before I could reply. "That doesn't fit either of us, does it?"

"No. Least of all you."

"Only when I want it to." She shifted her weight behind me, and the hard tip of the phallus prodded my opening. "You once said I looked beautiful with your cock in my ass, and I can honestly say I understand the appeal. Say red if you need me to stop."

Slowly, she pushed into me. I squeezed my eyes shut and forced myself to relax and push out, allowing her to seat the toy inside me, stretching my inner walls with a mixture of burning pain and incredible pleasure.

I groaned, unable to hold the noise inside. "Fuck…"

"Am I hurting you?" When I didn't respond, she stilled and laid a hand on my shoulder. "Lachlan, answer me."

"Don't you dare stop," I hissed, sliding my hands from the cuffs. When she didn't move, I rocked my hips to encourage her.

"And what if I do?" I heard laughter in her voice as she eased the phallus from my hole.

"You might get punished for being naughty." I flipped over, then wrapped an arm around her waist and pulled her off balance until she fell to her back next to me. Without giving her time to protest, I unbuckled the strap-on and tossed it away.

I cupped her round bottom and rubbed my aching shaft along the seam of her wet pussy. She cried out and her back arched as she ground herself against me.

"Damn." She dropped searing kisses along the line of my jaw as she reached down to position my cock at her entrance. "There was a TENS unit and soy candles in that drawer. I was so going to tease you, but I need you inside me."

"Wish granted." The lingering pain in my side vanished, and I surged into her welcoming channel, making her moan with pleasure. "The TENS unit is going on your sweet cunt, and I'll decorate your magnificent breasts with hot wax while electricity stimulates your clit. That ginger plug will be going in your cute ass."

"Promise?" Her short nails dug into my shoulders as she wrapped her calves around my waist and lifted her hips to meet my pounding thrusts.

"That and so much more." I took her mouth in a brutal, claiming kiss, then reached between our bodies to roll her clit between my fingers. "Come for me, love."

Tingles of warning shot up my spine, letting me know I wouldn't last. It had been too long for us, but I refused to come until Natasha did.

"Fuck! Lachlan!" Her screams of pleasure filled the room as she clamped down on me, her inner muscles squeezing my cock.

My vision darkened, and I stilled inside her, trying to drag her pleasure out. As if determined to make me lose control, she dragged her nails up my back and sank her hands into my hair and kissed me. The sweet taste of her, her breathless whimpers, and her scent of aroused woman and flowers sent me over the edge.

"Natasha..." I collapsed on top of her, then rolled to my side before I crushed her. "Fuck."

"Uh huh." She curled up against me and threw a leg over me. "Love you, but gonna sleep now."

"I love you more than my life, little slave."

———

"Is it stupid to be nervous?" Natasha asked as we strode to the front door of her mother's house.

"Of course not." I kissed the top of her head and tucked her hand around my elbow. "Just be yourself. She'll love you, no matter what."

"Be yourself," she muttered. "An assassin with a supervillain nickname?"

"Natasha..." I let my voice trail off but made the warning more than clear. "I—"

"Aatos, they're here!" Arja Korhonen, formerly Cherise Ashland, dodged her husband's attempt to keep her still and waddled to Natasha. Pulling her into an enormous hug, she said, "My dreams have come true, and I—"

A strange, almost pained expression crossed Arja's face, and she didn't finish her sentence.

"Mom?" Clearly on edge, Natasha slid a hand under

her skirt and retrieved a knife from a sheath strapped to her thigh. Keeping it hidden, she positioned herself between her mother and the road. "Are you okay?"

"You called me Mom." Giving Natasha a beatific smile, she looked down at a puddle spreading under her feet. "Aatos, darling, would you get my hospital bag and bring the car around? I'm afraid we'll have to skip supper."

Nine hours later, Natasha held her new sister while her mother and stepfather rested.

"So, anyway…" She smiled when the infant grabbed her finger. "I've been thinking."

"About what?" I adjusted baby Natalya's blanket to protect her from the breeze flowing from the overhead vents.

"Babies smell good." She brushed a kiss over Natalya's wispy brown curls. "I didn't know that."

"They do," I agreed. "What else are you thinking?"

Her smile faded and she looked up at me. "I'm going to finish my last assignments with Ella, then I'm retiring."

"All right." Although she'd unknowingly gifted me with something I desired above all else, I needed to make sure retirement was what she truly wanted.

"And what brought this on? I thought you liked being The Spider."

"I do." She repositioned Natalya in her arms and sighed. "My priorities are changing though. I'm going to ask Ella to keep me on staff as an analyst instead of doing field work."

"May I ask why?"

"I want babies, Lachlan. *All* the babies, and I want you to be their daddy. I want enough to field a rugby team, and if I can't give birth to that many, I want to adopt." She lifted her chin and met my gaze. "I want them to never have to think for a single goddamned second that I might not come home one day. I want to bake cookies and go to PTA meetings without worrying that one of the little shits will tell everyone their mama got shot again. I want us to share huge holiday meals where we all eat too much and fall asleep during football games none of us actually watch. I want to give them all the joy I never had, and I want to live long enough to watch them grow into the magnificent humans I know they'll become."

"I—" No words would come, and I blinked, hoping the ache of tears in my sinuses would fade. She'd laid out everything I never dared hope she'd give me.

"I want to live in a place where I won't have to worry about whether my sidearm is loaded." She laughed softly, and laying her hand on my cheek, kissed me gently. "I want a place where I don't even need a gun, but I know I'll probably carry one anyway."

I lowered myself to my knees and took her hand, then pressed a kiss to her palm. "Wish. Granted."

ABOUT RAISA GREYWOOD

USA Today bestselling author Raisa Greywood loves to write stories that make her readers wonder if they should laugh or cry. Or even better, do both at the same time! She takes special delight in turning traditional romance tropes upside down and shaking them until something fun falls out.

Raisa lives in the midwestern United States with two cats who share one brain cell, and her husband, who taught her how to write great enemies to lovers stories over thirty years ago, and who still brings her flowers.

Sign up for her newsletter or visit her website at www.raisagreywood.com

If paranormal romance is your jam, her alter-ego Minette Moreau has just the thing. Sign up for her newsletter or visit her website at www.minettemoreau.com

You can also buy many of Raisa's and Minette's books direct from their websites!

amazon.com/stores/author/B076FRRHT4

facebook.com/AuthorRaisaGreywood

instagram.com/raisagreywood

bookbub.com/authors/raisa-greywood

goodreads.com/raisa_greywood

tiktok.com/@raisagreywood

threads.net/@raisagreywood

ALSO BY RAISA GREYWOOD

Vindictive Queens

Breaking Donatella

Stealing Natasha

Club Apocalypse

Grim's Little Reaper

War's Peace

Pestilence's Cure

Famine's Feast

Death's Desire

Charon's Chaos

Evenings at Club Apocalypse Website Exclusive

Cherry Popping Daddies (Multi Author Series)

Emily (By Golden Angel)

Lottie (By Stella Moore)

Titania (By Raisa Greywood)

Holiday Daddy Doms

Jennifer's Christmas Daddy

A Valentine for Chelsea

Treats for Lucia

Zinnia's Solstice Daddy

A Daddy For All Seasons Website Exclusive

Black Light

Black Light: Roulette Rematch

Black Light: Saved

Dad Bod Doms

Henry

Happily Never After (written with Sinistre Ange)

Demon Lust

Blood Lust